BEAR

GHOST MOUNTAIN WOLF SHIFTERS BOOK 6

AUDREY FAYE

1

RONAN

My bear is being ridiculous and I have no idea why. I try not to wriggle like a cub as I stare out the window wondering what on earth has set fire ants loose under his skin.

Ames looks over at me from the pilot's seat. "Don't you dare shift, you big loot. This plane is barely big enough for you as it is."

It's not me taking up most of the room, but I'm also responsible for most of the gear tucked in behind us. "If you didn't put quite so many dents in it, your plane would be more spacious."

Ames's glare could strip the skin off a lesser bear, and probably has. "I need to put in a couple that are big enough to get rid of annoying poker players who think I should fly them all over the damn planet just because they drew to a full house when they were sitting on absolutely nothing."

Scotty had us both beat until that draw, which is why she made the dumbass bet in the first place. "You like flying me places. I'm charming and you get to see the world."

She rolls her eyes hard enough to bounce and raps on one of the gauges in front of her.

My bear snorts. That gauge hasn't worked for at least a decade.

She eyes me as she nudges the nose of the plane left so that we don't hit a mountain. "What's got your bear's shorts in a twist?"

Something big enough that even her wolf can smell it, and Ames's nose works about as well as her gauges. "No idea. He's not normally like this." That's an understatement. Very big bears learn to control themselves if they want to live in dens full of tenderness and fascinating ideas and fragile packmates. I haven't felt him struggle like this since our very first days in Whistler Pack.

I stare out the window again. There's nothing up this high that could possibly be affecting him, and not much down below, either. Just vast swaths of wilderness he can hardly wait to explore.

A hand pats my knee. "If you need me to find a place to put down, just say the word. Preferably before there's a bear-sized hole in my fuselage."

If I lose that much control, we're both dead. I mutter Russian poetry in the back of my head. Usually engineering equations are more effective, but I can't remember any at the moment. Which is a bad sign. Bears have several layers of primal instincts, but all of mine suitable for being in the presence of non-bears went to engineering school.

I inhale slowly, discarding the scents of yarn and chocolate and tool grease and the leftover Chinese food Ames had for breakfast. There's something else. The tantalizing smell of prey across a vast wasteland of ice and snow—except my bear has never been a hunter.

It's why I left.

"Down there." Ames nods at a second mountain that has come into view behind the one she nearly grazed. "See the rock that looks like raccoon poop? We land just in back of that, unless you want me to put down in Hayden's fire pit for fun and giggles."

My bear's eyes sharpen. The smell. It comes from there—from the glinting panes of glass and the strewn boulders and the fire-ant-sized shifters streaming toward the bare place where Ames means to set down her plane.

"Dude." Ames sounds almost alarmed. "You're smelling awfully furry."

Damn. I wrap both arms around my bear's neck and yank on his ears. Ghost Mountain is a pack full of strength and bravery, but it's also a pack far more fragile than the Whistler wolves, and he's a big, scary polar bear who needs to arrive with his very best manners intact or he'll never forgive himself.

He shakes his head, left to right, right to left.

I grit my teeth until they creak. "Tell me about angular velocity."

Ames stares at me as she does six things with knobs and pedals that are in far better working order than her gauges. "What?"

I manage to keep my growl reasonably polite. "Explain how airplanes fly or why you insist on runways the size of postage stamps or how internal combustion works. Anything you know that resembles engineering equations. Please."

She bumps against my shoulder. Hard. "There's an eleven-year-old kid down there who can tell you all of those things just as soon as I get this plane on the ground."

Reilly. My bear finds his first degree of calm. He will not scare the cub. He will show him how to fish and how to bisect an angle using only the rays of the sun and then he will tell him stories of ice and snow and bear courage.

I sigh. My bear keeps forgetting that we'll only be here for a few weeks—but I can remind him about that when we're no longer several hundred meters above the ground.

HAYDEN

We've had some highly anticipated visitors these past few months. Sierra and Sienna. My mom. Martha bearing photos of the new raven babies.

None of them made my entire pack zoom around like subatomic particles on a sugar high. I shake my head as

Reilly runs headlong into Kennedy and both of them barely notice. "Does Ronan have any idea that he's Ghost Mountain royalty?"

Kel snorts. "He's a polar bear. He expects the world to revolve around his presence."

It's hard to disappear into the woodwork when you're fifteen hundred pounds of apex predator. Fortunately, Ronan's generous heart weighs at least that much, too. He loves to be at the center, but he never lets himself be there alone. "How's Mikayla doing?"

Kel chuckles. "Shelley got her calmed down."

Feeding a polar bear has even Shelley tied up in a few knots. Which I trust Ronan to promptly undo. Some of the other impacts of his visit are going to take a little longer to smooth out, but Ronan always leaves a pack stronger than he found it, and he always starts with the people who fill his belly.

Eliza and Danielle arrive, both of them a little out of breath and covered in dust.

I grin. "I thought we were done pouring bags of concrete on each other."

Eliza rolls her eyes. "Don't ask."

Sanding, probably. Between getting the hot pools ready and the concrete-table prototypes made, there's been a lot of dust. I glance at Eliza's partner in crime. Danielle is on my list to worry about this morning. The big guy on the plane that's lining up for a landing is already most of the way in love with her cub, and she has plenty of reasons to be wary. The previous bear in her life wasn't a good man.

I wrap an arm around her shoulders. "You have choices, remember?"

She looks up at the plane and swallows. "He's smart and kind and Reilly really wants to meet him. I'll be fine."

If Ronan has a weakness, it's his desperate need for people to accept the warmth he so badly wants to offer. "If you need a break, use the hand signals." Kel will make sure a big bear knows all of them, even if he isn't the intended recipient. Ronan has always been his own best containment field.

Her forehead wrinkles. "He'll be busy on all the fancy engineering work. I can stay out of his way."

Not if her alpha has any say in the matter. Which I likely won't. Ronan acknowledges pack leadership in many things, but how his engineering teams run isn't one of them. "I don't think you and Indrani left him much to do."

Eliza snorts. "That's a good thing. Have you seen Reilly's schedule for this visit?"

Danielle's cheeks flush. "I told him that Ronan would need time to work."

Ronan will have no trouble rolling an eager eleven-year-old into his engineering team—or making sure that they all take time to have some fun. "Do me a favor and don't say things that will make a polar bear cry."

Her shoulders relax a little under my arm. "Glow is really good with the pipes, and Indrani has the cables mostly sorted. If he checks over what we planned and fixes our mistakes, we can probably do most of the work while he follows my son around."

Glow and Indrani both think Danielle has Albert Einstein hiding inside her brain, and Rio isn't far behind them. "I thought Scotty looked at your plans?"

Danielle's shoulders squeeze up around her ears. "He did, but he said Ronan needs to have the final say because boots on the ground will see things that he can't. He put some flags on the parts he wants Ronan to look at really closely."

Ronan doesn't need flashing arrows to sniff out trouble. "Did he say those parts are a problem?"

Eliza elbows her friend. "No. He said they were the parts that no conventionally trained electrician or plumber would ever dream of, and he wants me to steal Danielle's brain and put it in a bottle and have one of the hawks fly it down to Whistler."

Geek compliments are so weird. "Do I need to growl at him?"

"No." Danielle sighs. "He's a very nice man and he's trying to make me feel better, but I know that I don't have any formal training. I don't mind if people tell me what I did wrong."

Scotty has never dodged that kind of teaching opportunity in his life, but it isn't going to be my job to point that out. That honor belongs to the bear who is currently waving wildly at Reilly and Kennedy and Mellie as Ames brings her plane into what most pilots would politely call an emergency landing.

The shifters of Ghost Mountain swarm forward. Mellie heads for the cantankerous old pilot she's adopted as an extra grandmother. Everyone else reckless enough to brave the growl of the plane charges the big man who drops out of the side door and lands in a crouch as gracefully as a cat.

Reilly gets to him first, which probably had some pack engineering involved, but Kelsey isn't far behind and neither is Robbie, and they aren't nearly as awed. They both crash into Reilly and topple an organism with about a dozen limbs into Ronan's waiting arms.

The laugh that rolls out of my friend is almost as loud as the plane.

My wolf watches, astonished, as most of his pack reacts to the terrifying sound by pushing closer. I raise an eyebrow at Rio. Ronan sets off primal flight instincts, always. He's earned himself a lot of goodwill in this pack, but instincts don't understand yarn trades and fish stories.

Kel makes some quick hand signals at Ames that earn him a snarl, but the engines shut down moments later.

The reaction my pack is having to Ronan doesn't change in the sudden silence. Some wariness, some shyness, some shame and fear as the wolves who struggle with the presence of adult men try to acclimate to the very burly one who just landed. But nobody is panicking about the fact that he's a polar bear.

My wolf nods complacently. Smart pack. Strong pack.

He clearly doesn't remember the first time he laid eyes on Ronan. I step forward. There are formalities for visitors, ones meant to help soothe our wolves and sort out temporary hierarchies. Which don't actually seem to be necessary, but Ronan will appreciate them all the same.

He finally glances in my direction, a bear far too preoccupied with the joy in his arms to be all that interested in a friend he hasn't seen for months.

The woman at my side stiffens, and I realize that I forgot to let go of Danielle when I stepped forward. I hastily rectify that as the polar bear who just arrived for a visit glances curiously her way.

Which is when all hell breaks loose.

RONAN

Her scent slams into me first. The wild rightness of it catapults my bear through my skin and deposits him into her sturdy, competent hands before I take my next breath.

I yank him back frantically. I cannot go furry now. I know this with everything in the few shreds of aware humanity I have left—but they are few, scattering in the headwind of the oncoming vortex of polar bear who has found the first thing in his life that he truly wants to hunt.

The man who has shared a body with that bear for forty-four years panics. Nothing stops a polar bear's hunt. *Nothing.*

Puny humans step into my path. Some I know. Hayden. Kel. Rio. Another with a soldier's bearing.

My bear opens his mouth to roar.

A hand pats my arm. "My bear sometimes gets riled, too. It's okay. Do you want a honey berry bar, maybe? They're really good."

My bear looks down, gaping.

Reilly smiles up at him. "The new batch has blueberries in it, but I saved one with strawberries in case you like that kind better."

Holy hell. There are eyes drilling holes in me all over this pack, but I keep mine on the cub who might be the only creature in existence that my bear will let contain him.

The cub is hers. She has trusted me with his presence.

I breathe that message deep into the violence of a polar bear who believes he has smelled his destiny, and lay my hand over Reilly's far smaller one. "I've been waiting weeks to taste these honey berry bars." My voice doesn't sound remotely human. "I imagine that I'll be eating a lot of them, so I brought a small gift for the one who invented them."

Reilly beams at me. "That's Mikayla. She loves presents."

I do my very best to knit the remaining shreds of my humanity into something worthy of the look of adoration in those brown eyes. "I have a few other gifts in my backpack. Perhaps you can help me distribute them."

Ames snorts from right behind me, which tells me just how close I came to getting my ass kicked along with whatever frontal attack Kel was assembling. "My whole plane is full of crap."

Reilly grins in her direction. "At least you don't have to fly back with smelly fish this time."

Barking laughter from a woman who finds very few people funny. "True. Maybe I can take some jam, instead. This big loot ate my last jar."

"Jam can be arranged." The wiry elder who makes all of my favorite kinds steps forward, reaching up around my neck for a brisk hug and a pat on my cheek before she shoots Reilly a meaningful look. "Perhaps we should show our guests over to the picnic before Brown eats all the grilled fish."

My bear freezes in shock. She met his eyes.

She looked straight at the hunter and patted his cheek.

Myrna wraps her arm around mine and leads me away from the plane. "I hope you brought more purple yarn. We're rationing what we've got left, but the situation is getting dire."

I manage to take another breath, one that makes it all the way to my ribs this time. "There is no yarn of any shade of purple left in Whistler Pack. Aurelia made sure of it."

She nods approvingly. "Excellent."

I walk as steadily as I can, flanked by a bear cub and an elder who are calmly herding a polar bear grenade while he figures out how to stick his safety pin back in again. It helps that the scent tormenting my nose is behind me, no doubt with a wall of teeth and claws guarding her.

Shame floods the human part of my soul. I made promises.

Something bounces off of my head.

I stare at the pinecone that lands at my feet, stupefied for the third time in as many minutes.

Reilly giggles so hard it shakes his thin body. "That's how we tell someone they're being a dumbass."

Myrna snorts. "I thought we agreed that I'm allowed to use that word, and all wolves and bears and ravens still young enough to be in school have to find more appropriate synonyms."

"There really aren't any." Kennedy wraps her arm around Reilly's head from his other side. "Quit hogging the cute polar bear, Riles. I want to see him eat the fish Brown grilled up. I hear they're really spicy."

"Confirmed." Kel juggles a pinecone in his hand. "The fire-breathing contest will be right after lunch."

His eyes are the calm of a soldier who's glad he won't have to maim a friend today. I put abject apology in mine. He knows just how badly I fucked up.

Something that looks very much like compassion flickers in his in return. He nods to his left. "You know Indrani, but this is the rest of your engineering team. Danielle is Reilly's mom, so she handles bears just fine, and Glow somehow tolerates Brown, so we figure that she can put up with you, too."

I throw a war hammer at my bear's head just in case he tries to be stupid again. I smile at Indrani first. She knows me as a goofy, easygoing guy who tells very bad jokes about electrical wires, and I'd really like to keep it that way. "You've learned a lot while you're here. Someone must be a good teacher."

She meets my eyes in the way of ravens and smiles. "Rio taught me some stuff, and Brown, and Eliza. But Danielle taught me the most. She's amazing."

Glow nods, a wary young wolf who absolutely agrees with that statement.

The lessons of Whistler Pack reach for me, even as my bear's nose flares again. I smile at Glow. I like quiet wolves, especially if they don't mind hanging out with a chatty bear.

The wariness in her eyes diminishes a shade.

I wink at Indrani. "From what I've seen, we're all going to be working hard to keep up with Danielle."

Reilly's squeak is pure joy for my bear.

The hissing worry from his mom is another thing entirely.

Kel's pinecone hits just before I do something eternally stupid.

A small hand pats my arm again. "My mom is really smart."

My eyes travel the few, agonizing centimeters to the face that goes with the mesmerizing scent. The rosy cheeks and angular jaw are familiar. I've seen Danielle before, even said a word or two to her in the many video calls I've had with various members of this pack.

She smiles faintly, every line of her full of hesitation and worry.

My bear stammers, trying to find the best words. The first words. "Thank you for allowing me to spend time with Reilly."

Her eyes widen.

Reilly looks entirely horrified at the possibility I just spoke into existence.

Danielle nods a little and says nothing at all.

My bear frets. She is too small. Too contained. Cramped, almost. That's wrong. He can smell the size of her soul. She must have all the space she needs.

His poetry knifes into my ribs. For others to be the size and shape they're meant to be, he needs to be so very careful. That's the reason for the promises he made so many winters ago to the fierce, compassionate wolf who was willing to give him a chance. Promises that committed a bear to seeking forms of expression that work in a pack that cherishes kindness and honors softness and never permits strength to overpower consent.

This is such a pack.

My bear whimpers, a cub watching his first ice floe melt into oblivion.

I lean my head against his. He cannot hunt. He must not. But perhaps, if he is a very good bear, one day he will earn the right to ask.

2

HAYDEN

I lean against a tree and hold out one of the grilled-fish sandwiches that are making my wolf drool. "What the hell was that?"

Rio's smile is almost dopey. "That was nothing I ever thought I'd see in my lifetime. Two things, actually."

I bump his shoulder, and not particularly gently. "I'm hungry and there's a polar bear running amok in my pack. This is a really crappy time to be mysterious."

He looks over at Ronan, who's sitting in the middle of a bunch of pups. They're feeding him honey berry bars and bites of fish and waiting for the next wonder to emerge from his backpack. "He's settled. For now."

My wolf sits up, alarmed. "It's going to happen again?" Watching Ronan's eyes go feral easily counts as one of the most terrifying experiences of my life, and this hasn't exactly been a calm year.

Rio's shrug isn't at all reassuring. "He'll likely have it under better control, but this isn't going to be easy for him."

I let out some of the growl that I managed not to point at Ronan. Even alpha wolves know better than to poke a nearly feral bear.

Ears flicker all over my pack, and then flicker back to the cute polar bear again.

I shake my head as he pulls out tiny knitted baby things and says something to Indrani. For the new hatched babies of Desolate Inlet, no doubt. If Ronan is here for as long as Rio expects him to be, they'll have enough tiny knitted things for an entire flock of hatchlings.

Eliza leans in and asks him a question. I don't hear her words, but I can read the lines of her face and her wolf. One of the most submissive wolves in my pack, and she's already decided that Ronan is a friend.

"That's part of what I never thought I'd see," says Rio quietly.

I squint at a tableau that happens every day of the week in Whistler Pack. "He always charms everyone." It's in the core module of his polite-polar-bear operating chip. The one he somehow forgot to insert when he stepped off the plane. I've seen the wild side of Ronan's bear before, but never around the vulnerable. Never around the frightened. Absolutely never around pups.

Rio's smile is dopey again. "How did the pack react when he arrived?"

I squint some more. Some of us nearly went to war—

including Ames, who is over eating a sandwich with Brown and acting like chewing on a polar bear is just a standard part of her delivery service. Given how often she visits Ivan's territory, it might be. "He set off every dominant in the den, but since you're being mysterious, that's probably not the part you mean."

Rio takes a big bite of his sandwich.

I hate it when they decide I'm smart enough to figure shit out for myself. I play through Ronan's arrival in my head. The moments before the feral eyes. I sigh when the obvious hits me in the forehead like a pinecone. "You mean what happened when he laughed."

Rio's lips quirk. I'm not a completely stupid alpha. "That wasn't his inside laugh."

It wasn't. It was the loud one that takes up lots of space. The one he's very careful to keep away from new den members and anyone who might not handle his true dimensions. Which apparently isn't anyone here. They've all clearly decided that he's a cute bear who can be as loud as he wants. "Huh."

"He makes himself small to belong." Rio's eyes aren't those of a sentinel—they're the fiercely happy ones of a friend. "He maybe won't have to do that quite as much while he's here."

The part of me that loves a polar bear like a brother hopes like hell a sentinel's instincts are running true. The part of me that's alpha of a pack that still has far too many whimpers in the night shudders. Even the small version of Ronan is really big.

I look back over at our visitor as he pulls two brightly

wrapped packages out of his backpack, one for each of the pups who had a birthday in the last couple of weeks. Jade and Kelsey beam at him in unison, which causes puddles of melted wolf all over my pack.

I shake my head. They all saw the feral eyes, I know they did, and this is not a stupid pack. It might have a stupid alpha, though. "What am I missing?"

Rio chuckles. "They understand why Ronan lost his shit. You apparently don't."

I take a bite out of my sandwich and pretend it's chewy sentinel instead.

He grins. "Do you at least know *who* set him off?"

My wolf stops chewing.

Rio takes his eyes off of the polar bear and his bag of delights for long enough to toss a pointed look in my direction. "He's going to need your confidence that he can keep his shit together. Maybe put Kel on that, too. Or Kennedy. She's got a way with bears."

My wolf tries to take over my skin. I get a hold of his scruff. One feral shifter a day is plenty. "What the hell will you be doing?"

He smiles, his eyes traveling to a group of shifters over on the periphery. "Helping her."

I faceplant into a mountain that wasn't there a second ago. "What?"

Rio chuckles, but it doesn't entirely hide his concern. "Ronan's bear thinks he scented his mate."

I stare at him, not sure whether to laugh hysterically or puke. "That's a fairy tale."

He rolls his eyes. "It happened to your parents, dumbass."

I shake my head, trying to scrape it off the side of an invisible mountain. And then I figure out who Ronan's bear scented, and I smack right back into solid rock. "Oh, fuck."

Rio nods slowly. "Yup."

The part of me that has been Ronan's friend for most of my life takes over just long enough to grin like an idiot. The rest of me that has to keep my pack in one piece kicks his ass half a second later. "How the hell do we roll with that?" I can hear the alarm bells ringing in harmony in my head. Danielle has really good reasons to want no part of that, ever. There's a bear cub and a traumatized pack that will absolutely be in the middle of anything that happens. And the leading guy in the fairy tale is a polar bear with a heart as tender as Kelsey's flowers.

Rio smiles as Jade wraps her arms around Ronan's neck and hugs him tightly. "The way that we always do. We stand for pack. All of them."

I blink. That sounds a whole lot like a sentinel just added a polar bear to our numbers.

RONAN

I gave up many things when I left the north. I did it with my eyes wide open, and I did it for reasons that have made the intervening years very happy ones. I have no idea how to explain to my bear that the universe just tried to give one of those things back to him—and it's almost certainly a gift he can't accept.

My eyes stray to the wolf they cannot stay away from. She's sitting on the edge of the lunch gathering, tinkering with a pile of parts in her lap. The innards of a video camera, I think.

My bear sighs happily. Smart hands. Good hands.

I yank my eyes back to my backpack. There are a few small things inside it, yet, and plenty more on the plane. Perhaps Danielle will enjoy Reilly's robot.

She makes a quiet sound, one that carries easily to my ears through the dense noises of happy, excited pack.

I don't whimper, but it's a close thing.

Kel glances up from the admiring that he's doing of Jade's new music box. It plays a song that her daddy wrote for her, and her small fingers stroking it gently are making my bear sniffle.

I focus on those fingers, letting them soothe the volcano inside me.

My bear snorts. No self-respecting polar bear would be caught dead anywhere near a mountain full of fire.

I don't argue with him. I can feel the hot truth melting rocks inside me—the ones that I've used to contain him. Until today, I didn't truly understand just how many of them I'd piled up over the years.

I left the north because I was a bear drawn to soft things, because violence and the exercise of power weren't things that made my heart sing. Because I believed myself to be a different kind of bear. But what rises in me now—I've seen it. And I don't know if it will allow me to stay.

I shift my gaze to Reilly, who has been distributing gifts and documenting the story of this day on a well-used notepad. He, too, is a different kind of bear. One who deserves every gift I can give him, and most of them can't be put in a backpack or crammed into the tail of Ames's plane.

I take a resolute breath. Leaving is unacceptable. I would not be the only one who paid a steep price. "There's a box of books just behind my seat on the plane. Some on gardening and photography, and some with knitting patterns, and one on folding paper into lantern boats so we can have candle races down your stream."

His eyes shine. That was one of his special requests.

I take another breath. I can do this. I *will* do this. "There are a few engineering books in there, as well. And some really dusty textbooks on architecture and design."

The big, black wolf with a feisty toddler in his lap raises a mildly surprised eyebrow.

I ignore him. I was under strict instructions to bring only well-used books with me, and Scotty whined when I tried to steal his. "We have a library at Whistler Pack. These are books that weren't getting enough use." I don't mention that many of them only landed in the library long enough to get sprinkled with an appropriate amount of book dust. "I thought they might find a home here where they'll be properly appreciated."

Reilly looks properly horrified at the idea of books languishing in obscurity. "Adelina and Hoot really like gardening and I bet the photography books would help with taking better pictures for the newspaper. Robbie is our new cub reporter, which is funny, because he isn't a cub, but Myrna says that's still the right title. The knitting ones will probably be Eliza's, because she knows how to growl now, and my mom likes learning how to make things sturdy. Would the engineering books help with that?"

I can't really breathe anymore. Which is perhaps good. Inhaling has never been quite so dangerous. "I believe they would. Most people don't consider them very interesting, though."

Indrani snorts. "They put me to sleep better than Wrinkles's teas."

I carefully don't meet her eyes. She read half the books on my work shelf during her first weeks at Whistler Pack. "Some people like to learn from books. Others prefer to experiment and let their hands lead the way."

A box thunks to the ground beside me. Ames scowls like it might have contaminated her plane. "I'd advise reaching into the box carefully. There are enough twigs and dust in there that there's probably a mouse or two, too."

Not unless someone got really creative trying to make them smell less like polar bear. I hide a smile as Kelsey bends over the box, her eyes bright as she scans words that she likely can't read. Her fingers unerringly pluck out one of the knitting books, and then she's gone, heading straight for the knitter who wields a chain saw and pours concrete footings in her spare time.

My bear grins as she collects Kel on her way. Tiny bossy wolf.

A sneeze pulls my attention back to the box. Glow backs away sheepishly, a book on gardening in one hand that she's already passing to another young wolf I haven't met, and a second one on plumbing that she's carefully cuddling to her chest.

Kennedy bumps her shoulder. "That one looks awful. I can't believe you want to read about pipes."

Glow's eyes fill with guilt and yearning. "I can wait. I bet someone else wants it first."

Not unless this pack is suddenly full of dunderheads. I look over at Hayden, because he's the guy who used to deal with this kind of stuff at Whistler—but he just grins at another teenager who's obviously not staked out beside the box by accident.

Kennedy rolls her eyes dramatically enough that my bear sniffs to make sure she's a wolf. "You need to read it, because if I have to, I'll probably break out in really itchy hives, and I need to know whether to put pebbles or sand around the pipes that are going to run under the new den paths, remember?" Another eye roll for good measure. "Eliza and Danielle can't make up their minds."

My bear grins. He likes this one. She tells good stories.

Reilly elbows her. "Sometimes it's good to think things through instead of making mistakes."

She wraps her arm around his head fondly. "Mistakes are fun. You should try one this week."

I watch, fascinated by the young leader who's clearly

decided to stick her fingers in my engineering-team pie, and who hasn't so much as glanced at me to see if I care. Which isn't arrogance or youth or inexperience. It's a baby alpha who knows her packmates that well and expects me to deal.

I can always use someone like that on my team. "Pebbles and sand each have advantages and disadvantages, and they differ by environment. You have a couple of weeks to run some tests and see which ones will work best for each of your desired applications."

She stares at me, blinking slowly.

Reilly grins—and doesn't translate.

Good. This will be a fine team. "I'd advise testing at various water temperatures, as well. The pipes from the hot springs will likely behave quite differently than the ones from the stream."

Kennedy's eyes narrow into a look that says she's on to my meddling bear ways and her approval is only provisional. "I could maybe do that. I'll need some help, though. I only know how to do the shoveling part."

I have a good poker face for a reason. "Mistakes are fun. This is a good week to make some."

She studies me a while longer, with shades of Adrianna Scott in her eyes. Then she lets go of Reilly's head and reaches into the box. "Let's hand the rest of these out, Riles. Before somebody tries to make me read one of them."

She would read every last word if it would serve pack. But that won't be necessary. There are others who will read. I brought her something different. I reach into my backpack for one of the few items still left at the bottom.

Kennedy eyes the old-school recorder and small tapes like they're foreign objects, which they probably are. Technology this ancient was obsolete before she was born. Which is part of the message. "These are from Adrianna. They're copies of the interviews she did during her thesis work."

A soft, awed inhale.

Which is exactly the right response. I've heard the tapes. They contain conversations with submissive elders in packs all over the continent about the qualities of good leadership. There was magic in hearing those old, wise voices, even for an engineer. And more magic in hearing young, sharp, insightful Adrianna Scott asking the questions.

I place the tapes into hands that tremble.

Reilly wraps his arms around my neck and squeezes hard. "That's a really good present."

He smells like honey and slightly sweaty sunshine. I let bear and man and the place where we meet drink in the pure pleasure of what he so easily offers. "Wait until you see how much purple yarn we stuffed into the plane."

His giggles shake his whole body.

I close my eyes. He's wondrous. All of them are.

I need to be so very, very careful.

3

DANIELLE

I shake my head as a gangly bear cub trips over his own feet and somehow manages not to squish Robbie and Mellie when he lands, mostly thanks to an enormous white polar bear paw that bats them out of the way. Mellie yips with glee and goes back in for a second swat.

Myrna chuckles beside me. "They're all going to sleep well tonight."

I try to imagine the schoolhouse with a polar bear in the pup pile. "I'm not so sure of that."

She eyes me over knitting needles that already have the beginnings of a new purple sweater underway. "How are you doing?"

She's the fourth person to ask me in the last hour. I wish they would stop. I have no idea how I'm doing. I just want to find someplace quiet and fix the video camera that's acting up again, or maybe read a page or two from one of the books that were in Ronan's box. One of them has a whole chapter on electrical wiring in capricious environments. I figure that hot pools full of shifters qualify. "Who's the sweater for?"

Myrna grins. "Robbie, I think. Although Rio batted his eyelashes at me and said he might know a guy who would wear it if it accidentally gets too big."

My throat tightens. This pack used to have a line that defined things that were silly and weak and female. For months, the big men of this pack have been casually stomping it into absolute oblivion. "Kenny had flowers in his beard yesterday."

Myrna's lips quirk. "So did Brown. Although he was casting some longing looks at Eliza's chainsaw while he was getting decorated."

He's the only one who can wield it better than she can—and as far as I know, he hasn't touched it in weeks. "Is any man in this pack ever going to use a power tool again?"

She snorts. "Not likely."

I wince as Mellie nearly gets squished again. I have no idea how toddler dominants survive to adulthood. My son was so quiet at that age.

The old sadness rushes in. He had his reasons.

I watch as a bear far larger than his father bumps into Reilly's shoulder with just enough force to topple him over—and then mimics a grizzly cub's theatrics when Robbie and Ebony and Mellie tackle him in unison.

My wolf recognizes the lesson. Hunting as pack. She grins as a small white wolf clambers up on his prize, neatly blending in against fur almost the same color as his own. Mellie can't quite get enough purchase to climb, but nobody moves to help her. There are also lessons in knowing what you can't do—and in figuring out how to wriggle up against a polar bear's nose and make him sneeze, instead.

The huge pile of fur suddenly turns into a chuckling man, one who catches Robbie as he tumbles out of the air. Lissa's son holds his pale hand up to Ronan's much darker one, a clear question in his eyes. Ronan grins. "Some of us match our fur. Some of us don't."

Robbie signs a rapid reply.

Reilly laughs. "He wants to turn purple like his new sweater."

The big rumble from the man wrapping them all up in blankets should scare my wolf, but Ronan's laugh feels like a wild forest—so open and free that it has no boundaries at all. He signs at Robbie as he answers. "That would make it a lot harder to hide in the snow."

Reilly's eyes widen. "You practiced."

"Of course I did. I want to talk to everyone in this pack. How else will I get you all to laugh at my stories?" Another signed sentence, this one with no verbal translation, that sends both boys into giggles.

I stare. "He learned sign language."

Myrna shrugs. "Looks like."

My brain feels like it stuck itself in a light socket. "He's only here for a few weeks."

She nods and keeps knitting.

I shake my head again. I'm good at knowing what's

reasonable and sensible, and this isn't either of those things. I know how much time Reilly spends learning new signs and how to string them together. "Ronan is here to get all of our systems ready for the main den building and the hot pools."

Myrna makes a noise at her knitting that I can't decipher. "Nope. That's your job."

That's an argument I've had a hundred times. I open my mouth to have it again, but nothing comes out. My wolf is too distracted. She's busy watching a bear tell a story to two boys, entirely with his hands.

KEL

Darn bear. I scowl at Ebony, who happens to be conveniently in the vicinity. "Can you follow what he's saying?"

She grins. "Nope. Bad angle."

We're both fluent in the hand signals that protect perimeters and order the right number of hot dogs for lunch. Kelsey and Robbie and Reilly and Ghost have taught themselves something else entirely.

So, apparently, has a polar bear. "He has a lot of stories that aren't appropriate for five-year-olds. In any language." The current one has Robbie in near hysterics.

Ebony chuckles. "Okay. You go tell him to stop."

I scowl at her again. "How is your wolf so calm about this?"

She rolls her eyes. "I try to only get riled once a day. That happened about ten seconds after his plane landed, so now I'm chill."

That's not precisely the truth, but it's not entirely a lie, either. My wolf got hit harder than anyone else's. Probably because I know exactly what my chances are if Ronan ever decides that he truly wants to get through me. I also know that I'd hand him a newborn pup in the middle of a war zone. Which is a whole lot of cognitive dissonance for one puny wolf brain.

My wolf snarls.

I keep my important parts well away from his teeth. He's definitely still a little riled.

Ebony finishes stacking the plates that were left out on the grass to dry after lunch. "He's your friend. Other than drowning him in pups and making sure he's well fed, how do we help him?"

Rio had a fancy, esoteric answer when I asked him the same question. Mine isn't nearly so frilly. "We trust him to help himself, and we chew on his ass if he screws up."

She grins and starts collecting forks. "That's about what I figured."

Troublesome beta. "Does Danielle know?" I've been watching her, but the women of this pack are really good at hiding things from prying eyes.

Ebony makes a face. "I don't think so. Does Reilly?"

That's a complication that's already setting fire to my kidneys. "No, but he might get there faster than his mom does."

"Maybe." Ebony's eyes are on the polar bear who's telling a story with his hands that's getting bigger by the second. "Ronan is locking it down."

My wolf agrees. "Yeah. He does that." He helped a soldier drowning in pain to do it, too. I'm just not sure it's the right answer this time around. Some things lock down more easily than others, and what I saw in his bear's eyes might accept a cage, but it won't stay alive in there.

Unfortunately, the other alternative involves letting a polar bear run some experiments and make some mistakes. Which is absolutely going to set the rest of my internal organs on fire.

Ebony drops two dozen forks into the container that will corral them until we need them again. "He's got plenty of work to keep him busy."

A beta wolf's favorite strategy. "Did anyone tell him about Fallon's idea to run pipes up to the ledge?"

Her evil grin is a thing of beauty. "I think they were saving that until he got here."

A tricky engineering problem should take some of the edge off of Ronan's bear. A team who thinks that he plans to be in charge will hopefully do the rest of the job.

Ebony squints at Ronan's hands. "Isn't that the sign for vodka?"

"Yup." I pick up a stray fork that she overlooked and add it to her container. This week has more than enough dangerous objects in it already.

RONAN

She watches. She's quiet, but not alone. Her fingers itch for the books that Kennedy casually piled right beside her, but she watches my fingers instead. And when I got to the part of the story where the silly polar bears discovered jars of jam instead of the bottles of vodka they expected at the end of their treasure hunt, her eyes gleamed with a laughter that I badly wanted to hear.

She is not meant to be so quiet, I think.

I keep my gaze on Robbie's hands as he asks whether Myrna puts vodka in my special jam. I worked hard on my signing these past weeks up in the Arctic, but I haven't had nearly as much practice at reading them, and a polar bear knows better than to let himself get distracted. So does a good engineer. A man trained by Adrianna Scott to be a good packmate is a different matter, however.

He knows how to adore two boys and still let the data of pack seep into his soul.

Reilly giggles as Myrna strings together a very respectable signed answer to the important question of whether vodka belongs in her jam jars. I nod my approval. Both are sacred, but the thought of mixing them makes my bear want to hide his head in a nice, comforting snowdrift.

Ghost drops down beside Robbie, ruffling his head and signing with her other hand. I watch intently. One-handed signing is not a skill I have, yet.

She slows her motions, repeats them. Adds fingerspelling for a word, then repeats the sentence again. Reilly copies her motions, angling his body so that several packmates off to the side can see better. Robbie grins and fires back a reply I can't follow as the new signs make their way around the pack, one to the next, with repetition and careful corrections and pleased smiles from the knitters.

There are a lot of them this morning. I need to order up another plane's worth of purple yarn. Fortunately, I have a lot of willing Whistler Pack minions—and they really like purple.

A motion to my left catches my bear's eye. Someone in the trees, straining to see, but not wanting to leave the shadows. They smell vaguely of Kelsey and banana muffins.

I hold up my big left hand and sign Ghost's original sentence. She notices and repeats it. I try again, fixing the small error I made. She shoots me a quick smile as she takes the same basic structure and uses it again, changing one of the signs in the middle.

Robbie freezes, his eyes intent. A wolf ready to learn.

Reilly carefully copies the new sign. Hayden and Lissa are the first to pick it up this time. They bounce it to Danielle, whose graceful, sturdy hands move into a beam of light so the wolf in the shadows can see.

She smiles at me cautiously. One hand quickly fingerspells. *Cleve.*

My bear stills. I know of him. Grandfather. Ghost wolf. His favorite blanket is green and brown, and the new wool sweater Myrna will be making for him is orange with purple stripes.

I make slow, careful signs toward the trees. *Friend. Safe. No harm. I like muffins.*

Danielle looks down at her lap—but not before I see her smile.

A real one, this time.

RIO

I shake my head as Cleve inches a little closer to the big polar bear who just crash landed in his pack. His whole nose is sticking out of the trees as his wolf tries to learn the new signs.

My sentinel smiles. Signing started in this pack as a way to keep submissives and pups safe, and Kel built on that. We began turning them into something more for Robbie. Then Hoot saw Moon Girl signing a story to three ghost wolves on the big sunning boulders to the east of Moss Rock, and we began to understand just how much it might matter to this pack to have a language that can bridge the gap between spoken words and wolf howls.

I run through Ghost's first sentence a couple of times. My brain picks up new signs easily. It's not nearly as good at the dance of connecting them.

Ronan, who has clearly figured out the connecting dance, adds something in the middle of Ghost's new sentence that makes her snort with laughter. Robbie copies him solemnly, which just makes Ghost laugh harder.

I shake my head again. Ghost so very rarely lets herself be the center of attention, but she's no match for a polar bear who lives and breathes to see others take up space.

A generosity for which he is about to be richly rewarded.

Kelsey sneaks in under his arm, a pup who claims the center with no problem at all, but isn't on that journey now. Ronan's big hand strokes her hair as he adjusts her seat in his lap so Cleve has a better view of his granddaughter's graceful hands. Kelsey beams up at him, well pleased with her new accomplice. Then she stares straight into the shadows and places an order for more banana muffins. The ones with nuts and honey, because bears like those best.

Ronan turns to bear goop.

My sentinel snickers.

I tell him that he has a job to do, and it isn't watching Kelsey take over his duties. My eyes seek out the quiet wolf with video camera parts in her lap. When Ronan turns on the polar bear charm, he's awfully irresistible, and I want to make sure that Reilly's mama has all the energy and support she needs if resisting is on her agenda.

She isn't where I expect her to be, however. I keep the lines of my body casual as I search more diligently through the faces of my assembled pack. I don't want to ring alarm bells. Yet.

Kel's eyes join mine. So do Ebony's. Betas never need alarm bells to be audible.

When I finally find Danielle, tucked into the shadows of a big rock, it takes every bit of self-control I can muster not to bust up laughing. She isn't watching Ronan at all. Or messing with video-camera parts.

She's reading.

DANIELLE

Friend. Safe. No harm. I like muffins.

I'm trying to read the words on the page, because they're very interesting ones about the challenges of laying wiring that will survive the extremes of Canadian winters and the seasons that come in between them. I'm not succeeding. I keep seeing Ronan's hands, signing those simple words.

He's so not what I expected.

He notices the quiet ones and the ones who feel weak. He delights equally in Robbie's quick hands and my son's quick brain, and he very clearly spent dozens of hours before he got here teaching himself a whole new language just so he could make a couple of boys happy. He brought gifts that see right to the heart of each person they're for, including these books. Books from his personal bookshelves, I think. I saw his name, neatly printed, in the front of one of them.

Nothing inside me knows how to feel about that.

Friend. Safe. No harm. I like muffins.

I stroke the words on the page, just like Jade stroked her music box. I know better than to believe that all bears are the same. Brown is entirely different from my Reilly, and neither of them is at all like the man I walked away from nine years ago with my toddler son in my arms.

He was a bear who never would have begun a conversation by promising friendship and safety. A bear who never would have bothered to learn of the expertise of a scared wolf in the shadows, or grinned at a teenager who corrected his mistake.

I make a face at the words on the page. I don't know what to make of a man who has shown all of those things in less time than it's taken him to eat a couple of fish sandwiches.

Friend. Safe. No harm. I like muffins.

I sigh quietly. That he felt the need to introduce himself with those words is wonderful—and somehow also makes me sad. I saw my son spend the first ten years of his life trying to be a small bear. As big as he is, I think maybe that feeling lives inside Ronan, too.

My wolf snorts. She, for one, is glad of his manners. He maybe won't growl while he works like Brown does.

Silly wolf. The growl isn't the part of a bear that's dangerous.

My shoulders curl in. Always, the most dangerous part of a bear is what they do when they see softness.

She gently nudges my eyes back toward the big man sitting beside my son. She already knows what he does when he sees something small and weak and soft and scared.

Friend. Safe. No harm. I like muffins.

4

RONAN

I come around the bend in the path that Ghost set me on, and stop as I come face to face with the shifters I was seeking.

Judging from the alarm on their faces, they clearly weren't expecting me.

Danielle clears her throat. "We were just going over the plans for the hot pools one more time before we made a nicer copy for you to see." She tucks a wrinkled, taped, well-used roll of paper behind her back, along with the rest of my engineering team. "I'm sorry. We should have asked you to join us."

Indrani looks sheepish. The rest of them look ready to scoop up Danielle and her precious schematics and make a run for it.

If I let them do that, I'm quite sure that the sweet teenage beta who pointed me in this direction will make sure that I never see honey-glazed fish in my sandwiches ever again. "I would be very sad if you wasted your time making a fancy copy just for me. My schematics always look like the pups use them for tablecloths." Which is sometimes true.

Danielle's eyes fill with something that makes my bear grind his teeth. "They're hard to read. We made a lot of changes."

I nod agreeably, trying not to look like the ogre they're clearly expecting. "Of course you did. A good engineer's most important tool is her eraser."

Indrani sneaks me a grin. That was an acceptable answer.

Thank goodness for good-natured ravens. One who has clearly made friends with the rest of the team in her short time here, and that's going to make my job a lot easier. Once I figure out how to get a foot in the door, anyhow. I drag my eyes away from the schematics that I so desperately want to see and nod at the vista behind my huddled team. I can see hints of the hot pools, but not nearly enough. "Can I see the work site?"

Eliza looks scandalized. "It's covered in rock dust."

I feel like the engineering villain in a murder mystery. "Of course it is. I promise you, I'm a bear who knows how to take a shower after he gets dirty."

Glow and Indrani look at each other and snicker.

My bear huffs out an invisible sigh of relief. Two down, two to go. He bats his eyelashes at Eliza. She's a harder sell, but when he did that at lunch, she gave him an extra sandwich.

She rolls her eyes and hides a grin. "Sorry. It's just that we had it all cleaned up for you to see and then Brown showed up with a perfect rock for one of the cuddle seats. I only meant to sand it a little, but it got away from me."

I don't hide my grin. "I never have that problem. I'm a well-behaved engineer who never shows up for dinner covered in whatever project I'm working on."

Indrani giggles. "Liar." She elbows Eliza. "The second day I was at Whistler, he came to breakfast with yellow paint all over his hair and two of his fingers glued together."

I maintain proper bear decorum. "That wasn't my project. The pups were building racing cars. I just happened to be in the vicinity."

Eliza's lips quirk. "Did you glue any pups together?"

My reputation has somehow preceded me. "I got them unstuck before breakfast." I cast Danielle a cautious look. She deserves fair warning. "Pups and cubs who play with me sometimes get a little messy."

She studies me with something that looks almost like sadness in her eyes.

My bear squirms. Whatever I did to put that look there, I need to fix it.

I tell him to wait. To watch and learn. I don't know nearly enough about her, yet, and I want to be granted that privilege. Slowly, with every step of the way being one that she chooses.

She finally offers me a faint, lopsided smile. "Good."

I stare. That wasn't the answer I was expecting. Which means I've somehow underestimated her already.

Eliza shoots me a look that carries hints of sympathy and approval. "You make as much of a mess with the pups as you want. They're washable, and Reilly could use a little mussing."

Danielle snorts, far easier with her friend than she is with me. "You didn't have to get the fingerpaint out of his fur last week."

My bear's ears perk up. He likes painting.

I chuckle. I don't think he understands that he's going to be the canvas. "That will be easier in the winter. It flakes off quite nicely after it freezes."

Eliza's lips quirk. "Did they teach that in your fancy engineering classes?"

Not unless I'm setting the syllabus. "I learned that on my shifts in the Whistler Pack nursery. All pups who get covered in paint are sent outside to clean up. Swimming in the summer, rolling in the snow in the winter. Or playing with dry ice if Scotty happens to be around."

Four sets of eyes flash with interest.

I grin. Engineers, every last one of them. "I hear that there's more fish for dinner and I'm supposed to be catching some of it, so let's get started, shall we? Show me your hot pools, and then we'll take a look at the schematics."

I carefully don't look at Danielle as I say the last part.

Eliza elbows her. "If I have to show him my dust pits, I say that you let him see your drawings. Maybe he can help us figure out the corner that's got us stumped."

Indrani grumbles. "It didn't have us stumped until I opened my big mouth."

I look over at my intern. Thanks to an unexpected trip to the Arctic, she's spent more time in Rio's care than in mine, but my bear doesn't give up people entrusted to him that easily. Especially ones brave enough to show their vulnerabilities to help their team. "Tell me more about that."

She makes a face that shows both the teenager she was not long ago and the impressive young woman she's becoming. "Danielle had it sorted, but I thought one of the junctions didn't follow the rules that you and Ryder taught me, so I said something, and then it wasn't sorted anymore, but I think maybe she was right in the first place."

"You're the one who knows the proper ways of doing things," says Danielle staunchly. "We need to do this safely. It was good that you spoke up."

A leader who supports her team, even when she doesn't believe in herself. "Rules are useful, and a smart engineer knows when and how to break them. It sounds like you were having a useful and important conversation."

Two sets of eyes look at me suspiciously. Indrani's clear first—an intern who knows what it is to be mentored. Danielle can't quite get there, which runs tiny cracks through the glass encasing my bear.

I grab his ears just before he roars. That won't solve anything, and it will make people nervous and churn up a lot of dust. Instead, I step to the side and make room for

Glow, who hasn't said anything as she's herded us over to the pools.

Which are indeed dusty.

They're also magnificent.

I let my eyes roam, drinking in the genius of four women who know their pack very well and don't have the faintest idea just how many rules they've broken. My engineering brain catalogs all of it. I can see some fascinating places to poke my nose into, and a few tweaks to suggest. An extra drain here, a rock or two to buttress the concrete there.

But those can wait. The first act of this engineering team is not going to be one of documenting small, easily fixed errors. I let the wonder of the bear cub that I've never quite grown out of show in my eyes. "When do we add water?"

They all look at me like I've lost my engineering marbles.

It's water and rock. There aren't that many catastrophic things that can go wrong, and a polar bear can circumvent most of those by leaning on a few things to make sure that they're sturdy before the pups jump in. "We're engineers. We test things. So let's run some water in and figure out what we might need to fix."

A giggle squirts out of Indrani.

Good intern. I toss a grin in her direction. "I brought my swim trunks. And I bet that you know a few shifters who wouldn't mind getting wet in the name of science."

Eliza rolls her eyes. She thinks I'm a cute bear, even if I am a lot of work.

There's no way this team is afraid of work. Not given what I'm looking at. "This week is about making mistakes, remember?" I'm fine with making the first one, but this isn't it. I eye the two members of my team I haven't won over, yet. "Have you got a pipe from the hot spring that you can temporarily run over this way?"

Danielle exchanges a look with Glow that is clearly weighing their options—and my sanity. "Maybe. If we take the showers offline for a bit."

Glow wrinkles her nose.

I know how to bribe a pipes specialist. "I brought a blow torch. That should speed things up. And a few specialized fittings with valves that can be controlled by a phone app that Scotty designed."

Danielle sighs as Glow's eyes light up. "Did you also bring spares for all of those fancy parts in case we break them?"

I manage to smother my bear's roar of delight. "I hear that you're really good at fixing things." I do indeed have spares, and an extra blow torch, but those seem like unnecessary details to add. I very much like the story that's forming without them.

Indrani eyes the beautifully arranged and contoured rocks that will be a set of cascading soaking pools. "It will take us a few hours to get the water over here, right? We could maybe have a puddle for the pups to play in by sunset."

My bear wriggles his ears. Good intern.

Danielle groans. "Don't say that out loud or someone will hear you."

"Too late." Rio unveils himself from whatever cloak of invisibility he was using to sneak up on us. "Are we swimming?"

I eye him, curious about why a sentinel has come to mess with my team's delicate first steps. "The smallest pups might have enough water to swim tonight. You'll need to wait until sometime tomorrow."

He doesn't look at all discouraged by that information —or in doubt that the pools will hold water, and he's a very decent engineer under the gummy-bear thief. "What do you need?"

Danielle's squeak of protest has five heads swinging in her direction.

She doesn't look at me. She stares at Rio, a silent plea in her eyes.

He smiles. "A hot soak sounds pretty good to me."

She scowls fiercely, which tells me just how thoroughly the big, black wolf of death has earned the respect and trust of his new pack. "If we're really lucky, you might get to soak your big toe. Then a pipe will burst and the pups will all be covered in mud and the showers will be offline and maybe then you'll finally remember that we're amateurs and the engineer who's come to help us hasn't even looked at the plans, yet."

Oh, yes. This is a very good story.

Rio grins at me. "Lazy bear."

Troublesome wolf. One who knows his job in helping a very good story to form. "If a pipe bursts, we can turn it into a temporary water fountain. The pups will like that just fine."

His eyes glint with amusement that he mostly manages to hide before he offers Danielle an innocent shrug. "That sounds like a reasonable idea to me."

She snorts. "Says the man who thinks that wolf packs should have pet bunnies and orange gummy bears are a vegetable."

My bear rolls over on his back, enchanted. "The green ones do taste a little bit like broccoli."

Indrani elbows my ribs. Which she has to work hard at—her elbows can barely reach my ribs. "Mikayla makes spicy green beans that I bet you'll love. Now can we stop talking about vegetables and go play with all the new toys you brought and run ourselves a water supply?"

Easygoing, cheerfully reckless interns are the very best kind. I wrap an arm around her head. Carefully. Ravens are more fragile than most shifters. "Someone point me at the pipe pile. I'll find some assistants and start lugging them into place."

Indrani twists her head to look up at me quizzically.

I wink at her and stay quiet.

Eliza studies me, long and hard, and then she dusts off her hands. "I'll show him the pile. Glow, do you want the fat silver ones for most of the pipe run, or the black ones?"

Glow tips her head side to side a few times and finally signs. *Silver*.

Trickier to manage, but better suited to the job at hand, and she's not showing any doubt. Good.

Four heads turn to look at Danielle. My bear joins them.

She scowls, but she's already thinking. "We can tap in at the heat exchanger. I'll just need a minute to get the wiring out of the way."

She's not getting herself out of the way that easily. "The smart valves in the joinery that I brought will need wiring. And a satellite signal, if you happen to have one available."

Rio manages not to roll his eyes.

Silly sentinel. I always bring toys to bribe engineers.

Danielle stares at the ground for far too long before she finally nods. "I can do that. Just let me know where everything needs to be hooked up."

I will not allow her to think herself unworthy in any way that I can prevent. "I think there are instructions in the valve boxes." I grin and toss my free arm over Eliza's shoulder. "While you and Glow take care of that, we'll go move pipes and find our swim trunks."

Indrani, still cuddled against my ribs, giggles. "Maybe we should put those on first. I think this is going to get wet."

It might. Which is a fine thing. One that needs to get started, so I do what bears do best and drag my two most cooperative teammates off into the woods, very sure that a sentinel is following us.

Eliza dares a quick glance back at Glow and Danielle. Then she looks up at me, a warning in her eyes. "If you let them fail, I will borrow Myrna's frying pan and see just what it can do to a polar bear's skull."

Rio snickers behind us. "Ronan, meet Eliza, the most submissive wolf in this pack."

I grin, very pleased with the story thus far. "In that case, remind me not to make any of them mad."

Eliza's eyes shutter. "Glow and Danielle are my friends."

My bear names several very specific things he'd like to do to the idiots in her past who didn't respect her properly.

I suggest he start with not adding himself to that list. "Have I given them a task beyond their skills?"

Her eyes clear some. Cautious. Thoughtful. "No."

She's a smart, straightforward wolf. I like her very much. "Do you have suggestions on how I can help them to succeed?"

She blinks.

I smile as gently as I can. "I don't know them very well, yet. You do."

She takes a deep breath. "Send Shelley to help Glow. She'll do fine as long as her wolf stays steady. For Danielle, go see her after she's taken everything apart and she's starting to hook it back up. Tell her what she's done wrong. Not a whole pile of criticism or anything, but she won't believe you if you just point out the parts she got right."

Moral support for one teammate. Gentle, specific mentoring of the other once she's had a chance to develop a plan in solitude. Excellent, easily executed advice. I nod at the wolf who gave it. "Thank you. For your insight and for being willing to share it with me."

Something in her straightens.

I wrap my arm back around her shoulders. I haven't

figured out all the inner workings of my new team just yet, but some things are obvious. The pipes are Glow's. The wiring and the overall plan are Danielle's. The enthusiasm and helping hands are Indrani's, and the hot pools are Eliza's. "We're going to fill your pools with water today."

She makes a sound so full of doubt and hope. "Maybe."

I grin and keep walking. I don't need to bother with trying to convince her.

I'll let the first pup splashing in the first puddle do that.

5

HAYDEN

Darn bears who arrive with a bang and leave mud all over my den.

I shake my head as Reilly and Hoot trot past us carrying shovels. They're following Kennedy, who's pushing a wheelbarrow half full of pea gravel. "Promise me that no teenagers will get encased in concrete today."

Ronan's cheerful chuckle shakes the ground under our feet. Heads all over camp lift up and grin at him like he's a very cute bear. "I don't think we're making any concrete. It wouldn't have time to set before we fill the pools."

Trust a bear to ignore the point of a rhetorical question. I elbow him, mostly in case he needs it. I know that he's hanging out with me because he's trying to keep himself from peering over Danielle's shoulder while she plays with the really fun stuff. He already carried every pipe that we have over to the hot pools.

He'll have plenty of volunteers to help him carry most of them back to the supply pile tomorrow. This pack has no problem doing things the long and winding way, especially when they're getting serenaded by bear stories as they work.

The banana muffins with extra honey probably didn't hurt, either.

Ronan scans the den as far as he can see, which is a lot of it from this vantage point. "You use a lot more passive security than Whistler does."

It's not judgment in his voice—it's slightly desperate curiosity from a bear who needs something comforting to do and finds that in some of the same places as Kelvin Nogues. Ronan isn't a soldier, but he's an apex predator. One who chose friendship over power, but some instincts don't get easily laid to rest, and protecting home turf is definitely on that list.

I survey our new den through his eyes. It's a nightmare of ways to get in—or it would be if they couldn't all be easily watched from a couple of convenient high perches. Which most ground-dwelling shifters would overlook, but Ronan spends way too much time hanging out with the Whistler Pack security crew to be that foolish. "Kel tried getting past our lookouts when we first set up the inner perimeter. He failed."

Ronan's eyes widen fractionally. "You have some very sharp-eyed sentries."

My wolf preens.

I sigh. He forgets how they acquired those skills. "I spent the first couple of weeks here thinking we were desperately short of teeth and claws. Then Kel pointed out the obvious. You can probably talk Ebony into putting you on the ground-patrol rotation if you want, but this den is largely guarded by its submissives, and they're damn good at their jobs."

A slow smile. "You're also very good at yours."

I lean against his shoulder. "Didn't expect that, huh?"

He snorts, but he leans into my weight, letting me offer him the comfort of a wolf. "You've been a leader waiting for your pack to find you since you were ten years old."

Darn bears and their penchant for mythology. "I was an overgrown juvenile with an arrogant wolf and some really patient mentors."

A dimple quirks in his cheek. "Is that how you're spinning it?"

It is, and a bear doesn't get to alter every story to suit his liking. "Are you going to ignore your new engineering team all day?"

He sighs heavily. "They mostly don't need me."

I imagine Scotty and Rio already told him that. "Of course they don't. You've been neatly feeding them help through Indrani for weeks."

He surveys the shifters below us who are throwing together a dinner that can be eaten while optimistically watching *very* big bathtubs fill. "I've been teaching her as I can. She's got a quick mind and a good eye for detail."

Professor bear. "She knows that she's your conduit.

She's done a good job of pretending to be a cheerful intern who just happened to know something useful about whatever they were trying to get sorted, but I don't think anyone actually believed her. Just so you know."

He smiles. "There are a few tricks I can show them, but mostly they just need to trust what they already know. Eliza was born to work with rocks. She's got a feel that can't be taught, and she bosses her crew around like a wolf who knows right down to her bones that she's valued by her alpha."

This conversation doesn't get to be about me. Even if he's absolutely right about some of the more annoying aspects of what wolves need from their pack leadership to be able to thrive as their full selves. "Glow doesn't ask many questions, but she watches."

He grins. "Shelley was asking the questions. Glow learns with her hands."

He spent almost an hour with the two of them while the rest of us cleaned the dust off a lot of really big rocks. Which seemed like something that would have been easier to do once the water showed up, but Eliza had other ideas, and smart alphas don't argue with submissives who have that particular look in their eyes. "Glow might need to head out to the woods for a bit. She's spending more time at the den lately, but her wolf gets shaky if she pushes too hard. It's good that you're signing with her. Talking shuts her wolf down faster."

A faint smile. "She left on a run with Ebony after we finished the last of the tricky joins. If I miss any other cues, please throw one of those very annoying pinecones at my head."

He's about as annoyed by the pinecones as I am when Robbie wakes me up with nose kisses. I study him out of the corner of my eye and contemplate the one member of his engineering team that he's carefully not talking about. Which is a line that an alpha might respect, at least for a day or two. Sadly for Ronan, I'm also his friend. "Are you okay?"

His shoulders hunch a little. "Yes."

I bump against him. Wolf-speak at bear volume. "Your bear got hit by lightning. Don't be an idiot."

He sighs. "I will do my best."

Fuck. If he's misunderstanding me that badly, he's not nearly okay. "I meant that you shouldn't clam up and try to be a tough guy. Don't make me send Lissa to pry out all of your secrets." I probably will anyhow. She's frighteningly good at it, and she's ready to die for the bear who spent his unexpected Arctic vacation learning her son's new language.

His smile is tinged with the wild generosity of spirit that made my mother give a gangly polar bear a chance—and with sadness. "She is exactly what I would have wished for you. Robbie, too."

The sadness claws at me. It pulls out words that aren't wise. Ones that might throw chaos at my pack. "Be yourself. Let her see you. You never know what might happen."

His chuckle is real and shakes the ground under our

feet again—and it's somehow still fragile. "You haven't seen my new swim trunks."

The alpha worries. The friend lets him deflect. For now. "I'm sure they'll sear my eyeballs." Which won't stop anyone in my pack from seeing his soft heart. The shifters of this pack have all met evil, and it somehow means that they all see right through Ronan's scary parts.

He waves down at Kelsey and signs something about his honey-berry-bar requirements for the night.

She giggles up at him and shakes her head.

He gives her a bigger number.

She considers, her head tilted like Fallon when she thinks. She shakes her head again, new giggles already working their way up from her belly.

Ronan makes a face and doubles his first number.

She grins and dashes off. My wolf watches her go, the wise young pup of his pack who isn't letting a polar bear be small—and hopes like hell he won't ever have to say differently.

DANIELLE

I try to spit the red wire out of my mouth, but not the black one, and end up landing them both in the mud instead. I make a face and collect them up. This part could really use an extra pair of hands, but I have everything spread around me and my brain isn't ready for help just yet.

Glow is as happy as a clam with her fancy new fittings and a blow torch that made her sigh with delight. I can't get there. I'm too worried. Too sure that I'm doing this wrong, which is silly. We're just running a few temporary pipes and wires to a new location, and we do that all the time.

I contemplate my muddy wires and sigh. There are so many feelings swirling around inside me, and they're making it hard to think.

My wolf mutters. She thinks that chewing on a nice wire or two would help immensely.

I roll my eyes. I already had that conversation with Mellie. Some of the cables are fat and pretty and just the right size for pup teeth.

My wolf scowls and tucks her nose under her tail. *Not a pup.*

She isn't, but she isn't helping me feel like a grown-up, either. I've worked hard these last few months to find my feet. I want to be mad at a polar bear for pushing me right back off them again, but this isn't his fault, either, not one little bit. There's a mess of history and insecurity tangling inside me, and I can't seem to get it sorted any better than these wires.

My wolf casts a pointed look at my hands and snorts.

I follow her gaze and sigh again. I've managed to get everything but the black wire connected while I wasn't paying attention, and I'm not sure that one is actually necessary. I reach for my electrical tape. I should at least wrap it and tuck it out of the way so that Mellie doesn't nip at something that will make her fur stand on end.

A hand motions near mine. "That's not necessary. That wire won't be live unless we connect it to something, and it looks like you've got a plan that won't do that."

My cheeks go instantly hot and itchy. "I guess I messed up somewhere."

A long silence as a big man crouches down on the other side of my jumble of wires and pipes and junction bits. "Your hands don't think so."

They don't, which is maybe a lot of the problem. I scowl at the black wire. It's the easiest thing to blame for how I'm feeling.

Ronan clears his throat. "Is it okay for me to be here?"

He says the words easily enough, but my wolf hears something different. The invisible sound of silent, futile wishing. My eyes come up. I know that sound. I heard it from my son for far too many years. "Of course it is. You came to help us."

He shrugs, his gaze carefully aimed over my shoulder. "If you're uncomfortable having me join you, or you would rather work alone, I can go elsewhere."

The careful formality of his words slices through the tangles inside me. He doesn't know how to do this, either. I don't know why, and I don't know how a few pipes and wires could possibly be troubling a bear who has three engineering degrees and teaches classes at the big university down south, but this is my pack and he's an honored guest and I want him to feel comfortable here. I take a steadying breath and hold up the black wire that doesn't seem to have a home. "Care to tell me what we do with this?"

He offers me a lopsided grin. "Cut it off?"

Silly bear. One who clearly isn't going to give me the answer. Scotty and Bailey are like that when they're helping Reilly to learn.

I take a deep breath. I want to learn, and it's okay to make mistakes. Even if neither of those things feel very comfortable at the moment.

I pick up the instructions and set them back down. I'll study them later, but they're just going to tangle up my brain again. I put my hand on the top junction box, the one that will re-attach to the heat exchanger once I've got this sorted. "Everything's straight up here, I think." I look at the bear sitting calmly on the other side of my mess. "Would you mind double-checking my connections? I don't want to electrocute a pup."

His lips quirk. "You're talking to the guy who accidentally glues them together, remember?"

My wolf snickers. She liked that story. "I figured that part was bear exaggeration."

He sighs, just like Reilly does when he's feeling bashful. "Nope. One hundred percent true." He waves a hand at my junction box. "Besides, if I look at that, I'm going to beg for a tour of your whole heat-exchange system, and then we won't get the pools filling by moonrise and Hayden will chew on me for making the pups cry."

I aim a wry glance up at the darkening sky. "Bears maybe shouldn't make promises like that when their team hasn't done this before."

His eyes meet mine, dark and incredulous. "You're the ones who built a heat exchanger out of spare parts from the hardware store."

My cheeks get hot and itchy again. "Those were all we had." The one HomeWild sent for the school wasn't big enough to add the showers or the cook shack.

He throws up his arms in an excellent imitation of a Mellie tantrum. "Of course they were. And your system is still so ridiculously brilliant that half of the nerds I know want to kidnap it. Scotty plans to enter the damn thing into an engineering innovation contest. Has he even told you that, yet?"

I stare at the bear with fire in his eyes. Fire that should probably have me running, because I've seen that kind of fire before and it was never good.

But I can also hear the invisible sound again.

The silent, futile, wishing one.

RONAN

If I don't get my bear under control right this minute, Hayden is going to do more than chew on me—except it isn't my bear waving his arms around. It's the human part of my soul. I yank on his ears. He needs to behave. *Now*. "I'm sorry."

Danielle stares at me like I'm a stray black wire she can't quite figure out.

I close my eyes, chagrined and ashamed. "I'm usually

better at this. And far less obnoxious. I apologize. Profusely."

A whiff of surprised breath. "You need to stop that, you know."

My eyes fly open.

She shrugs, her hands starting to work on her wiring again. "We're not fragile."

Chagrin morphs into embarrassed regret. I haven't taken this many wrong steps since my first days in Whistler Pack, and at least back then I had an excuse. "I know that. You still don't deserve blustery Ronan." Even if she's handling him exceedingly well. Which has my bear's absolute attention.

She snorts, her hands competently assembling the work in her lap. "Have you met Brown?"

He came to find me, with warning in his eyes and a rough growl that made Kelsey giggle and pat his knee. I pick up one of the secondary junction boxes and try to steady the mess inside me. "Do you mind if I work on this one? I do better if my hands are busy." I wait for her eyes to look up. My bear already cherishes the delight that sometimes appears in them when I surprise her. "It's why I like to knit."

Her face softens. "Reilly loves all the bright yarn you send him."

I soak up the gift in her words and connect a wire to its downstream cousin. "Adrianna stopped yelling at the crafting guild about our storage issues sometime last month. It's been an excellent deal all around."

She reaches out a hand toward my wiring and pulls it back again, biting her lower lip.

I pause what I'm doing, yanking my brain back from its gooey consideration of brightly colored yarn and wolves with lovely smiles. It doesn't take long to work out the issue once I'm paying enough attention. She's changed the default wiring running to the secondary boxes. A sensible upgrade if this were going to be permanent. Which is interesting, or it will be if her assistant doesn't cross his wires. "Oops."

She watches me as I switch things up to match her changes. I keep my hands calm as I work. It's far harder than it should be. "I like the way you think."

Wary, uncertain eyes.

Fuck. "About wiring. This is a good change. One I've been trying to convince the plumbing company to make. Your opinion will add some weight."

Startled eyes.

I gesture at the far more complicated box in her hands. "Did you make any other changes?"

Her eyes go back and forth between my hands and hers. "Just ones that will let me make alterations at the junction instead of at a control panel." Her cheeks flame again. "I haven't built one of those for the heat exchanger yet."

No wonder Scotty wants to kidnap her and all of her creations. "No smart engineer puts in the control panel until the very end. Just imagine who might come along and start turning knobs and flipping switches."

The uncomfortable heat in her cheeks eases some.

"It's easy enough to make manual changes for a while. Besides, this heat exchanger is only temporary. You're going to help us build the real one."

Sure, I will. Right after I move to the rainforest and start eating crunchy bugs for breakfast. I hold up my correctly wired junction box. "Are we ready to hook this thing up and test it?" The pups will be getting restless, and so will their alpha.

She looks down at her hands, apparently surprised to discover that everything has been neatly assembled.

It takes an act of supreme willpower not to stick my nose in her lap so that I can see everything she's done. "Glow and Indrani ran some water through the pipes to test the welds. They should hold so long as we keep the water pressure under control." If not, we'll have some unauthorized water fountains. Which likely won't upset anyone except for the women who did the welding.

Danielle's lips quirk. "How did you get Glow to put down your blow torch?"

It stopped being mine about three hours ago. "I'm not sure if she has, yet. Last I saw, she was showing Kennedy and Robbie how to turn forks into spoons."

Danielle stares at me, wide-eyed.

I grin. "Hayden was supervising."

She rolls her eyes.

I grin bigger. He found himself such a good pack. "Kel is supervising Hayden."

She makes a wry face. "That might work."

I maybe won't tell her what Reilly's doing. I hold up my pair of secondary junction boxes. "These should do.

We can add another one in the morning if we need to balance the loading."

She looks at the gear in my hands for a very long time.

I don't think I messed them up, but something is on her mind. "What are you thinking?"

She sighs—and doesn't quite meet my eyes. "You're so easy with this. With letting us run an experiment and seeing what happens and not worrying about the details." Another pause. "I was just wishing that I was better at doing that."

I open my mouth to give the engineer's answer. The mentor's answer. The very fallible human being's answer rises up and shoves them aside instead. "I worry."

She considers me with the same careful look that she used to study my junction boxes.

I smile a little and offer her the rest of the fallible human being's answer. "But not about this. There's not much that can go wrong tonight that can't be fixed by a polar bear sitting on it."

Surprise lands in her eyes a heartbeat before her laughter bubbles up like an unauthorized water fountain.

Which is when the pups find us.

6

RIO

I pause in the shadows, drinking up the magic of this night. There are only a couple of inches of water in the smallest hot pool, but the pups are already in heaven and so is the big polar bear lounging on the edge keeping a watch over the beginnings of our moonlight soak.

Reilly looks up at the woman of the hour, joy gleaming in his eyes. "It works, Mom—it really works."

She smiles at him as she fiddles with the wiring closest to the hot pools. "For now."

He grins. "If it breaks, Ronan gets to sit on the first water fountain and I get to sit on the next one." His glance over at the lounging polar bear is full of the kind of hero worship that would terrify me if I didn't know every spiral of that bear's DNA.

Danielle's eyes follow her son's gaze and then slide back to the work in her hands.

My sentinel watches with interest. I heard her laughing earlier, and I saw her work alongside Ronan to get the wiring next to the pools set up. Her competence didn't surprise me. That she allowed her diffidence to be chased away by a polar bear's growl absolutely did. I would normally attribute that to Ronan's excellent team-building skills, except there's diffidence in him, too.

My sentinel approves.

An elbow lands in my ribs, none too gently.

I look down at the pregnant raven who frequently dwells in our shadows. She's got a fluffy towel in her arms and bare legs poking out from her voluminous sweater. "I don't think the pool is quite deep enough for grown-ups, yet."

She grins. "It will be."

Her raven seeks warmth like my wolf is drawn to joy. "Is Ben still doing his water dance?" He's in charge of keeping marauding teenagers from attacking the pipes running down from the hot spring. Or something like that. With Dorie leading the water pirates, it could have turned into any number of kinds of improvisational chaos by now.

Our pack does not have boring elders.

Fallon snickers. "It turns out that Dorie has an aversion to small wolves who have very good aim with their sand buckets."

I don't ask. Fortunately, making sure that Mellie doesn't turn into a holy terror is Kel's job, not mine. I just enjoy the easy amusement in my feathered packmate. She still has days when being at the den is hard, but that just makes her a really good role model for the rest of us who sometimes struggle. "Is there anything I should be doing?"

She snorts. "Nope. Cori is fierce when she's in charge of the troops."

I grin. Nobody messes with a pregnant wolf who might still puke on them if she gets mad. Which means the hot pools are well supplied with snacks and tea and bedding for whoever might want to try to get some sleep tonight.

I don't think that's going to be a very big group.

Ravi starts strumming off in the distance, and bright eyes turn in his direction. Someone set out glow lamps, so I can't actually see him, but I can feel his happiness as he picks out the notes of our collective mood. It's a tune that's pretty and lively and full of collective anticipation, and the lounging polar bear swings his head happily in time to the beat.

Kelsey catches Ronan's nose long enough to give him a big kiss. She signs something about oceans and swimming and sharks and a water fight and then runs back to the edge of the pool that's slowly filling.

Robbie, who's sitting right in the middle of the growing puddle, looks up at her and beams pure bliss into the universe.

Kelsey shimmies down a rock to join him, clad in a bathing suit that somehow manages to glow, even in the dark. Kel catches her as she lands, mostly to give himself something to do. Jade yanks on his free arm, complacent in her certainty that he can easily handle two things at once. "My want more water."

Danielle shakes her head from the pool's edge. "It's coming, cutie. Remember the story about how long it takes a river to fill the ocean?"

Jade scowls, clearly not a fan of that particular tale. "My Reilly make it go faster."

Reilly has possession of the app that controls the pipe valves. Sadly for impatient pups, he's under strict orders not to blow anything up.

Which doesn't stop him from shooting his mom a pleading look.

Danielle shakes her head.

Robbie sidles up next to Reilly and signs something that I don't quite catch, but it's clearly a big wish with a bow on top.

Danielle sighs at the two of them—and then glances at the lounging polar bear.

Ronan keeps cheerfully bobbing his head to the music.

My wolf rolls his eyes. Troublesome bear.

Kennedy and Hoot splash into the water behind Robbie, copying his signing and the wistful, hopeful look on his face. Kel grins and joins them.

Danielle signs a long, fast, exasperated response that warns of explosions, flooding, and a whole lot of mud to clean up in the morning.

Her audience looks delighted by every single one of those possibilities.

The polar bear keeps bobbing his head to the music.

Myrna and Shelley lean against each other and snicker.

My sentinel thinks that maybe he should do something, but he doesn't have any idea what that might be, and there's no room left in the puddle for him to join Robbie's signing brigade.

Danielle mutters under her breath and looks around for her team.

Glow shrugs from her spot under a tree where she's listening to Ravi and holding a very dopey Braden. The pup is cuddling her new blow torch on his way to sleep. Indrani sticks her head out from a high ledge. She waves a pirate sword in one hand and a fork in the other and casts a wordless vote for flooding and explosions. Eliza captures the fork and tosses it to Ghost, and together, they do a victory dance. Silently, so that they don't startle Braden.

Three team members acting very much like their fearless leader has this handled and they can keep going about their possibly questionable pack business without a worry in their heads.

Lissa sits down beside Danielle and pats her shoulder.

My sentinel approves. Lissa doesn't know a thing about wiring or water pressure or the kind of welding mistakes that can happen when beginners play with blow torches, but she knows all about walking with the needs of her own heart.

Danielle's wolf steadies.

I watch.

So does the polar bear.

Danielle takes a deep breath. Two. Then she meets her son's eyes and nods. "Dial it up, kiddo. Just one notch to start with. Send out scouts to make sure each weld is holding, and if they are, you can do two more."

Surprise flares in the polar bear's eyes.

Pride flares in Lissa's—and a challenge for the polar bear.

My sentinel grins. Good alpha.

Reilly's designated scouts scramble out of the pool, swords and forks abandoned as they follow the trail of pipes, looking for any signs of leaks or fountains or marauding invaders who might have stumbled across Kel's perimeter since dinner.

Kel doesn't join them, mostly because he has a small girl in a sunflower-yellow swimsuit sitting in his lap and looking up at him sternly.

I grin. The big, black wolf of death might need to take an extra perimeter shift tonight. Kel is always happiest in the water, and Kelsey Dunn knows it.

Ghost is the first scout back, signing at Robbie too fast for me to catch. It doesn't matter—the look on his face says plenty. Reilly picks up the sat phone that he carefully stashed well above the water line and taps a couple of times.

The water running out of the nearest pipe changes from a trickle to a steady flow.

Danielle holds her breath and keeps her eyes on the pipe trail.

The polar bear holds his breath and watches Danielle.

RONAN

I know how to make mistakes, and I know how to watch other people make them and give them a nice, squishy polar bear to land on if they haven't learned to roll right back up to their feet after a mishap.

This feels different. I don't want this to be a mistake. I want the wolf of the lovely smile and quick, steady hands to find victory in her hunt.

Owl hoots emerge from the dark, and Reilly pumps his fist into the air. "Pipes are holding, captain."

The fond look in Danielle's eyes would have brought me to a standstill at eleven years old. The bear cub on the receiving end hardly notices. Which is as it should be. He has never doubted that his mother loves him. I am fiercely glad for him.

I watch as he carefully dials up the pressure in the pipes, the pups cheering as the flow into the pool increases, and then increases again.

He dutifully sets the phone aside and hoots at the invisible water sentries. The return calls aren't ones we use in Whistler Pack, but judging from the happy grins, all is well up the pipe trail. Reilly opens his mouth, perhaps for another report to his captain, but gets cut off as a white pup dashes through the water and shakes spray all over everyone in striking distance.

There's a gangly bear cub in the water a second later.

Kel, who is a smart beta, holds up Kelsey so that she takes most of the incoming. Hoot promptly dumps a bucket of water on his head, which, judging from his reaction, didn't come from the nice, warm water running into the pool. He sets Kelsey on her feet and turns, vengeance in his eyes.

Which is when Hayden arrives, making more joyous noise than all of the pups put together.

My bear quivers. He wants to play. He knows he can't. He gets too big when he plays. They aren't used to him here, yet.

Cold water splashes against his face.

I stare at the teenager who just tossed the contents of her toy bucket at an apex predator.

Kennedy cackles, baby-alpha delight in her eyes. "There's more where that came from, lazy pirate. Get thee away from our water treasure, or your hide will be forfeit."

My bear licks the dribbles off his nose. Good water. Tastes like fish.

"Ha." Myrna brandishes a bent sword in my direction. "You can't scare a polar bear with water, Kennedy Jones. What kind of pirate are you, anyhow? You have to threaten his jam treasures."

Kennedy snickers. "I thought *he* was the pirate."

Myrna shrugs and adjusts her eye patch. "Somebody's the pirate, and there will be no jam for any of them until this pool is full of water right up to my eyebrows. Hear that, head-engineer matey?"

It takes me a second to realize that she's not talking to me.

Danielle's reluctantly amused laugh is music to my bear's ears. "You're not very tall, so that might happen by morning. It would go faster if you could keep my son from splashing the water out of the darn pool as fast as we're putting it in there, though."

"Right." Myrna holds up her sword again, an avenging angel about to make a rather bedraggled proclamation. "Reilly Arkadian, guardian of the pipes and eater of honey, leave some water for the rest of us to play with. Captain's orders."

The grizzly cub in the center of the splash zone pauses in his wreckage and looks around sheepishly.

My bear sends a pleading look to the captain.

She scowls at me—but the dimples in her cheeks tell a different story.

I watch her cheeks. The treasure I hunt lives in those dimples.

She blinks, once. Twice. Then she lets loose a sigh that would do a polar bear proud and waves a hand in the general direction of the satellite phone.

Indrani whoops and dives for it. A few seconds later, the rush of water out of the terminal pipes is audibly louder.

I don't look to verify and neither does Danielle. She just stares at some point off in the distance as the ever-present caution in her eyes wars with something deeper.

Something like the dimples, but more vast, seeking to find enough space on this dark night.

I watch. I have seen glaciers crack from such forces.

The touch of a sentinel brushes against my fur.

I growl. He will stay back. This is not his to do. It is hers.

Surprise from the big, black wolf.

My bear stands his ground. She will choose the time and space of her own cracking, or she will choose to stay attached to the cliff. Ice has its own majesty. It cannot be engineered and it should not be rushed. It is to be respected.

More surprise, and not from Rio, this time. From a sturdy gray wolf who somehow caught the edge of my answer to a bossy sentinel.

Her eyes glisten.

I nod with as much solemnity as a polar bear can manage.

Which is when a grizzly cub and a baby alpha decide that I've had enough time to be a lazy pirate and a torrent of water hits me right between the eyes.

DANIELLE

He looks so surprised. That's all I have time to think before Kennedy's wildly waving hose soaks my wolf and has her spluttering along with half the pack. Spluttering and looking around accusingly for whoever installed the unauthorized water source.

Indrani streaks through with Hayden hot on her heels and casts me a sheepish look. "My alpha made me do it, but don't worry, we tapped into the stream, not the heat exchanger." She gasps for breath and takes a sharp left into the fray. "Brown built us a pump. It's really cool."

It's not cool. It's freezing cold.

My wolf ducks as Kennedy takes aim again—and then a huge white paw smacks down on the hose and stops the flow of water in its tracks. A terrifyingly toothy grin, and then a second paw bends the hose and aims it straight at a baby alpha's nose.

Kennedy backs up, alarm in her eyes and a waterfall of giggles flooding up from her toes.

The polar bear flicks the hose.

My wolf spies shadows sneaking up on his blind side. She dashes in and cuts Ghost and Ebony off at the pass. Sneaky betas.

A squealing howl that says the hose didn't miss its intended target, and then I'm somehow in the middle of a water fight with a polar bear on my team and the rest of the pack on the other side.

Ronan's paws wield their endless supply of freezing cold water with alarming accuracy. I keep my eyes on the fragile, twisting hose that's the most vulnerable part of our weaponry. I have no worries about the pump. Brown doesn't build things that break.

Apparently, that's my job.

Kel tries another nefarious sneak attack that almost works, but a shadow slinks out of the dark and growls at him.

My wolf chuckles.

Grandpa Cleve has always believed that fights should be fair.

Hayden tries a frontal attack that results in a really wet alpha and most of the pack laughing so hard they can barely breathe. Ronan, smart enough to know who the biggest threats are, wraps the hose around Robbie and Hayden, and then aims the two of them and the hose nozzle they're wearing at Lissa, who stumbles backward into Kennedy and knocks them both into Reilly's lap.

Which is when I find out what it sounds like when a polar bear laughs.

Or rather—what it *feels* like, as every inch of Ronan shakes, from his gaping mouth to his paws to his fuzzy, adorable, oddly small ears.

The ground quivers, and so do the atoms of my wolf.

Pack responds in the only way that wolves know how to meet that level of contagious joy. Myrna's howl hits the sky right alongside Kelsey's, and Ravi's musical voice joins them a heartbeat later. Lissa and Hayden add the call of alphas, and a quiet, rusty howl joins in from the trees a moment later.

My heart sings. Cleve.

The elders speak, Myrna and Dorie and Tara responding in unison. Welcome to the one in the trees—and admonition. He will not stay away from the songs of pack so long, next time.

Rusty acquiescence.

More notes join our story. Innocent pup tales of hawks and berries that might be hidden under the wood pile. Teenagers finding their way. Grown-up hearts rejoicing in freedoms found and responsibilities gained and silly pups who can dream of berries and feathered friends.

My wolf seeks out the note that matters to her most.

Reilly's growling howl is bright with happiness, a bear cub who has found his place and his way to serve his pack and an older, wiser bear to idolize, and he doesn't remember the first time in his life when he tried that and it didn't work out at all.

Robbie's howl from right beside my son is a story accompanied by the movements of a wolf who knows that his body can say just as much as his voice.

Ronan rumbles just beyond them, low like Brown, but gentler, somehow. Softness, if softness came in the size of continents.

I tip back my throat, adding my voice to pack. There's an odd note in my howl. My wolf wrinkles her nose as she hears it, mystified. She didn't put it there. She doesn't mind it, exactly, but she doesn't know where it came from.

I swallow. I know what it is, even if she doesn't.

It's the feeling that was pressing against my ribs, earlier. It found a way out.

The first unauthorized water fountain of the night.

7

RONAN

I look up at the sun, still weak by soft southern standards, but more than enough for a bear born to long northern winters to see by. I've always loved the hours that come between night and day. They speak to my soul in ways that sharper light or its absence never have.

I wrap an extra loop of tape around a pipe join that would be holding perfectly well if an alpha hadn't tripped over it. That's the story I'm going with, anyhow. Hayden knows better than to get in the way of a good embellishment, and the wolf who actually tripped over it was carrying a sleeping pup at the time. A polar bear might have charmed her so that she didn't notice what her feet had kicked up.

Which worked out very nicely. I got a sweet kiss from a small boy who smelled of maple syrup and mischief, and Layla and Miriam got to be the inaugural occupants of the hot pool's cuddle seat.

That part isn't embellishment. I saw the photo that will grace the front page of the next edition of *GhostPack News*. I hope Reilly puts it out today. There are enough inquiring text messages on my phone to cover the walls of a den far larger than this one. This pack is loved well beyond its borders.

I tug sharply on the pipe join to make sure it doesn't need anything beyond a little reinforcing tape. Likely the weld would have held without my interference, but a bear needs to keep his hands busy, and my knitting basket had a pup sleeping in it.

My bear stretches his paws to the sky. He loves the crispness in the early morning air. Sleeping on a warm floor was disconcerting.

I roll my eyes. It was only for a couple of hours. He was all nice and cozy and snuggled in pups after telling them a bedtime story, and the mated pairs deserved a little more private time in the hot pools. There was nothing I could do about Myrna sneaking away from the schoolhouse with a very bearlike gleam in her eyes, but alphas who can't deal with elder tricks should just turn in their leadership badges.

I pick up my tape and tools and make my way along the pipes, looking for telltale signs of moisture or less obvious hints of stress. Another half day or so to completely fill the pools and we'll be able to turn down the flow. Then maybe I can convince my engineering team to show me the innards of the heat-exchange system they built.

I've been such a patient bear.

It was worth it, though. The hot pools are wondrous, even half-filled and with rather more cold water from the stream than the engineering team originally intended.

I grin. The mates cuddling in the pools last night didn't seem to mind.

My bear grumbles. He likes cuddling.

I roll my eyes. He's calmer this morning. For now, it's enough to be close to Danielle. To learn more of who she is. To enjoy her cautious smiles of victory and her tenacious guarding of his flanks. That was entirely unexpected. As was the assistance from the elder wolf in the woods. Two who believe in fairness, even for a silly polar bear with a hose.

A wolf steps out of the trees to join my quiet morning walk of the pipes. That doesn't surprise me. It does surprise me that I didn't hear her coming. I study the quiet teenager who has earned Kelvin Nogues's respect and a place in her pack's beta ranks. He says that she still isn't entirely comfortable with her badge of leadership, but she's absolutely wearing it this morning.

She watches my feet as we make our way in the direction of the heat exchanger. "You walk like Kel."

Interesting. "I should. He taught me most of what I know."

A faint smile. "Ivan is arrogant. You aren't."

I can't believe that the most feared bear of the north is

having casual and apparently charming conversations with the wolves of this pack. "I can be. So can you. We're just quieter about it."

Her eyebrows fly up—and then she pauses. Thinking.

Another faint smile. "Thank you."

A teenager who can understand the nuanced layers of a bear compliment. No wonder Kel likes her. "Have you come to help me or threaten me?"

She nearly trips over her own sneakers and casts me a rueful glance as she untangles herself. "Both."

Honest and complicated. I brought seeds for her garden. I will perhaps send more interesting ones, next time. "Both are appreciated."

She laughs quietly. "How can you say that before you even know what I'm going to say?"

I could probably write it out for her. "You care for your pack. Anything you say to me that furthers that goal is welcome."

A long silence. "Reilly talks like that after he's been video chatting with you."

Help and threat, both. "He's special to you."

A very teenage shrug. "He's in my baby pack."

He's a very fortunate cub. "So is Kennedy, and yet you didn't send her to make the threat."

She casts me a sideways look. "Do I need to?"

I snort. "I've been friends with Kel for almost thirty years. I know better than to underestimate submissive wolves."

She pauses. "You knew Kel, then. Before. And Hayden's dad."

The knives in those stories find their usual places in my ribs. "When I came to Whistler Pack, I was a very uncivilized bear. Adrianna agreed that I could stay, but it was the two of them who helped me with what I needed to learn to make that possible."

Fists pushed a little deeper into pockets. "That was Shelley, for me. And Bailey."

One I've met. The other is a legend I will seek out soon if she doesn't come to find me. "Then we've both been given truly fine gifts in our lives."

She looks up at me solemnly. "I want that for Reilly, too."

Blow landed with force and precision, little beta. "He hasn't had an easy life thus far. He deserves for who he is to be seen and encouraged and treasured."

She walks several more silent steps, weighing my words. Then she bumps against my arm.

My bear exhales a sigh of relief. Sisters can be fierce guardians.

I crouch down by a pipe join that doesn't need any attention, but my hands need to check, all the same. "Are you offering help and threat concerning Danielle, as well?"

Ghost's cheeks turn a little pink. "No. I figure Kel will probably do that."

"He will." I wait until she meets my eyes. "But he would have spoken for Reilly, too. It says something important that you got to me first."

Her lips quirk. "That I'm a nosy, annoying beta?"

I grin. That, too.

KEL

I glance over at the woman beside me, watching the same duo that I am. She isn't carrying her daddy's frying pan, but the weight of it is in her hand, all the same. "See? Beta wolves never sleep."

Myrna snorts. "When Reilly wakes up, he's going to write a story about last night, and somewhere in there he's going to put the real story together, because he's a very smart bear cub."

I'm surprised it didn't happen last night. It was right there to read in a polar bear's eyes. "I don't think there's anything we can do to prevent that."

Myrna hefts her invisible frying pan. "Does Ronan understand how badly Ghost could hurt him, or should I go add a few words?"

I roll my eyes. "I hear that some packs have mild-mannered elders who knit and help young wolves learn their manners."

She grins at me. "That sounds like the most boring job description of all time."

That's what I said about returning to civilian life. "Betas like boring. It lets us sleep at night."

A friendly elbow to my side. "You don't sleep. You should take a long, hot soak today and drink one of Wrinkles's teas and see if you can do something about that. We need you sharp for when your friend over there makes these next few weeks interesting."

I raise an eyebrow. "It might be Danielle who makes things interesting."

A thoughtful chuckle. "You're right. It just might."

Danielle handled Ronan just fine yesterday, and not by building a really big brick wall between herself and a dazzled polar bear. Which makes it a whole lot harder to guess how this is going to roll, and even more difficult to guess where a smart beta should be standing.

Somewhere he can't get squished by a polar bear, probably. Although I imagine an irate or scared or fascinated Danielle could make a fair number of things blow up, too. Which is why I'm lurking in the woods with our most troublesome pack elder. The one who walked over to the hot pools last night and handed out mugs of fertility tea, stroked Kenny's fur like a pup when he dreamed of his son in the dark, and is ready to go to war on behalf of her favorite bear cub this morning.

Troublesome and entirely indispensable. Especially if we've got a polar bear doing unnecessary pipe inspections.

CLEVE

I'm too old to believe in magic. I tell myself that as I breathe in the mists drifting up from the hot pools. I can see them properly, now that the sun has come up. This ledge is small, but it's got a good view.

I'll bring Rennie soon, if I can. She always loved the water.

The pools are empty. Wrinkles and Brown came for an early morning soak before they headed out to the far orbits. Now there's just Danielle, working on hooking up some wires to the glow lamps that the juveniles set out last night. The ones that help human eyes see in the dark. They annoy my wolf, but that didn't stop him from hanging out in the trees half the night, listening to pup laughter and teenage shenanigans and rumbling bear growls.

The big bear is nowhere in sight. I saw him earlier, inspecting the pipes. His scent is still here. It made Danielle scowl, but she wasn't afraid. My wolf isn't either, even though he should be. There's a terrible predator in our midst, and much of my family is the living and dead shards of the last time that happened.

I breathe in more of the magic mists. My wolf is not afraid—and when I went up to Rennie's caves this morning, she was outside waiting for the sunrise.

I move a little, trying to keep the warm spot on the rocks under my gimpy hip. A hot soak would help. Maybe one night when the pools are empty. In the meantime, I'll keep my eye on the big bear who plays with the pups and looks at me with gentle eyes and talked to himself as he left a small gift down by Danielle's wires this morning.

I didn't see what it was—but it made Danielle scowl harder.

I won't say what happened after that. An old wolf knows how to keep a secret or two.

RONAN

"Do you think we filled enough buckets?" Reilly surveys a row of them almost as long as he is tall, all chock full of fish. They won't be wasted. Brown was already firing up his smoker when we left.

I shake out my bear's fur before I shift. He's had a really good morning. The streams in Whistler Pack territory have strict limits on how many fish can be caught so that we don't rob any of our neighbors of food or the streams of their ability to continue to be fruitful. The same rules apply up here, but there are a lot more streams and far fewer neighbors. "We can always come back for more tomorrow if we don't have enough."

Reilly shakes his head absentmindedly, still counting buckets, or maybe fish. The cub is an excellent mathematician. "We could go someplace else. Wrinkles says that we have to give each stream time to recover from having a bear terrorize their fish."

I already know better than to cross Wrinkles. "That's wise. It probably gives the fish time to get lazy again, too."

His grin is quicksilver fast. "That won't matter for your bear. You're really good at fishing. So is Brown. I'm still learning."

I bump against his shoulder as we pull on our shirts and the jacket Shelley made him put in his gear bag. I'll have to let her know just how hot Reilly's metabolism is going to run now that he's heading for puberty and his growth spurt. I felt like I was on fire half the time, and I slept in a cave lined with ice. "I have bigger paws and a lot more practice. You can fit in the small places where they like to hide, and you're good at predicting their likely escape routes. We make a good team."

His eyes shine.

Mine probably are, too. Reilly has been a wonderful tour guide. We sniffed at half a dozen streams before we chose this one, ducked under a waterfall just the right height for a polar bear shower, and explored a thicket that will be a berry patch for the ages, come summer.

I already promised to come back when the berries are ready.

I pull a container of sandwiches out of my rucksack. We ate plenty of fish, but I've never been convinced that my bear and my human share the same stomach. "Hungry?"

Reilly sniffs. "Did Shelley make those, or Adelina?"

I'm uncertain why that matters. They smell delicious. "Adelina, I think. She's the one who growls if you get too close to her coffee cup, right?"

Reilly giggles. "She growls a lot, but she's really smart and she likes science and she puts extra honey on my oatmeal."

A wolf who loves him, then. I hand over one of the

sandwiches. "I like growly wolves. They help steady my bear."

He takes the sandwich, his eyes thoughtful. "My bear doesn't really like it when people growl at him. Maybe because the wolves who used to do it were pretty mean. He doesn't mind Adelina, though."

I strangle my apex predator before he can make promises about raining retribution down on the assholes of Ghost Mountain. Kel made it clear months ago that I don't get to be at the front of that line. Ivan said the same thing more recently, although I think the order of his line maybe isn't quite the same as Kel's. "Your bear is different than mine. It's good for you to know what he likes and what he needs."

Reilly looks a little disgruntled about that for a minute. Then his eyes clear. "Your bear is more like a dominant wolf, maybe. Kennedy needs people to growl at her, too. Hayden does it all the time. And Kel, when she steals his muffins."

Smart baby alpha. Smartass, too. "Do you steal hers?"

He makes a wry face. "I try, but I'm not very good, yet."

That, I can help with. Bears move differently than wolves, even when we're human. But that's for later. "Shifters all have to work out a balance between our humans and our animals. Bears can be tricky. Mine wasn't very happy about living close to the city so that I could go to university."

The fascination in his eyes is instant and bright. "Is that why you moved to Whistler Pack?"

This is a story I've told often. It's rarely felt this important. "That was some of it, yes. Learning called to me, and I was struggling to find my place in the north. Adrianna invited me to join the university student group in her pack, and even though I was a wild bear and I had a lot of work to do to learn how to be a good packmate, I knew that it was work worth doing." A pause as I let myself fully remember. "I felt like I belonged. From the very first day."

A long, slow nod. "I bet that was a really good feeling."

I know Reilly has a good pack at his back. That apparently isn't going to stop my bear from pledging his undying loyalty in defense of this cub. "It was the very best feeling. Then I learned how to be a good packmate and a good engineer, and I saw how those things could contribute to my pack, and those were some pretty good feelings, too."

He smiles and looks down at his sneakers. "I felt like that when we put up the walls for the school."

He wasn't the only one. I could feel the vibrations of Jules Scott's touchdown dance all the way up in the Arctic, and Scotty researching engineering scholarships, and Ryder sending drunken texts to everyone on her contact list. I reach out a big arm and hug him in tight to my side, this bear cub I fell in love with months before I ever met him. "Could you hear me cheering?"

He giggles. "Nope. You'll have to try harder next time."

Troublesome cub. "That will be in a couple of weeks

when the main den arrives. I'll be close enough to make the ground shake."

Reilly's eyes widen. "I won't be team leader for those walls." A pause. "Will I?"

Bless Jules Scott and her maniac schemes. "Sure you will. Do you think we did all that training just to have you laze around and eat all the best sandwiches while the real work happens on the next building?"

Hesitant glee—and then a big thought. One that stiffens his spine and squiggles him out from under my arm. "What about my mom? Aren't you the boss of her team, now?"

Spoken like a cub raised in a wolf pack. Hierarchies matter. I speak to that first, even though I can hear the other layers in his question. The ones that maybe he can't quite hear, yet. "That will be up to her."

Surprise.

His pack hasn't always been a good one. I plant a guidepost so that he can work the rest through himself. "What she wants matters."

Reilly tilts his head like a raven. "Most of the pack thinks she can be the leader."

Of course they do. But that isn't the answer this gentle grizzly cub is hunting. "Wolves see that as a compliment, but not everyone wants to lead. In most circumstances, I don't."

More surprise, but it disperses more quickly this time. "You lead the engineering teams sometimes. And the craft guild. Aurelia says that's mostly about being a goof-ball, though."

Some day I will explain to him how a tiny, cheerful wolf managed to get a polar bear elected when his name wasn't even on the ballot. Or Rio will do it. That story still makes him cackle. Especially when the guild has refused to hold new elections every year since. "We all lead some of the time, but I like to spend most of my day doing other things. I bet you have wolves like that in this pack."

He nods solemnly. "And bears. And ravens."

I met Fallon last night. She was snarky and funny and she adores her mate—and it was entirely clear why Ivan idolizes her. He will be enchanted that his gift made her cry. "What about you?"

Reilly makes a dozen faces in quick succession. "I don't want to be a pack leader. But I like it when I can be in charge for a little while. Especially if we're learning. Or building something."

To an engineer, those are the same thing. "Good. Then we have the right bear in charge of the walls for the main den building."

He eyes me carefully. "Mom will do the wiring, right? Scotty showed me some diagrams. They looked really complicated, but she can do it."

There might be some who doubt that, but none of them are bears. "Of course. But she might do it as the team leader, or as the subject matter expert."

Reilly's agile brain grabs for the words before I even get them all of the way out. "What's that?"

I grin. "It's kind of like being a beta. They know everything and fix all the stuff that the leaders screw up."

He giggles. "Moms do that, too."

My heart squeezes. His does. "Yup. There are lots of ways to be a useful wolf or bear. Like hauling a dozen buckets of fish back to the den before they get stinky."

He snickers and eats the last of his sandwich. "Brown says they're stinky two minutes after he catches them, and after that they're only good for smoking or grilling."

Brown is a very smart bear. "I bet he still eats a couple of these. They're particularly tasty."

A happy cub rubs his very full belly.

I grin at him. "Think we've stayed away for long enough?"

He shakes his head wryly. "I can't believe you got us kicked out of math class."

It was a really small differential equation. Multiplication tables are boring. "We'll take Bailey some fish. That should get us back in."

Reilly rolls his eyes. "Nope. But figuring out how to help Stinky remember his multiplication tables might."

They really need to make the third-grade math curriculum more exciting. "Have you tried using rows and columns of cookies?"

A long sigh. "Yup. He just guesses and then eats cookies until he's right."

Smart pup. One who can clearly work both multiplication and subtraction in his head if it will make someone laugh. "He sounds like someone we need to recruit for our engineering team."

Reilly manages to look excited and daunted at the same time. "You heard about the skunk story, right?"

I grin at my best bear cub.

He sobers. "We should ask him if he wants to be on the team. Because what he wants matters."

I rub his head as gently as I can. "Always."

Unless you're a really big bear.

8

HAYDEN

It takes a really long time for my mom to stop laughing. Which is fair. Lissa is still snickering every time she looks at me.

My wolf scowls. He knew there was something wrong with that tea.

I sigh. He thinks that all tea smells like dirty socks. "Is there any alpha business we need to attend to, or did you just call to make fun of your only son?"

My mom grins and holds up her mug, which is almost certainly not full of tea that will make her fart unceasingly for the next six hours. "Do I need a better reason?"

I roll my eyes. "No. But you probably know all of our news already." From possibly unreliable informants, however. Reilly is our usual keeper of the pack sat phone, but he was off fishing. At least Robbie just called my mom. Last week, Mellie talked to half of the alphas in the province before a snickering Kendra bothered to let Ebony know that we had an electronic menace on the loose.

One last squirt of giggles and my mother manages to look mostly sober. "How are you doing?"

She isn't asking about me. It's also an interestingly general question. Ames is back in Whistler Pack territory, but she can be surprisingly tight-lipped at times. "We have a visiting polar bear, I have a toddler dominant who is best friends with a hawk alpha, and I can't stop farting. How do you think we're doing?"

The giggles threaten again, but the alpha of all alphas manages to tamp them down. "That sounds like a fairly typical week."

I roll my eyes. "Maybe for Whistler Pack."

She takes a sip of her tea, studying me over the rim of her mug. "Something on that list is actually niggling at you, and it's not Kendra or healer pranks. What trouble has Ronan managed to cause?"

She swears that she can't read minds. Jules and I have never been dumb enough to believe her. I'm oddly reticent to spill Ronan's secrets, though. "He got Reilly kicked out of math class."

An amused eyebrow. One that says she knows I'm dissembling, and quite possibly why.

This is why I'm a terrible liar. Between my mother and Kel, there was never any point. "He got a little shaken when he arrived."

Crisp, sharp eyes. An alpha who takes her responsibilities seriously, even when they're hundreds of kilometers away. "What happened?"

I shrug, which won't fool her at all. "His bear slipped out a little more than usual. He's got himself locked back down. Mostly. My pack is rolling with it just fine, so you don't need to go all alpha on him."

Both eyebrows raise this time.

My wolf growls. Good pack. Strong pack.

She smiles gently. "That isn't the part that surprised me, Hayden. Of course your pack is handling it. They know what evil looks like. They won't find a speck of it in Ronan, no matter how much of his wild he inadvertently lets them see."

Something inside of me that has been tense for two days eases. "Some of them have been poking at him and making sure he doesn't have a chance to entirely lock himself back up again."

An impressed blink. "Really."

That answers one question, although Ghost's moves smelled more of Kel than of Adrianna Scott. "He learned sign language. To talk to Robbie."

Her eyes soften. "I know. I tried to keep up with him, but I wasn't stuck in the Arctic with nothing to do for twenty hours a day. It's a beautiful language. It appeals to my wolf."

The part of me that fiercely loves a small white pup is having trouble speaking. "How many of you are learning?"

She shrugs. "Most of the pack, I think."

The part of me that still deeply loves the pack of my

birth knows what that means. What it needs to mean and should mean and what I want it to mean. "I'll bring Robbie and Lissa for a visit. Soon."

Happy-mom eyes. "When you're ready."

There are a lot of things weighing on the timing of that decision, but nobody understands every last one of them better than Adrianna Scott. "You should have seen Robbie in the hot pools last night, trying to splash like a bear."

She chuckles. "You got pretty good at it, as I recall."

I had excellent motivation. I spent most of Ronan's first year at Whistler Pack half-drowned. "You should come visit. Have a soak with the other elders."

The look I get over the rim of her mug is an excellent reminder of why nobody messes with my mother. "I might join Jules. She'll be coming with the next delivery. I assume you've figured that out already."

Kel got there faster, but that's because I was distracted by my green-eyed wolf instead of paying attention to her spreadsheets. "Yes. She's already been assigned to Reilly's wall-building team."

A soft smile. "She'll love that."

I roll my eyes. "I'm not an entirely clueless big brother."

Another smile, more amused this time. "Indeed, you're not. You are a polar bear's friend, however. I imagine you're worried that will cloud your judgment."

I grimace. "He's a polar bear. He's dangerous as fuck."

She looks at me for a long time. "You don't believe that. And far more importantly, neither does your pack."

I blink at her. Adrianna Scott doesn't downplay threats, ever. Even ones she hasn't been fully briefed on. "He believes it."

She takes a long, slow sip of her tea before she answers. "Perhaps it's time for him to reconsider."

RONAN

Eliza sees me first. "It's good of you to show up."

I don't have to work very hard at a bashful grin. "Sorry. Fishing got away from me yesterday." And learning all about Brown's new smoker. And making a deal with a southern bear for some honey that I think the smoker of fish will like.

Eliza snorts. "Fishing, and honey tasting, and robot building, and teaching Braden his first bad word."

Myrna was the one who actually said the bad word, but it was right after she discovered the science project we had cooking on the stove. That didn't stop her from taking a walk through our gravity-defying slime, however. "There was a schedule for my day. A good engineer knows not to mess with one of those."

Indrani rolls her eyes and bumps my bear. Good raven. "There's also a schedule that says our main den building is arriving in two weeks and the fancy guy they sent from HomeWild is supposed to look over all of our plans so that we can actually get to work and have the pipes and wiring ready to go when it gets here."

I grin. "I can do that. So long as it doesn't get in the way of fingerpainting after lunch."

Danielle closes her eyes and shakes her head.

The vulnerable place I spent all of yesterday trying to get under lock and key pops right back up to the surface.

Eliza elbows Danielle. "That means we have a couple of hours to walk him through the plans, so maybe get on that, fearless leader."

A scowl. "I'm not the leader. He is."

I don't think so, and neither does the very competent wolf who built the finest natural hot pools I've ever seen. "I'm only here for a few weeks. Someone needs to lead the team after that. It doesn't have to be you if you don't want to be, however."

Danielle catches her answer before it lands in her eyes. Almost.

A key slowly turning in its lock.

It takes every bit of restraint I collected up yesterday not to add a swipe from a polar bear's massive paw. This isn't mine to do. Locks and keys are sometimes necessary, holding one door closed so that freedom can enter through another.

Danielle's team doesn't appear to be constrained by such philosophical musings. After a moment of pungent silence, Glow growls.

Indrani folds her arms over her chest. "What she said."

Eliza's eyes hold hints of sympathy, but her tone is all

business. "You've been the team leader for months. We've all done our parts, but you're the one who figured out how it all comes together. No bear gets to walk in here and take over just because he's a man with really fancy tools."

Tough words—but she's shaking as she finishes them.

I lean against her shoulder as carefully as I can. "What she said."

The answer that glinted in Danielle's eyes earlier goes to war with every cautious instinct of a submissive wolf. She finally lets out a sigh worthy of a bear. "I want to learn. I need to learn. I don't know that I should be the team lead until I've done that."

Good enough. She's turned the key. Now a polar bear can throw his very substantial weight around. "Hayden's a brand-new alpha who doesn't know half of what he needs to know to properly lead a pack."

Four sets of eyes glare fiercely.

I grin. "Fine. He's a brand-new alpha who's doing ridiculously well and you're all helping him get there. But he's still got a lot to learn, and I bet he'd tell you that himself. Just like I have a lot to learn about using a hot spring as a heat source and Shelley has a lot to learn about just how many cookies a polar bear can consume after a good fishing trip and Indrani has a lot to learn about how to wield a hose properly in a water fight."

My favorite raven intern snickers. "Don't let a polar bear chew on it first?"

My bear looks at her regally. "I did not do the chewing. That was Mellie."

Glow grins silently.

I glance at Eliza to make sure she also approves of my antics, and then I focus on the wolf who still needs to fully own her choice. "I know how to be a team lead. I also know how to be the walking instruction manual, or the guy you bounce ideas off of, or cheerful manual labor. So long as I get to go fingerpaint after lunch, I'm good with any of those roles."

Her dark eyes stare back at mine.

Sometimes it's really hard to tell the difference between being a pushy asshole and holding space—and the vulnerability I can't quite keep locked down is clouding the hell out of my judgment. "Generally the right answer is whatever you want deep inside. Expertise and big muscles and smart thinkers are easy to add to a team. Leadership isn't about any of those. It's about wanting to see the whole and make it better."

Danielle's eyes drop to her hands. "I'm better with wiring and repairing things."

Those are forms of seeing the whole, too, but that isn't what she means. I take a deep breath and dive into icy waters. "Being your den's resident expert on those two things is a very fine life. If that's what you want."

DANIELLE

I don't know what I want. Except every time I try to form those words, my wolf snaps at them with her teeth.

She knows they're a lie.

I wasn't sure of that until the bear with gentle, implacable eyes suggested that someone else could lead my team once he's gone. My fingers clench and release in my lap. It's an old habit. They're seeking something to do. Some way out of the tight place.

"You don't need to decide right now." Ronan rolls to his feet and dusts off his hands on his blue jeans.

Eliza looks up at him and raises an eyebrow. "It's not time for fingerpainting, mister."

He grins. "I know. But I've been a really good bear, so can I see the heat exchanger now, pretty please?"

His eyes are shining just like Reilly's do when he's excited. I shake my head, not wanting to dull the shine, but knowing it's inevitable. Our heat exchanger isn't fancy. It isn't even very sturdy. "It's just temporary."

Ronan manages a pout worthy of Mellie after the hawks leave. "Nobody has even let me peek at it."

I take a deep breath. There are a lot of reasons for that, but the biggest one is that I'm unreasonably proud of what we built from guesswork and spare parts. Which is foolish. He's only here for a few weeks, and I need to stop dithering and let him help us. "I was reading one of the books you brought. I think we should just start with a fresh design for the permanent one."

Indrani looks at me like I just suggested starving the pups.

I swallow. She spent a lot of hours working on the heat exchanger with me. "We can use what we learned on the first one, but follow good engineering principles, this time."

She wrinkles her nose. "We followed them. Some."

We broke so many rules, and there's math in those books that I don't even know how to do. "We could do it properly."

"There's no such thing." Ronan shrugs as we all look at him. "The books try to make it seem that way because it's the easiest way to teach young engineers. You've done your learning by building things and seeing what goes wrong and developing the kind of instincts that only come with years of experience." He smiles a little. "I would really like to see what that kind of experience built."

I meet his eyes. If I'm going to give up my pride, I need something in return. I want to learn. "I want you to tell me every single thing that's wrong with it."

He doesn't even hesitate. "Deal."

My wolf stares at him. He means it.

Indrani snorts and pokes her elbow in his ribs. "I did the part that runs hot water to the shower, so if that part sucks, be nice. I'm just a lowly intern."

I scowl at her, and at the big bear beside her for good measure. "Everyone loves the showers. You spent days making them just right. You did a fantastic job."

She leans against Ronan and folds her arms across her chest. "The school floor is amazing and the hot pools are fantastic and even washing dishes is pretty awesome. If we're judging how well we did based on results and all."

My wolf blinks.

Eliza chuckles. "What she said."

I shake my head. My whole team ate feisty cereal for breakfast, but we won't learn if we hold too tightly to what we've already done. I meet the eyes of a polar bear. "You promised."

He nods solemnly. "I did. I'll tell you the whole truth of what I see. Every last wart and weakness."

I tell myself that it will be worth the dents in my pride to learn.

I make my way to my feet and head over to the heat exchanger. It takes a while to work the cover off. I look over at the bear who's standing patiently as I undo the bolts. "One feature we need in the new design is easier entry for maintenance. Something that's still secure and will keep the pups safe, but simpler to access."

He nods agreeably. "A building would provide that. A smaller version of what Brown built for the kitchen, maybe."

Indrani grins. "That's already in her plan."

Ronan's lips quirk. "Hush, intern, or I'll never get to see the pretty machinery."

Somehow, those are the words that make me feel better. Under all the fancy degrees and big projects and technical papers is a bear who is a bit like me. Who likes to play with things and see how they work.

Who thinks my heat exchanger might be pretty.

I bite my lip so that I don't apologize for the maze of spare parts he's about to see. Our local hardware store doesn't have all the options I've seen online. Not in the discount bins, anyhow. I try to decide where to start and point at the far end of the big pipe that runs through the middle. "This is where we're connected to the intake from the hot spring, and here's where we return the water back underground."

His eyes sharpen as he steps in closer. "How are you down-regulating the pressure?"

I make a face. "With a really small intake pipe, mostly. That's one of the things I wasn't sure how to do properly."

He nods. "That works. It's fast and reliable and easy to trade out for a more complicated solution when you need one. Have you got a couple of failsafes in place in case the flow changes suddenly?"

The ants running around inside my chest slow down a little. "Yes. There are two overflow pipes with valves that will open if the pressure gets too high. We'll need to change them out regularly because of the mineral build-up."

He leans in until his nose is almost touching the bowels of the heat exchanger. "So here's the pipe from the hot spring, and here's where it passes heat and energy to your cold-water system and your battery hookup. Why the copper coils? Wait, did you bend that pipe yourself?"

I blink. He's working out what we did faster than Reilly does his math homework. "Glow did. We needed something that fit tight against the main pipe, and copper's a good conductor. It needs insulation, but we weren't sure how to do that and keep it safe and accessible for repairs."

Ronan shrugs. "The hot spring provides way more heat than you need, so keeping it efficient isn't a big priority. This is excellent design." He smiles at Glow. "And really excellent execution."

She spent days getting that pipe bent just right. I'm realizing just how much of my team's work I'm trying to throw on the compost pile along with mine. "Maybe we can re-use the coil she made."

Ronan snorts. "If I'm the team leader, we're re-using this whole thing." He looks over at me and grins. "If you're the team leader, you can make your own choices, but you deserve fair warning that I'm a really opinionated polar bear and I think we should keep this beauty."

I stare at him. "It's just temporary."

His lips quirk. "Says who?"

Indrani grins. "Says our team leader."

He eyes her sternly. "Don't push."

She rolls her eyes. "Don't be a mean polar bear."

He chuckles. "The connection to the shower looks terrific. Particularly the care you took in making sure that the water cools off before it gets anywhere near a pipe that a pup might dig up. In case the opinion of a mean polar bear matters."

Indrani blinks at him, sheepish and proud and speechless.

Which makes two of us.

9

KEL

I shake my head as Reilly points his hose at yet another splotch of bright paint on Ronan's fur. It's a losing battle —Mellie and Jade are still gleefully planting handprints on his other side. "Is this going to happen every day that he's here?" This is only day two of painting a polar bear, but the enthusiasm isn't exactly waning.

Ghost grins. "Shelley might run out of fingerpaints."

There are hawks who will gleefully fix that, and they don't seem to charge Mellie delivery fees. Which isn't my problem. The bear cub merrily wielding the hose is, however. I eye the teenager who has decided that she's in charge of making sure he makes it through this visit in one piece. "Reilly seemed happy after his fishing trip with Ronan."

Her lips quirk. "He's fine."

I'd accuse her of being a tight-lipped beta, but I know

who she learned it from. "Do any adults need to get involved, or does your baby pack have it covered?"

She snorts. "Kenny's an adult. Mostly."

If they're trusting him with Reilly's vulnerable places, Kenny has gotten a lot more solid than he's let me see—but he's also still got the kind of wounds that old soldiers know about and teenage betas maybe don't. "Kenny might need some space at some point. If you need help, ask for it."

Ghost sighs. "Ebony already gave me this speech. And Lissa. And Shelley."

Oops. I only knew about one of those. "Sorry. We all love Reilly. It's making us a little stupid."

Her lips quirk again. "As long as you know it."

Smartass. One who just got in from a run to the far orbits, so we have work to do that doesn't involve repeating what three smart wolves have already said. "Any news from the base camps?"

She smiles. "Teesha wrote some music for one of Terrence's poems. He's hopelessly embarrassed. I got a recording."

I shoot her a look, pretty sure I'm about to say shit that I don't need to say, again. "Did you also get his permission to share it?"

She rolls her eyes. "Duh."

I aim a scowl that used to regularly make soldiers quake in their boots. "Pretend that you weren't born good at this beta stuff and let us double check your work every so often. It makes us feel useful."

She leans against my shoulder. "You could let the

pups use you as a painting canvas. I bet you would look great with some streaks of lime green in your fur."

I shake my head. "You used to be such a quiet wolf."

A soft, amused huff. "I still am, mostly. This is a good pack to be that kind of wolf."

I rest my cheek on the top of her head. "Yeah."

She watches the painted-bear antics for a while, gathering her next thoughts. "I stopped by the heat exchanger on my way back."

I raise an eyebrow that she can't see. "Ebony tried earlier. She got chased away by a raven holding a wrench."

Ghost giggles. "You guys must be doing it wrong. Indrani shared her sandwich with me."

The best intel comes through connection, always. "Are they managing, or do I need to kick a polar bear's ass so that he actually does some useful work?" He's likely the best judge of that, but betas exist to doubt everyone's judgment.

Ghost shakes her head. "They're good. Glow was humming and Danielle had that look that means she's thinking really hard and the fancy new gauges that Kendra dropped off are already installed."

Good eyes can collect a lot of useful intel, too, and she got a look at more than Ebony did. "Do we have any idea what happened yesterday?" Eliza just patted me on the head when I asked.

Ghost smiles. "Ronan got it right."

That much is obvious. Something big changed right around lunchtime. Ronan's mostly been goofing off since then, but the body language of the three wolves and the cheerful raven who worked deep into the night and started up again before dawn this morning is speaking loud and clear. They're intent and proud and busy and oriented toward their leader. Who isn't a polar bear. "Do we need to send in food? Or wolves who know how to wield tools and keep their mouths shut?"

She pats my arm. "Eliza will let us know."

If engineering teams have betas, that position has been filled. "She did let me know that they'll need to drain the pools the day after tomorrow to clean them and fix a few small issues. Which means we need to clear out the pups, including the really big one with yellow fur." The pups have at least taken some naps. I'm not sure Hayden has been dry since the first pool filled.

Ghost reaches into her pocket for a honey berry bar and offers me half. "Already covered. Bailey will take the school kids out to Hidden Creek. Lissa's going, so Hayden should, too, or he'll just sit by the hot pools looking sad and lonely."

That will take care of most of the pack. There are an awful lot of adults enrolled in school. "I'll threaten him with reorganizing the kitchen cupboards if he doesn't go. Shelley says the plates are too high for the pups to put away properly."

A long pause that isn't about plates or alphas who pretend to have maturity issues. "Will Ronan come?"

Smart beta. One with her young eyes wide open. "That depends on a lot of things. You just got back from the far orbits. How do you think they'd handle a polar bear running through their turf?"

Silence as she thinks through the layers. "Ivan has done it."

Interesting angle. "Ivan and Ronan aren't much alike."

A longer silence. "I don't think that's true."

That observation would rile the hell out of both of them. I keep quiet. There's more where it came from, and it feels important.

Ghost shifts her weight, seeking literal firmer footing for her murky thoughts. "They're a lot different on the outside, and they've decided to matter to the world in really different ways. But they both look at Kelsey and their eyes get soft. And when they rumble in our territory, even the ghost wolves feel safer."

I move to where I can see her eyes. I'll pick my jaw up out of the dirt later. "Say that last part again."

She shrugs, looking at me uncertainly. "I ran past Ruby's turf. I stayed up on the ridge like you told me."

Unlike a baby alpha who will be washing dishes for the next week. "Did you see her?"

A nod. Happy eyes. "She was down by the river chasing crows like Stinky does."

Ruby has been having more good moments lately, small stretches of time where she's more than a broken wolf who bleeds nothing but violence. Chasing crows is better than good. "Did you tell Hoot?"

Ghost swallows and nods.

That wouldn't have been an easy conversation. Hoot

wears all her emotions on her sleeves, and the broken wolf chasing crows by the river is her mom. I wrap an arm around the young beta who delivered the news anyhow—and who knew to do it before she found me. "That's really good to hear."

A long, shaky breath. "I think it matters to Ruby that Ronan is here. The pups are safer. They're really safe even with you and Hayden and Rio, but Ronan is different. He makes the ground rumble."

I shake my head. Betas are supposed to be on top of everything, and I totally missed this angle. Polar bears are the scariest predators in the world. I wasn't overly worried about this visit, because Ronan knows how to make space in a wolf pack for a well-behaved polar bear. I forgot that Hayden already made that space when he stood in front of Banner Rock and read the high court's proclamation and banished Eamon Martins into the care and keeping of a polar bear. One who growled and made the earth shake—and told us, right in our bones, that we were safe.

Ghost is right. In that respect, Ivan and Ronan are exactly the same.

Something that a soldier who nearly drowned in his own failures should have realized. It's a big part of why I count a polar bear as my brother. I squeeze Ghost's shoulders. "I've known Ronan for a really long time. Too long, maybe. I didn't see that. I'm glad you did. Let's make sure that Stinky and Hoot are really visible on the run, tomorrow." We don't actually know if Ruby remembers her pups, but they remember her.

Another slow breath. "Hoot wants to see if Grady will come."

Grady is so full of anxiety and darkness that he can hardly handle his own shadow. Which seems like a dumbass thing to throw a polar bear at, but I got dragged out of the darkness by an arrogant juvenile wolf who used every flavor of dumbass in the universe. I consider. "Maybe. Check with Rio and Wrinkles."

Ghost shoots me an innocent look. "I thought that could be your job."

Not a chance in hell—I smelled the tea Wrinkles was brewing this morning. "I need to help Reilly get paint out of Ronan's fur."

Ghost leans against my shoulder again and snickers under her breath.

Which means I get to talk to a healer.

RONAN

I set the wheelbarrow handles down gingerly. I'm not sure how it made it over the several kilometers of rocks and tree roots between here and Rio's truck. It's rusted and wobbly and older than Cleve.

Hayden stops his much newer and larger wheelbarrow beside mine and surveys the growing pile where we dumped the last two loads of pea gravel. "Think this is enough?"

That isn't up to us. Kennedy is supervising construction of the new paths that will cover up the permanent pipes and wires running from the heat exchanger to the main den building. We're just manual labor. Which clearly isn't bothering the alpha wolf beside me. Probably because he has the wheelbarrow that actually works.

I tip out my load on the pile and grin at the small avalanches it causes. I didn't meet pea gravel until I came to the south. It still delights the cub that lives inside my bear. "We should make this big enough for the pups to slide down."

Hayden snorts. "Because sliding down a polar bear isn't enough fun?"

That's a really good game, especially when there are attentive catchers and a polar bear can shake and rumble. "It would provide sliding variety. And it could be a physics lesson."

He rolls his eyes. "That's the same angle Reilly uses. Anything can be school if you try hard enough."

I do like that bear cub. "Does it work?"

Hayden chuckles. "Usually. Bailey's a science nerd, and the teenagers have gotten really good at tossing out just enough disturbingly inaccurate facts to reel her in to teach whatever lesson they're pretending to not want to learn."

The teenagers of this pack drink up knowledge like water. Which makes a polar bear want to melt an iceberg or two so that they can keep drinking. "You lead far differently than Adrianna, but when it comes to letting the young people of this pack be one of its greatest strengths, you remind me of her very much."

He exhales slowly. "She always said that was something she learned from my dad."

I saw Adrianna Scott rend the limbs from the van that took the life of her mate. It took every bit of the self control that she helped me to acquire for an anguished polar bear not to join her. James was the very best of men, and losing him severed something precious from far too many that I love. "He knew how to help the young ones rise up. She knew how to funnel their energy in service of pack. You do both."

Hayden looks at me, his eyes wide and vulnerable and proud. "I have help."

So did they. "Does he visit you here?"

The small nod of an eight-year-old boy who never entirely let his father go. "Yes. Mom sends him sometimes, I think."

The Russian hearts of most polar bear shifters might not understand such things, but my genetics took a detour through a couple of Caribbean islands and a great-grandmother who read palms for a living. "I imagine that he whispers to Kelsey and steals muffins from Cleve and tells Robbie stories with his hands."

Hayden huffs out a breath that carries the scent of tears. "A few months out of range and you're going to sit on me all at once, huh?"

It's what polar bears do when they love. I huff out a breath of my own. "Sorry. I didn't mean to push quite that hard."

"You can tell me that my dad would be proud of me anytime you want." He bumps against me hard enough to knock over a lesser bear. "Especially when you're showing enormous restraint with your engineering team."

I blink. Hayden rarely gets such things wrong. He must be distracted. "I'm not. They showed me the plans for the new system. It's excellent. I can't wait to see it finished."

He studies me for long enough to make my bear squirm. "You don't feel any urges to tinker or tweak the design or take the old heat exchanger apart to see how all the pieces fit together?"

Troublesome wolf. "I have eyes. I saw everything I needed to see."

His lips quirk. "How many pieces is Scotty custom machining that neither of you have bothered to tell Danielle about, yet?"

I pick up the handles of my entirely inadequate wheelbarrow. "A design of beauty deserves to be constructed from beautiful parts." Besides, he had most of them made already. Her design diagrams were quite precise.

Hayden shakes his head and navigates around a tree on a path that wasn't built for side-by-side wheelbarrows. "Do I need to prepare Lissa for the cost of parts with decorative dragon welds?"

I grin. "I think he's sending a wolf, a bear, a raven, and a very cute baby rabbit."

He groans. "Who told him about our pet bunnies?"

I give up pushing my cantankerous wheelbarrow and sling it over my shoulder, instead. "Kennedy, I think. Or maybe Ebony."

He snorts. "Interesting that you name two wolves who can beat me up."

I'm not an entirely dumb bear. "Darn. I was hoping Kel hadn't taught them all the good stuff already."

He laughs, and I can hear James Scott in the sound. "They were both menaces before we got here. Kel's just adding a few decorative touches."

I smile. He's a wolf, so he can be forgiven for not understanding. "Sometimes those are what matter most."

He casts me an oddly opaque look. "Like an engineer who throws out all of his careful plans for the week and decides to run water into some half-finished hot pools, instead?"

That was an act of pure self-preservation. My bear needed a distraction. "They were finished. Mostly."

He snorts. "Eliza was ready to kill you."

My bear has some thoughts on how he can maybe make that up to her. Hayden isn't the right wolf for that conversation, however. "It's easy to become too careful with a complicated project."

A long silence. "Yeah. It is."

I glare at him. "I was talking about engineering."

His lips quirk as he wheels around another inconvenient tree. "I wasn't."

10

RONAN

I thought hard about the right wolf for this job. I'm still not sure that I've chosen wisely, but I don't know Ebony or Kenny as well as I should, and Rio will set me straight if I've misjudged.

He looks up with an easy smile as I approach. Then he smells what I'm bringing with me and sets down a scale model of what looks to be the design for Kendra's new nursery.

I scan it as I sit down. She's a very particular hawk. "I like the way you've shored up the tower supports."

He grins. "I build everything so a polar bear can visit. You know that."

Kendra's babies are fuzzy and fierce. Of course I'll be visiting. Although that feels oddly far away, somehow. "She would expect no less."

A sentinel's eyes study me with as much care to detail as Rio puts into his designs.

I let him look. Doing so isn't explicitly part of the promise I made to Adrianna so long ago, but there's never been anything but compassion in Rio's eyes, even back when they belonged to a young hotshot.

Whatever he sees eventually satisfies him, at least for the time being. "Shelley says that I'm supposed to yell at you about the slime in her kitchen pots, and then I'm supposed to get the recipe because the one she found on the internet didn't work nearly as well as yours did."

Shelley is a lovely wolf. One who has a fine touch with ginger snaps and watermelon seedlings and bears who haven't had enough cups of coffee. "She probably didn't add enough corn starch."

Rio's lips quirk. "Please don't make me talk to Shelley Martins about corn starch."

I grin. I've missed his dry wit and squishy heart. "Fine. I'll do that. You can have a nice chat with Bailey about fixing the science module on bridges."

His eyebrow slides up. "What's wrong with the bridges module?"

I throw up my hands. It likely won't keep him from sniffing out my agenda, but a bear's got to try. "It doesn't have any field trips, the students only get to build one bridge, and it doesn't even have to hold up a pup, much less a polar bear. What kind of an educational experience is that?"

His lips quirk. "Clearly one that doesn't meet your standards."

It shouldn't meet anyone's standards. Bridges are one of the best inventions of human history. They deserve proper respect, and in this case, they're also a very convenient means to an end. "Reilly and Adelina have already worked up a model for a tree bridge. A proper one. It's very elegant."

Rio chuckles. "When did you find time to help out with science homework?"

When I was on my way to find a bucket of coffee and spied them scowling at their textbook and some intricately arranged small branches. "Adelina has a good mind for structures. Scotty would enjoy her, but Reilly says she won't talk to him on video chat. He thinks that maybe she doesn't feel smart enough."

The big, bad wolf of death raises both eyebrows this time. "Let me guess. You're figuring that if you complain loudly enough about the science module on bridges, Scotty will materialize and fix two problems?"

I grin at him. He's always been a smart wolf. "Something like that."

Rio snorts. "You don't need to work nearly so hard. He's been angling to come up here. A simple invitation would do quite nicely."

Silly wolf. I sit quietly. He's got enough of the story to work out the rest.

He adjusts a strut on his tower model before he looks over at me again. "How many bridges has Scotty built in Whistler territory?"

It isn't the number that matters, but wolves tell stories differently. "At last count, over a hundred." Everything from tiny fairy bridges to ones big and strong enough for a herd of polar bears, and every single one of them is in a special place or holds a special memory or acts as a tangible reminder for those who built it.

My bridge is a simple one, built about a year after I arrived. It runs from north to south and is carved with words of learning. Adrianna's is embedded with shards of metal from a van. Kel's is a tiny wisp of a bridge sitting in a patch of sunlight. Hayden's is under water most of the year, and Jules's is a series of steps that helps small pups to escape the nursery.

I inhale deeply. I'm not wrong about this. Scotty should come here. His work is a gift to any pack—but perhaps especially to one with a lot of wolves trying to find their way home.

An arm settles around my shoulder. "It's a very good idea. He can come with the den delivery. It will give everyone a chance to build something that matters, even if they can't make it all the way to the den."

My bear rumbles happily. A sentinel's approval isn't always necessary, but it's a fine thing to have. "I'll set it up."

"You do that." Rio ruffles my hair, just like he does with the pups. "Now tell me about the idea that actually requires my help."

I stick an elbow in his ribs. "I don't need your help. I've got people in mind."

He scowls and releases my head. "Seriously? You don't want me or Hayden? You're no fun."

They need to be here at the den in case I'm wrong. "I

want to go talk to a young wolf. Damien is his name, I believe."

RIO

I'm an idiot for not seeing this one coming. Polar bears have tunnel vision, but Ronan learned how to use two shovels at the same time long before I met him. "He lives in town." It's a cautious opening. I'm not at all sure that a visit from a polar bear is what Eliza's son needs.

Ronan scowls. "He lives with the other assholes who chose to leave."

There's zero chance he hasn't hunted down most of that story. Not when it regularly puts sadness into the eyes of someone on his engineering team. His teams at Whistler regularly add shifters with sad eyes onto their rosters just to give him an excuse to intervene. "They need some time away."

His eyes narrow. He's always respected my sentinel, but that doesn't always extend to agreeing with him. "They need to feel pack ties. They can't do that while they're drinking too much beer and talking the kind of smack that keeps their souls tarnished and their claws weak."

I eye him carefully. "Kennedy wouldn't have used those words, and she's the only wolf besides Kel who has permission to keep an eye on the assholes in town." Very restricted permission. Kel trusts her skills. It's her dual needs for justice and redemption that worry him.

Dark eyes. Determined eyes. "I spoke to Ivan."

Damn. My sentinel has never had a good read on that relationship, other than it being a very complicated one. "He's a smart man who doesn't understand pack." Especially wounded pack.

"He will not intervene."

The certainty in Ronan's tone has my wolf sitting up sharply. Ivan is the closest thing the polar bears have to an alpha. "You might consider doing the same."

Ronan taps the interior edge of the tower on my model. "Two struts there would be more aesthetically pleasing."

I scowl at him. "Not if you're a hawk with a really big wingspan."

His lips quirk. "Use curved struts."

Damn. That's an excellent idea, and it would solve a couple of other niggling problems I've been trying to cut and glue my way around. "Jules will have my head. Production on this is already tight."

Ronan grins. "It will give her a chance to fight with Kendra. They both enjoy that."

They do, especially over something they both want done in the first place. "Fine. You tell Jules. She's still cursing at me for leading her idiot big brother into the woods and standing idly by as he claimed a pack with nowhere decent for anyone to sleep."

Ronan raises an interested eyebrow. "Was that actually your fault?"

I shrug. I don't think so, but sentinel woo doesn't always announce its intentions, before or after the fact. "He got here. That's what matters."

Ronan nods. No one has ever had to explain woo to a bear. "He holds the center. That's his job. Yours is to bring wolves close enough to feel their alpha's call. So why have you left Damien rotting in town?"

There are reasons, but looking into a polar bear's eyes, I can't find a whole lot of conviction that they're still good ones. Which is Ronan's gift to a pack and his curse. He makes things happen. I huff out a breath. This doesn't feel like a tunnel that a sentinel should barricade. "Who are you taking with you?"

He smiles faintly. "Kel, since he'll just follow me anyhow. Kennedy because she's Damien's friend, even if she's really mad at him. And I was thinking maybe Kenny, too."

Fucking polar bear. I shake my head. He's put way more thought into this than he has into our new heat exchanger, right down to the metaphorical curved struts. "You realize that you could just walk into town and roar and Damien would come with you, right?"

He snorts. "It sounds like I need to roar at the others."

That's been the conundrum since the day Damien left. We've always had the power to make him come home. He's never felt like he had the power to choose it. "He was young when Samuel took over."

Dark eyes. Listening eyes.

I sigh and give an interfering polar bear what he wants. "His mom is a very submissive wolf. She did more to protect him than he understands, but the guys in town are the closest thing he knows to a safe harbor, and they don't exactly value independent thinking."

Ronan nods, a bear confirming the elegance of his design. "I only intend to open the door. Kennedy and Kenny will help him walk through it."

They're a hell of an interesting tag team to try it. "What's Kel's job?"

Ronan flashes me a very dangerous grin. "Someone has to keep the rest of the assholes safe."

I hide my wince—and my wolf's wholeheartedly approving growl. My sentinel takes longer to weigh in, but he likes the feel of this plan. Especially the bold sensitivity that will ask Kennedy to be vulnerable and Kenny to use his claws. Smart bear. Astute, tricky bear. "I'll tell Hayden that his pack senses might be tingling."

Ronan eyes me carefully. "Do I need to be the one who does that?"

For a guy who didn't grow up in a wolf pack, he understands them exceedingly well. "No. He'll be delighted. He's wanted to drag all of them back here for ages."

Something sharp glints in a bear's eyes. "Why didn't he?"

Lots of reasons. I pick the one that will tell Ronan where he needs to be standing if Damien does come home. "They teased Reilly. They thought he was weak."

A polar bear's paws hit the ground. Running. Hunting. Seeking vengeance.

I watch the eyes of the man who has fought harder

than anyone I know to acquire that bear enough discipline that they could both be happy. His eyes are filling with compassion, even as his polar bear roars. Ronan understands all of the reasons a young wolf might try to make himself bigger at another's expense.

He shakes his head, his eyes clearing. "Reilly will be fine. He's a bear who knows his worth and that his pack loves him, and if he forgets for a moment or two, there are many who will remind him."

He isn't looking for a sentinel's agreement, but I offer it anyhow. "Yes. Damien will be trickier. Eliza might wobble, as well."

Ronan snorts. "She won't let that stop her."

My human blinks. My sentinel ponders. Perhaps the bear is right.

My wolf just grins. Eliza is bossy, now. And fierce. And at some point in the near future, she will get to stand in front of a polar bear and tell him to stop roaring at her son.

Which is classic Ronan—adding a curved strut where a straight one would do.

MYRNA

I won't cry. I won't.

I stumble my way to the pools, their wild, clean scent drawing me in even though I can hardly see. I set down the sandwiches I was bringing to fuel Rio while he worked. I manage to shuck my clothes before I fall in fully dressed, and I get a hand on Brown's sturdy railing to guide me to the already familiar steps.

I sink down and let the water wrap around me, warm and fierce and holy, as my tears fall, because promises made away from the holy waters don't count here, and I'm alone.

I cry for Eliza, who was forced endlessly to her knees as she tried to protect her son.

I sob for Reilly, who listened to so many words that tried to steal his worth and his right to take up space, and I let my tears fall for the men who said those words, too.

They're assholes—and they are pack.

I scrub my cheeks, but my tears aren't done yet.

I have more. For Kenny, and for the boy he never saw grow into a man. For Evan, who had to leave us to begin the walk of forgiving himself. Reese says he's doing well. I let more tears slide down my cheeks for that, too. For friends who are not pack and love us anyhow.

A slow, wobbling pair of tears scald my cheeks before they drip into the water.

I don't name those ones. I'm not ready.

I sniffle over a man I haven't met yet who builds bridges in the forest of his home and sent Kelsey a picture of one that made her eyes shine. I shed tears for a hawk alpha who loves a splash of whisky in her huckleberry jam and the wee hawk grandbaby that will be joining her in the spring.

I swipe at my nose so that I don't add snot to the holy

waters, and then I give up, because water that comes from the heart of a volcanic river can handle a little snot.

I cry for the enormous black wolf who carries within him both goose down and steel, and for Shelley, who truly loves corn starch, and for Adelina, who has a dream so small and well hidden that only a polar bear could have scented it.

Another slow, scalding tear comes.

I shake my head fiercely. I'm not ready.

The waters wrap around me, warm and fierce and holy.

I sniffle defiantly. I have work to do before I can be ready. I need to hug Damien once a polar bear roars him home and then make him scrub every pot in the kitchen. I'll probably have to give Eliza a good kick in the pants, too, because what our sons choose is sometimes entirely our fault and sometimes far beyond our control. And then I'll pull out my daddy's frying pan and cook us all a breakfast that tastes of history and hope, because that's what I do when moments need to be burnt into our pack history.

My nose drips again into a volcano's tears.

I'm not ready, but perhaps when Scotty comes to visit, I will build a bridge.

Just in case anyone decides to come home.

11

RONAN

I need some new projects. I'm not used to this restless, aimless feeling. There's always something to keep a polar bear's paws busy at Whistler Pack. There are plenty of tasks here, too, but I finished knitting the cozy nest liner for Fallon's chick, and Glow pointed her blow torch at me when I tried to help with burying the new pipes, and Reilly is busy figuring out how much ocean levels would rise if aliens tried to hide some really big spaceships underwater.

Fifth grade has improved a lot from the version I had to sit through.

I sigh. I do have emails from Jules with work that needs reviewing and approving, but I was hoping to avoid that fate. There are far too many polar bears on our current client list, and every one of the design tweaks that I need to review and approve is a reminder of how big we are. How heavy. How much space we take up simply by existing.

I frown. Those are old thoughts. Old beliefs. Ones that don't belong in these days where I've been given the freedom to splash in warm waters with adorable pups and fish until my belly is full and laugh long and loud by the fire without seeing wariness in a single pair of eyes.

I expected to have to be so much smaller.

I scratch at a stray itch behind my ear. I'm getting melancholy and adding embellishments that aren't true, and that's not a good place for a bear to be, especially when he's feeling restless. I really do need to find something to do. I survey the horizon and put my nose to good use. Surely there are teenagers in the woods I can stalk, or a mama who needs to be convinced to acquire more of my yarn in exchange for some time with her pup, or some big rocks that need moving.

My bear grins as he scents something better than any of those options. I squat down and wait for my small friend to emerge from the trees. He shifts to naked boy as he runs, which is an impressive feat for a pup who only found his wolf a few short months ago.

I open my arms to catch him. I'm not as warm as when I'm in bear form, but judging by how fast Robbie's hands are already moving, he'll be back in his own fur soon enough. I study the motions of his hands and hypothesize a few details based on body wiggles and bright eyes. "Finn delivered a package to Reese and dropped one off for us since he was in the neighborhood."

Kendra's mate defines that term even more loosely

than a polar bear. "Or that's what Dorie thinks, since he nearly dropped the package on her head instead of delivering it like a reasonable bird."

Robbie grins and adds an excellent approximation of Dorie's scowl.

I chuckle. Cats know how to embellish stories almost as well as bears. "Was there something good inside the pouch?"

Robbie nods solemnly and makes a couple of the signs that we've invented for the special pipe fittings he's been fetching for Glow. He's modifying the signs, though. Whatever's arrived, he doesn't quite have a name for it—and Glow just stared at it and wrinkled her nose.

I'm pretty sure I know what's arrived, and bless Scotty for sending them this fast. Either Finn lost at poker, or this pack has even better terms from the hawk couriers than I do. "That sounds like something Danielle needs to see."

Robbie grins cheerfully and replies with a few flicks of his fingers.

Excellent. They fetched her first.

I contemplate my informant. "Is she wrinkling her nose?"

He makes a different face. A thoughtful, focused one.

That looks promising. And catches my bear's attention, because nothing about that look suggests that I'm needed. "Who sent you to fetch me?"

A big kiss and a wiggle heading for the ground, and then a small white wolf dashes back into the trees, leaving an answer in his wake that has the full attention of the hunter who has stopped pacing inside my ribs.

Apparently a sentinel has decided to mess with my day.

DANIELLE

It's such a fancy part. I want to dislike it for that reason alone, but it's shiny and sturdy and elegant and I can't stop touching it. I hold it up against the new system schematic Indrani drew, instead. I can see what it will fix, what it will change and make so much easier—or I can see most of it, anyhow.

My fingers itch. They don't know how to alter this kind of schematic properly.

I sigh and reach into the oversized box where we keep most of our tools. I dig right to the bottom for the aluminum tube with the rolled-up papers that I was hoping not to need again. I slide them out of the tube, making a face at their mangled condition. That's what happens when you erase and redraw your plans so many times that you almost wear through the paper.

I flip through them, finding the one that I need. And the ones that it attaches to, because if this changes what I think it does, then we're going to need to make some alterations downstream, too. Quickly, before Glow gets to the pipes she's supposed to be laying next.

I line up the papers that show the section from the

heat exchanger to the primary junction that will serve the school and the main den building and the viewing ledge and anything else we build close by. We weren't going to run the wires and pipes for Dorie's camp that way, but I think that with this new part, maybe we can.

I eye the meager instructions that came with it. The doodle of the spaceship is pretty, but not at all informative.

I sigh and look away. It doesn't matter. My hands already know what the part can do. I just need to work out how it changes everything else. I set it down on the first paper, the one that shows the outflows from the heat exchanger and the temperature controls and a junction box that looks like it might belong on a spaceship. I touch them all as I imagine the flows of water and electricity. Battery exchange here. Detour to the outdoor showers, there.

A huff of breath over my shoulder. "These look interesting."

I close my eyes and sigh. Darn bear. "I was just checking a couple of things before I update the new schematics."

Silence as my heart beats loudly in my ears. "These look like schematics."

I can feel shame rising. Guilt. A hopeless sense of inadequacy. Old feelings, but ones that still have far too much power. I take a deep breath. It doesn't make the shame and guilt and inadequacy go away, but it lets me talk around them. "I didn't know how to do proper engineering diagrams before Indrani got here. She's teaching me, and she helped me make the ones for the new systems, but this is how I used to think things through."

A big hand reaches around me. Tracing lines on my papers. Pausing at the tricky points. Studying them. "You don't think like an engineer."

I shrink down inside the collar of my jacket. "I know."

A choked-off growl nearly topples me onto my mangled diagrams. "That wasn't an insult, Danielle."

My wolf stares at Ronan's hand, wide-eyed. The rest of me tries to breathe, even though the big, scary polar bear wasn't growling at me. He was snarling at himself.

"These are—just *look* at these." His finger traces the path of something that took me three days to properly untangle. "An engineer thinks about a schematic like a hawk flying overhead. They seek a view from up high enough that they can see the whole project at once. You don't do that."

I make a face. That's why there are so many papers and why they can't all be spread out at the same time, because they don't all belong in the same dimensions. But I don't say anything. I don't want the bear to growl at himself again.

His voice broadens into wonder. "You think about pipes and wires from the inside. Like a mouse would. Or a repair bot."

My lips quirk. There was one of those in the last science fiction story that Reilly gave to me to read. "So I'm good at being small and invisible and focused on the tiny details?"

A surprised huff of breath—and then a wry chuckle. "That wasn't what I meant, but none of those are insults. Many engineering projects fail because the people in charge have no idea how to think at that level."

Something inside me likes those words and is irritated by them at the same time. "That's why people like me exist. To help those of you who are good at flying up high."

He snorts. "Right. That's why you're designing the new systems for your den and I'm lugging around wheelbarrows of pea gravel."

I wince, even though he doesn't sound upset. "You don't need to do that."

He grins. "Pea gravel is fun. I think we're going to make the pile into a slide tomorrow."

Conversations with this man never go where I think they're headed. "I guess I'll know where to find my son, then."

A long pause as a bear's eyes look down at my papers—but I don't think that's what they're seeing. "I don't seek to replace you in Reilly's heart, but I know that I can be a large presence. If it squeezes your sense of connection with your cub, all I need is a word or a hand signal or a nod and I will back off."

My insides suddenly feel like water trying to flow both ways in a pipe. Ronan is a large presence—and he's a man who sent acres of yarn for my son's blanket so that Reilly could begin to learn to take up more space. I take in a breath and let it out again, and say the truest of the words colliding inside me. "Do you really think that Reilly's heart is that small?"

A sheepish, apologetic smile. "No. It isn't. Which is something that a cub only learns when they are deeply loved."

I'm not sure that's true, but it's a compliment that makes my cheeks warm, all the same. "He's an easy kid to love."

RONAN

She's amazing, and she has no idea. "He's a grizzly bear who shares a soul with a meek scientist. Laying the pipes and wires to properly support that is far more challenging than anything you'll ever need to build for your den."

She blinks at me. Then she swallows and looks down at her hands. "A lot of people have helped. Ever since I came home, but especially since Hayden and Rio and Kel came. These past few months, he's finally gotten to be a real bear."

The old ache blooms behind my eyelids. I can't make it go away, but I can speak to the ache that lives inside her. "He has always been a real bear. It can take us a long time to figure out what to do with how big we are. Reilly fills his space beautifully. That's the work of a lifetime, not a few months."

She lets out a breath very slowly.

Her bear cub gave me the most important clue, and I

didn't pay enough attention. His mom likes to build sturdy things. "You didn't have any fancy parts to work with, or any books with useful diagrams, or any engineering specialists to help you find your way. But even when this pack was under unimaginable pressure, you made space for Reilly to stay curious and soft and true to his heart."

I look at the woman whose drawings scattered on the ground around us are an ode to nuanced, adaptable, resilient sturdiness. "I didn't have that until I was a grown bear."

Horror lands in her eyes.

My bear wants to roar. To proclaim his strength.

I remind him of the hardest lesson. Sometimes strength is quiet. Open. Vulnerable. Soft.

He rumbles, but he subsides.

Danielle's head dips. "Maybe we did well enough. But it's done Reilly a lot of good to see those same things in you."

My bear turns to snow—the clingy, lazy, almost melted kind.

I grab his ears before he does something entirely ridiculous like try to crawl into her lap. "It did me a lot of good to see those things in Reilly. You're raising a wonderful cub. I'm honored to know him."

Her cheeks turn a pretty color that makes my semi-melted bear even less likely to return to solid form anytime soon. "Thank you."

I need to get us back to safer ground, the kind where a watery bear can't cause a landslide, but I somehow can't make myself leave this place of awkward hearts and stumbling words and pink cheeks. "Will you also accept my compliment about these wondrous drawings?"

She looks down at her diagrams as if she's surprised that they're still there. Then she squares her shoulders. "Will you show me how to update the schematics? The proper ones? I've been reading the books you brought, but I haven't got it all straight, yet."

That's because I brought entirely the wrong books. "I'll make you a deal."

Wary eyes—but somehow still vulnerable ones. "What kind of deal?"

I'm in so much trouble. "I'll teach you engineering. Not from the books. They start in the wrong place for you."

Her nose wrinkles just like her son when he's confused.

I touch her glorious drawings. "We'll start here. We'll look at the beauty and wisdom of what you already know. Then we can add what might be helpful."

She blinks at me.

My bear whispers very dangerous promises. I do my best to ignore him, which isn't easy. He's a big, warm, yearning puddle. I reach out and place my finger on one of her pages. "Why did you split the water flow so many ways, here?"

She shrugs, even as her eyes focus. "To control the water pressure."

I do my best to sound like a competent engineering specialist. "This method will require more maintenance."

Her eyes come up to mine as her backbone straightens. “We don’t mind the extra work.”

I smile, at her answer and her backbone. “Exactly.”

She blinks at me again.

I grin. She makes sturdiness so very interesting. “You built this to the strengths of your pack and your team.” Every centimeter of this design sings of a submissive wolf’s instincts. Soothe the power. Protect the den. Put in the work. “You also put every one of those pipes that I would have considered extraneous to work doing something useful.” More flows into the hot pools. More comfort. More future flexibility for packmates who might need a place to retreat away from the main den buildings or a spot to warm aching bones. Sturdiness as a prime directive of design, wielded by a wolf who deeply loves her pack.

Danielle nods cautiously.

I pat the papers. “Here’s my part of the deal. I would like for you to teach me how to do this. To think like this.”

She stares at me and doesn’t quite manage to hide the horror creeping back into her eyes.

I sigh. It’s entirely justified. I’m going to be a terrible student. “I want you to show me how to imagine a system from the perspective of a repair bot instead of that of an engineer or building contractor or architect.”

Reluctant amusement slowly mixes with the horror. “You want to learn how to be small and invisible?”

My bear nods agreeably.

Dumbass. I grin at her. “See, you have the far harder job.”

She shakes her head, but the amusement hasn't left her eyes, and it maybe isn't quite as reluctant, anymore. "Is this kind of dealmaking how my son somehow ended up with fifteen laptop computers and a life-sized robot?"

That was one of my better deals. It's been a good year for bear negotiations. "Would you like a robot? I have another one. It has a couple of parts that got a little chewed, but I'm sure you could fix those up in no time."

Her lips quirk. "Some of us have serious work to do or the new den building isn't going to have any heat or water."

I try to look meek. "You can always put me to work to keep me out of trouble. But I want to use these diagrams. They're pretty."

The sigh that comes out of her is a glorious mix of disgruntled, exasperated pleasure. "They're a mess."

They're papers that bear witness to history and the chaotic, uncertain beauty of their birth. They're priceless. "I'm an engineer. If I don't get my hands on something messy at least three times a day, I get cranky."

Her dimples press deeply into her cheeks. "Fine. Brown was supposed to be helping Kenny and Robbie upgrade the connections to the cook shack, but he went fishing." She picks up a paper without even looking at it and shoves it into my hands.

My bear wants to nuzzle in against her cherry red ears and never leave.

Instead, I take the paper. "On it. Anything else?"

She looks ready to dig herself an underground cave and move there for the winter, but she clears her throat and nods. "If you don't mind taking a look at the oven while you're there, one of the fuses is being temperamental again. Shelley will probably give you a burnt cookie or two for your troubles."

My bear struts. She's entrusting him to care for the pack food supply.

I remind him that we have no fucking clue how ovens work.

He bats at me with his paw. It's time to learn.

12

HAYDEN

Shelley collapses against my side, giggling helplessly. She wheezes in a breath and tries to speak, and then just starts laughing again.

I grin down at the wolf who didn't laugh for weeks after I got here. "I take it that Ronan hasn't managed to fix the oven, yet?"

She waves her arms around, possibly approximating some kind of bear theatrics.

Kennedy ambles over, ducking the mixing spoon that's trying to tell the story. "Does this mean we don't get any more cookies until the new kitchen stuff gets here?"

That would make my belly very sad. "I saw Reilly go in there with the pack phone, so hopefully they're Googling repair instructions." If that fails, I already put in an emergency call to Reese to see if we can borrow one of his ovens. He didn't even laugh. The cats might be more addicted to Shelley's cookies than we are.

Shelley manages to regain partial control of her vocal cords. "That oven is so old that the instructions are probably written on the wall of some cave."

Kennedy elbows me. "I thought Ronan was a really smart engineering bear."

He is, but nobody at Whistler Pack would ever let the engineering team anywhere near the kitchen appliances. That's probably how the first rocket ship got accidentally made. "Be nice, or that very smart bear will figure out how to hack into your math lessons and make you learn calculus."

She gives me a look that she absolutely learned from my mother. "Calculus is cool."

I don't even want to know. "So are cookies, so give me a report, since I can't get any good information out of Shelley, here." Our chief baker and mural painter is still wheezing periodically as she leans against my ribs.

Kennedy grins. "Robbie has learned some more curse words. Kenny tried to leave the repair zone, but Cleve growled at him from the woods. Reilly asked Adelina to call Scotty to see if he could help, but they got distracted talking about bridges."

I have no idea if Scotty knows anything about ovens, but he's definitely not going to prioritize anything that mundane over a wolf who might be talked into sharing his obsession for rendering truth in bridge form. "Do we have a dinner plan that doesn't involve a functional oven?"

Shelley snorts from her spot against my ribs.

Right. Engineers can't fix ovens and alphas definitely shouldn't try to mess with kitchen schedules. "Is there anything else either of you needs me to know before you go back to snickering at a polar bear?" If it was any other shifter, I'd be worried, but I have absolutely no doubt that Ronan is gleefully turning his repair debacle into an object lesson for every wolf, raven, and bear who happens to wander through the kitchen.

The curse words are just theatrics. Mostly.

Kennedy's eyes turn solemn. "I went with Hoot to find Grady."

I wait for the rest. Kennedy's wolf is really dominant, and trust is something that Grady can't hold on to, most days. He can handle Hoot and Fallon most of the time. The rest of us, it's a crapshoot. I never go anywhere near his trees without Lissa.

Shelley is waiting attentively, too. Grady ate one of her cookies last week.

Kennedy takes a slightly shaky breath. "We told him about the run tomorrow. He didn't say no."

Shelley smiles. "That's good. That's really good."

Kennedy nods. "Yeah. He bumped against Hoot's shoulder while he was walking in circles, and he asked for another cookie and a new blanket." Another breath that she lets shake. A baby alpha who's learning to let us see her tremble. "He was singing one of Kelsey's songs when we left. One of the new ones."

Damn. "That's good. That's really good."

Shelley swats me with her mixing spoon. "I already said that."

Kennedy giggles, which was likely the point. "Be nice to your alpha."

My wolf lolls his tongue. Good pack. Feisty pack.

I roll my eyes at all of them. "I'll just go see if Eliza needs any help moving big rocks."

"Good." Shelley taps my arm with her spoon again. "I have some sandwiches you can take out to her crew, and some fresh lemonade."

I grin. An alpha's work is never done.

FALLON

I grit my teeth. Good bird. Nice bird. Do not bite the wolf who brings us tea in the pretty mug.

My raven screeches. She wants coffee, not the tea that smells like mushrooms and tastes like boiled underwear. And she wants bacon. Which she can't have because she ate it all yesterday. Mikayla went to town to get more, but she isn't back, and besides, a polar bear broke our oven.

The strange flutters in my belly happen again.

I put a hand over them. "I know. You don't like mushroom tea, either."

Ben's eyes get all soft and goopy like they always do when I talk to the demon child in my belly. "Is she swimming again?"

I scowl at the poor, foolish man who picked me for his mate. "She's a bird. She hates swimming."

Brown snorts from his whittling stool.

I ignore him. The idea of my demon chick having to live in a cramped ocean for five more months is almost as awful as knowing that I'll have to stop flying soon. "She's just using up all of her energy so that she'll be a lazy, sleepy baby after she's born."

Wrinkles settles a cup of tea in my hands. "You just go right on believing that, dear."

These wolves have no idea how close they are to pecked eyeballs. "I thought healers were supposed to reassure their pregnant patients and keep us calm and fat and happy."

She chuckles. "That's Ben's job. Mine is to tell you the truth and make sure you can't reach any sharp objects when you go into labor."

There goes my whole birthing plan, whatever that is. I only made it three pages into the book Cori gave to me to read before I ran away screaming. I'm not scared of pain. It's the part about being totally out of control that I can't handle.

I probably should have thought of that before I let my mate put a demon chick in my belly.

He nuzzles against my cheek, his soft scruff ruffling my feathers and soothing everything else. "Want anything from the kitchen?"

The kitchen is only thirty steps away and it's covered in oven parts. "Tea that doesn't smell like mushrooms?"

Wrinkles leans over and takes a sniff of my mug.

"Your nose is still on the fritz. It smells like mint and rose petals."

My nose is a weak and feeble thing compared to any wolf's. I have no idea how Cori is surviving this pregnancy business. She hasn't even stopped puking, yet. I take a deep breath and rub Ben's scruff and try to ignore the smell emanating from my tea. Clearly the tiny flyer in my belly is going to suck at woodcraft. "Maybe one of the laptops so that I can check on our trades?"

He smiles against my cheek. "Done. Want to head out to Hidden Creek after that?"

He gets me so well. Tomorrow's daylight run to a place that we all know doesn't exactly require a scouting expedition, but every single day that my raven can still take to the skies is precious, and watching a sexy wolf run through the snow below me is one of the few things I actually like about winter.

I shiver. We don't have snow at the den, yet, thank goodness. Although it might look pretty from the hot pools.

My bird sighs happily. She adores the hot pools. I need to find a few shinies at the creek to thank Eliza for keeping the coolest pool at a temperature that works for pregnant mamas. Cori hardly ever turns green while she's soaking. A few new shinies for trading wouldn't be a bad thing, either, and I'll have a willing wolf to carry my treasures home.

He kisses the top of my head and unwraps his arms from around the sweater that makes me at least twice as big as I really am. "I'll be back soon. Don't let Wrinkles put anything in my soup."

The soup that she's been stirring all morning weirdly doesn't smell like mushrooms, even though I'm pretty sure I saw some go in the pot. It's a huge cast-iron deal hung on a tripod over our fire, which is big enough to keep even a raven warm. "Are we feeding everyone today, or is Brown really hungry?"

He doesn't even growl, which is worrisome. He's been uncharacteristically mellow since Ronan came to visit. Cheerful, almost. It's unsettling.

Wrinkles scoops the ladle up to her nose and sniffs. "Dorie might bring her crew over. Molly wanted to see how I make my frying-pan dumplings."

That would explain why all the guys except Brown are finding somewhere else to be. For whatever reason, grumpy bears don't make Molly shake. Even Ben makes her really nervous, but Brown can frown and growl and snarl and she just acts like he's part of the forest.

Maybe it's a bear thing. The freaking polar bear in the cook shack doesn't seem to be worrying anyone, either. "Can we have fried onions with the dumplings?"

Brandy snickers from the spread-out blanket where she's making snowflakes out of shiny paper with Kelsey. "My baby niece is so weird."

I scowl at her. "Wrinkles's fried onions are delicious and they don't smell like mushrooms."

Kelsey walks over and puts her cheek on my belly. "Maybe my cousin would like some apple slices."

Those actually smell halfway decent, but I'd eat them

even if they smelled like boiled underwear because it makes Kelsey's eyes shine every time I do it. "Those sound pretty good."

She runs back over to the blanket and digs into the snack bag she brought with her earlier this morning, along with the shiny paper and a pair of scissors as big as her head. "Ravi helped me cut this one up, and we sang it a song so that it would be a really happy apple."

I try not to think about food having emotions. "Was it a song with real words, or the kind where Ravi just wrinkles his nose a lot and expects us to understand?"

Her rolling giggles settle something inside me that nothing else can reach. "No, silly. That was the baby bunny song."

I grin and take a handful of apple slices from her container. "I'm a raven. We don't speak bunny." Or apple, or any other of the myriad languages that the wise and terrifying small cousin of my demon chick speaks.

Kelsey pats my belly, like she's maybe reassuring its inhabitant that the world is a nice place full of songs and shiny snowflakes and apple slices. Which is a good thing. My psyche runs more toward life lessons about bunkers and backup exits and how to land on your toes so that the floors don't squeak.

I have no idea how to raise an upstanding citizen.

Wrinkles eases the mug I've been holding out of my fingers and takes a sip. "Maybe Kelsey can fetch you a nice glass of cold water from our new tap."

Brown mutters something under his breath about

frozen pipes and foolish luxuries as she runs off, happy to have an important task.

Wrinkles just chuckles. "You looked at Danielle's design yourself, dear, and even you couldn't find fault with it. I, for one, am happy to have hot and cold water right here at our camp."

Kelsey stops to pat Brown's cheek as she collects a big glass from the dish shelf.

I shake my head. Mint-and-rose-petal tea would be so much warmer.

My bird caws. The tiny tyrant wants water. With ice. Pretty, shiny ice.

I groan as quietly as I can. That one is Ronan's fault. I never should have let my demon chick listen to a polar bear's bedtime stories.

DAMIEN

I glare at the screen of my crappy phone.

They all just fucking need to leave me alone. Which I've said, in really small words that even dumbass wolves should be able to understand, but none of them are hearing me.

Today they've apparently all decided to chew on me at once.

I growl. I should just delete everything.

My wolf whines. He likes the messages with pictures

of home. He misses the forest. And smells that don't make his throat sore and his nose itch.

I remind him that we don't have any skills to get a better job and he needs to suck it up. I'm lucky I got this one. I don't really know how to mop floors, either, but the jerk who hired me is mostly too drunk to notice.

My hand curls into a fist around my phone. I hate that smell, too. Even my bed smells like stale beer, and I stopped drinking that crap weeks ago. It tastes like garbage and it doesn't help me forget a damn thing.

I glare at the texts. The worst of them will be the one from Reilly. I bet the pack doesn't know that the little shit is sending me stuff. Dorky pictures and stupid stories. Because he's young enough and cute enough that he got to stay.

My wolf whines again. He remembers when a grizzly cub used to follow him around in the forest.

Stupid fucking wolf.

I delete Reilly's text. I can't handle him trying to be nice. Nice is weak. Nice gets your beer stolen and your head cuffed and makes your rent money mysteriously disappear.

Kennedy's text probably isn't much better, but I kind of like that she can beat the shit out of everyone. Watching her flatten Baird was one of the very few parts of the last four months that didn't entirely suck.

Heck, make that the last six years.

I throw the phone onto my sad excuse for a bed, drop my head into my hands, and groan. I'm exactly the pathetic asswipe that Baird tells me I am. He reminded me just this morning as he grabbed my lunch and headed out the door.

Jerk. He's probably not even headed to work. He says he'll get paid the big bucks to haul idiots out of the ditch when the snow comes, but I'm pretty sure that's just an excuse to make me pay more rent while he waits on little white flakes from the sky to make him feel important.

I sigh and make an actual effort to dig my head out of my ass. I need to get to work. I leave my phone where it is. Evan will eventually give up on trying to convince me to take a class at the community college with him, and Kenny is probably just sending me a list again. One with all the crap I can do if I come crawling back on my hands and knees.

I can't. Not ever. I saw my mom do that too many times.

I yank my jacket off its hook and swear as the hook comes out of the wall. Nothing works. Everything breaks.

Story of my fucking life.

I hate this. I hate my entire existence.

I just don't know how to fix it.

13

KEL

I shoot a glare at the polar bear who did the same damn thing that I did last night and apparently doesn't plan on letting it slow him down at all.

Rio bumps against my shoulder. "You can stay home, old man."

There isn't a single beta in this pack who believes that, including the other one who went along on our late-night trip to harass a guy holding a mop. I have no idea why a daylight run to Hidden Creek is setting off all of our spider senses, but it definitely has. I eye the guy who has better radar than any of us. "Are there any particular reasons that I need to be worried, or just the usual?"

Kennedy snorts on her way by us, a small white wolf tugging on her jeans. "We're taking a polar bear on a run in the woods. What could go wrong?"

We could lose Robbie, for starters. The snow is a foot

deep at Hidden Creek. "Are all the ghost wolves where we think they are?" She did a patrol loop this morning to check.

She bends down and growls at Robbie, which would be a lot more effective if she wasn't also scratching his itchy ear. "Next time maybe don't hide in Wrinkles's medicine cupboard, silly."

Rio grins and scratches the other itchy spot by Robbie's tail. "I bet he'll have lots of good hiding places today."

I roll my eyes as all three of them look delighted by that prospect.

Kennedy pats my shoulder. "Don't worry. If he gets lost in the snow, Ronan will find him."

I shoot her a look that won't do a damn bit of good. "You mean Ghost will find him while a dumbass polar bear tries to build an ice cave." There isn't nearly enough snow for that, even at Hidden Creek, but looming failure has never daunted Ronan in the slightest.

Kennedy grins. "Or that. Don't worry. We've worked out some special owl hoots for this run. Robbie knows all of them and he knows that he has to use them with Myrna a lot because she's his special buddy and she gets easily distracted."

Myrna will lose a pup shortly after Ronan becomes a serial killer, but buddies are a smart idea. Probably not one Kennedy came up with, but she's very good at coaching Robbie.

The small white wolf in question, done with standing

still, licks her knee. Then he bounds off, presumably in search of his friends. Kennedy glances back long enough to make sure she's not needed, and then there's a pile of clothes on the ground and a lithe brown wolf bounding out of them.

"Show-off." I couldn't have done much better myself, but she doesn't need to know that.

Rio chuckles. "She's been practicing for weeks, ever since Ebony did a lightning shift to catch Mellie before she fell down that crevice."

Ebony was crazy fast—and three wolves still beat her to the streaking toddler, including an elderly one with a crotchety hip. Keeping the pups safe is not what's making the back of my neck itch. I look around, cataloguing potential problems. "Is Cleve coming?" Even his hip should manage today's pace, and he got at least half a dozen personally delivered invitations.

Rio's eyes gleam with satisfaction. "Yes. He's at the front with Layla and Miriam."

Those two promptly adopted him after he saved Mellie from some nasty bruises. "Good. They'll keep him busy." And away from the left flank where Hoot and Ghost are hoping to have Grady join them. Keeping the Dunn psychics from overloading each other is one of today's trickier challenges.

It's also a really good problem to have.

A sentinel leans against my shoulder. "Trust your pack, old man."

That nickname needs to die, even if it's disturbingly accurate. "We're throwing a polar-bear-sized spark into a parched forest. My job isn't to trust. It's to have the damn fire extinguishers ready."

I don't actually expect a response, because we've had this conversation and I'm not actually all that concerned about Ronan's participation. Common sense says that taking an apex predator on a run in the woods through the turf of some of our most traumatized wolves is lunacy. The pack's reaction to his actual presence in our midst says something entirely different.

I'm still bringing my fire extinguishers.

Rio surveys the gathered pack, just like I'm doing. He just has a different sensor array. "There's going to be a fire, today. When it happens, you need to let it burn."

I try to keep the horror out of my eyes, but he'll know it's there anyhow. "Are you fucking kidding me?"

He grins. "Nope."

Sentinels are evil, but if he's telling me to park my fire extinguishers, he's not expecting danger. He's letting me know, in his usual delicate fashion, that I'm about to have an acutely uncomfortable day and I need to deal. "Go poke holes in Hayden's happiness. I have shit to do."

He squeezes my shoulder, which is a lot more alarming than talk of letting the forest burn.

As he walks away, I watch to see who's tracking his movements. Kelsey, because she's got sentinel radar and because she loves the big jerk. Kenny, because he's jumpy as hell after last night and his baby pack didn't crawl out of their sleeping bags early enough this morning to set him right. Shelley, because the need to run is stronger in her than in any wolf I've ever met, and she knows we won't go until Rio gives the signal.

Ronan isn't watching the big black wolf of death, however. He's cheerfully loading up an enormous pair of rucksacks with everything the pups and mamas and teachers and kitchen crew think might be necessary for a run in the woods. I have no idea how even half the crap they've gathered is going to fit, but I have no doubt that Ronan will find a way.

I sigh and look around for my own gear. It's almost time to go. I still don't know what's setting off my beta alarms, but I'll just have to keep my eyes open. Last night a polar bear roared. Today, something entirely different is on the move.

RONAN

I can smell the snow. It's faint, buried under the smells of sub-arctic forest that my bear acclimated to long ago, and the less common smells of the lunch he carries over his broad shoulders.

The weight is nothing, and Kelsey's delight at being able to bring so many apple slices for Fallon lit a bright and shining glow inside my ribs. I look over at the tiny red wolf who has already dashed between my paws a dozen times. That, also, feeds the glow. I usually have to work to earn such trust. This small one, she gifts it.

My bear would carry apple slices into war if she wished it.

Another pup tumbles through my paws, this one paying far less attention. No matter. I swat Mellie into the air because it makes her yip with glee, and because her alpha is ready to catch her. Pup basketball wasn't a game I imagined playing on this run, but Reilly set me straight this morning.

They have heard the stories of Whistler Pack shenanigans. He had a list.

My bear rumbles his approval. The cub is focused. Observant.

I snicker and hope he remembers that when we're trying to make an ice cave out of a snowball's worth of snow. That, too, was on the list.

He grins. Maybe a bridge of ice. One big enough for the pups to stand on and roar.

I chuckle and swat Jade toward her alpha a lot more gently than I tossed Mellie. A bridge isn't actually a bad idea, and it might convince Bailey to reinstate whatever she did to my login for the bridges learning module.

Apparently we aren't supposed to re-write the provincial curriculum.

I veer to avoid the large tree that's trying to get in the way of my romp and nearly squash Kennedy as she drops down from one of its branches. She rolls under my belly, a fancy piece of footwork that has Kel rolling his eyes and Dorie cackling overhead. They're part of the crew traveling in human form alongside packmates who can't find comfort in their fur.

That somehow finds a warm place inside my ribs, too. This pack has such ease with each other. Such lack of demand to be anything other than what is real and true. Belonging that is freely given, not earned. It tugs at me. I brought clothing and boots so I can travel human on the way home. I hope to walk with Terrence for a while. He writes poems that wreck my soul wonderfully.

Teesha says I should maybe not tell him that quite yet.

Two wolves dash in front of my nose, and they're not pups this time. One is Layla, who gave me a big hug last night before she snuck off to the hot pools with her mate. The other is a wolf I don't know, but I can tell by the look in her eyes that she didn't mean to get this close to a polar bear.

I slow my walk and keep her in my peripheral vision. She circles, eyeing me.

A word comes through the earth. *Molly.*

My heart gladdens. The young stray that Cleve found in the woods. Adelina wasn't sure she would come today. Too many big men.

Molly runs in a wide arc, circling. Layla stays close behind.

An enormous black wolf joins them.

I can see others in the pack changing position, too. Dominants and males getting out of the way.

My bear moves to join them. He is very big.

More words from the earth. *Stay.*

I want to growl at the sentinel who is talking to my paws, but that would only scare Molly. Instead, I stare into her gorgeous brown eyes. My bear would know who she is, this brave one whose is edging toward him.

I grab his ears and try to turn his head away. She is a wolf. A submissive, scared one. They do not stare into the souls of big, scary men, or bears.

He ignores me. Instead, he walks very slowly toward the wolf who has stopped moving and turned to face him.

Pack wraps around us, loosely, gently, leaving many exit routes.

My bear stops. The last steps are hers.

Stillness. Wariness. Determination.

I look into deep brown courage. *I see you, little one.*

Amusement. Two dashed steps and a warm tongue on my cold nose, and then Molly is running straight through the middle of her pack with Layla at her shoulder as Dorie whoops in the trees and an alpha howls his joy and a grizzly cub falls over in the dirt beside me, laughing his head off.

My bear only stares at the running wolf, stupefied.

She licked his nose.

DANIELLE

My wolf shakes her head as a polar bear bats at her cub with a paw big enough to slice him in two. She isn't worried. She just saw that bear's heart, and it is kindness to its very depths.

I want to tell her that there are parts of a man's heart

that she has never understood, but that isn't true. Reilly's father wasn't a bad man. He was just one without enough control over the big, brash needs of his bear. Ronan isn't that man, and as I watch his newly wet nose shining in the sun, it's suddenly so very clear that he isn't that kind of bear, either. Or rather, he is. Big and brash—and unfathomably kind.

Which somehow makes all of the difference.

I jump as a howl sounds from the front of the pack. Lissa, teasing those of us with lazy legs and reminding us that we're out in the forest on this crisp winter day to run.

Kennedy dashes past me, her hiking boots crunching the last of the dry leaves. "Anyone who licks a beta's nose gets the biggest cookies."

That's a good game. My wolf grins and looks around. Kenny won't be expecting a sneak attack from a submissive, but he doesn't scare her today. Not after what he did in town last night. I heard Kel talking with Hayden this morning while I was saving Shelley from the flashlight-wielding robot wired to her oven.

That was how Ronan solved the oven light's corroded wiring issue before he went to town to try to scare Eliza's son home.

My wolf crouches, her sights set on Kenny's nose. The robot was funny. She will win a cookie and give it to the polar bear. He likes cookies.

My brain stutters as her full intentions register.

She sneaks into the shadows. Kenny sometimes forgets to look there.

I grab my wolf by the scruff and shake her.

She shrugs me off. Not now. She's busy. She wants a cookie for the big, white bear. He's sweet with Reilly and he sings pretty songs and he's very warm and cozy to sleep beside in the pup pile.

The stutters in my brain trip over each other and land in a dazed pile. I rode on a teacup ride at a fair, once. I'd almost have myself gathered up and then the cup would spin wildly and my stomach would head for the hills again.

I have no idea how my wolf got her paws on the controls for my teacup.

She drops to her belly, her focus entirely on the hunt. She makes eye contact with Dorie, up in a tree. The cat is a good hunter. She will help catch the beta wolf.

I bang on the inside of her head. We are not hunting cookies for a polar bear.

She considers my words and dismisses them. Cookies are a worthy courting gift. Fish are too hard to catch.

My teacup isn't even attached to the ride anymore. I spin helplessly as my wolf turns her head to watch a polar bear and a grizzly cub use their combined paws as a scoop to toss Mellie into Ebony's arms. The naked toddler squeals and licks her beta's nose before she shifts back into her fur.

My wolf grins. Good hunting. Smart bears.

I plaster my face to the windows of my teacup as it zooms through outer space. I need to find my clothes. I could walk with Eliza for a while and talk about the pipes for Dorie's camp. Or I could tell Lissa about the owl shifter in Manitoba who's got a nearly new set of batteries to trade.

My wolf snorts as Kel streaks by with Eliza and Lissa hot on his heels. This is not time for talking.

An enormous black wolf settles into a crouch beside me.

I gulp. He sees too much, and my intergalactic teacup has way too many windows. I don't know who designed it, but they didn't read any of the engineering books and they absolutely did not look at how much glass costs in Lissa's spreadsheets.

His cheek nuzzles mine.

I lean against Rio and borrow some of the strength he's always willing to lend, and then I catch my balance and bring my teacup back to the ground. I smile as Shelley and Glow flank Kenny in a hunting maneuver as old as wolves.

They turn as a unit and look at me, the message in their eyes unified and unmistakable. The kill is mine, if I want it.

14

RIO

I expected fire today. I had no idea that Danielle's quiet, sturdy wolf was going to be the one to set it.

My sentinel snorts. It's always the butterfly wings that flap and upend the universe. Today, Shelley made giant cookies and Layla chased a squirrel and Molly licked a polar bear's nose. A whole herd of flapping butterfly wings.

It isn't butterflies moving now, though. It's engineers.

Eliza stations herself where I can see her and Danielle can't. Putting my sentinel on notice. I'd better get this right. Indrani and Fallon settle on a branch overhead, ready to put out fires—or fan them.

Then a small red wolf walks into the center of us all and tips her nose up at the sky.

I don't question Kelsey's instincts. Neither do her alphas, who arrive at her side moments later. Hayden's big yellow wolf sounds a low note under the red pup's high one. Lissa listens quietly for a moment before she adds an undulating howl full of empathy that shakes the wolf beside me down to her bones.

The alpha pair of this pack is not afraid of fire.

I add the voice of a sentinel to Kelsey's song, singing messages from the earth of incoming snow and softening seeds and a mysterious, crystal-clear image of a teacup twirling high in a night sky.

Kelsey's melody line giggles. She gives the teacup a spin with her nose.

Danielle's breath shudders.

Ah. The teacup is hers, then.

More stories join in. Molly's, bright and surprised and beginning to uncover very old pain. Ravi's joy for the child he holds in his arms and the one he will see arrive in the spring. Adelina, who can't unsee the bridge that has formed in her head, and Kenny trying to staunch the blood oozing through his newest cracks.

I put stern words into the earth. He needs to let it flow.

Braden howls cheerfully about the berries that will come in the summer, and Kennedy's wolf offers up its opinions about math, and Ghost tells the daybright sky about a poem that broke her heart and stitched it back together again.

A low growl begins. The words of that poem, rendered by a polar bear who knows how to speak wolf. The raw song of a soul aching to match the shape of the body it inhabits. Of a body that no longer knows what shape it is meant to be. Of a fragile, daring flicker of belief that perhaps belonging is not a shape at all.

Pack hears the rumbled words. Cherishes them.

Terrence, his cheeks fiery red, sits down hard, a poet entirely undone.

Teesha, who got him here, lets her tears fall unheeded.

Ronan's growl reaches out to soften Terrence's landing and catch Teesha's tears.

I cup my hands around the fragile, daring flicker and blow a sentinel's breath over the tiny flames.

RONAN

I watch helplessly as an enormous chunk of ice breaks off the glacier that lives inside my bear and falls into the waiting sea. I didn't mean to crack myself open. I only meant to honor the poet and his poem.

I shudder as pack voices wrap around each of us who know what it is to feel at war with your own shape. It slashes at me that Reilly is one of them. A bear cub who had to be small for far too long. Another chunk of ice falls off of my glacier. *I see you, bear who will be big.*

Kelsey's high song rises in defense of her friend. He is already the perfect size.

My bear laughs, dazzled by her, even as his cracks widen.

Kennedy bumps against a grizzly cub, giving him

permission to be as big as he wants. Hoot and Ghost promise to run with him in the woods, always, and Kenny rolls his eyes and scowls and grudgingly tells Reilly that somebody needs to get big enough to sit on Kennedy and it might as well be a bear who usually thinks before he acts.

I let my tears fall to the earth. It isn't poetry—but it's a love letter to a grizzly cub all the same.

My glacier heaves as the fault lines spread.

DANIELLE

I want to go to my son, to wrap myself around him and hold him tight like I've done for so many years, but my wolf can see the truth. He is ready to be in the world outside of my arms. Reilly's baby pack is holding him, walking with him, ready for him to get as big as he needs to be.

It is a different bear who stands alone.

My wolf riots inside me. The silent yearning in the big, white bear is the very same as the one in her son. Why can't everyone see? He is so sad, this big bear who believes he needs the biggest wolf pack on the continent to hold even his smallest self, and it's not true.

I gasp for breath, but there's no room for air inside my ribs. They're too full of my wolf's surging violence. My teacup shatters into a billion smithereens as she attacks it with her teeth.

I stare at her teeth and shake. I don't know what to do. I don't know what she needs me to do.

She crouches, growling, over delicate porcelain shards. *Help him.*

I don't know how. I've never known how. I can fix almost anything, but I don't know how to fix a bear.

She snarls. My hands know how.

I can't breathe. I don't know what she's talking about and the song of pack is circling around Ronan's pain and we are so willing, but we don't have any idea what to do.

Use. Your. Hands.

The words are sharp, slashing teeth.

I hold my hands up, frantic and helpless. And then I stare as a pencil somewhere deep inside my brain starts to move. Slow lines at first, and then faster ones, because my wolf is right and my hands know and this is a schematic that I've already drawn, over and over again until my eraser almost went through the paper.

Ronan is wrong. He doesn't need a big pack. He needs something sturdy. Something that puts his big flow into a lot of small pipes where it can be useful and make warmth and spread joy.

I reach out for the confusion of my pack—and their love. I know how it could work. I know how it could be done.

It isn't a wolf who answers first.

It's a grizzly cub.

My hands tremble. Reilly would be right in the very center of this design. My son. My beautiful, gangly, gentle boy. I don't know if what I've drawn is good enough. Safe enough. Proper enough.

My wolf's teeth snap. She understands this drawing. She knows each of the parts and all of the tools and where to take care. She knows how the big bear can be big. She will tell pack.

I try to argue, to ask her to wait, to be careful, to be cautious, to be sure, but I don't have any breath.

She tips her head up to the daybright sky and begins her song.

HAYDEN

Sweet holy fuck.

My wolf stares, gobsmacked, as the solid, efficient wolf who never rocks any boats howls a song and launches an iceberg at the damn *Titanic*. A white, furry *Titanic* who has spent all of his adult life engineering himself into being unsinkable.

Which should terrify me, because I can see Ronan's eyes.

But I can also see hers.

RIO

My sentinel stands witness as a quiet, competent wolf hunts a polar bear's single, most unshakeable belief all the way back to its lair. The one that says full-sized Ronan won't ever fit anywhere, at least not in any of the places that his soft heart has ever wanted to reside.

I listen to Danielle as she hunts—and I bow my head. Courage comes in as many shades as the green of a forest, and today it lives in a grizzly cub's mama. Danielle's wolf didn't just set her human on fire—she's pointing flames at a polar bear, too. Wielding her tools with workmanlike precision to melt the ice that protects the fragile lines of poetry written deepest in Ronan's heart.

My sentinel has always been able to see them, but I've never been able to free them. Ronan has never given me permission.

Apparently I just needed a better blow torch.

Awe blazes inside me as Danielle offers up an answer to those fragile, daring, sacred words. Her answer isn't the pretty version that Kelsey would have set to music, or the dramatic Russian one that Ivan might have penned. It lacks the fierceness that Adrianna would have put at its core, or the technical flourishes and pretty welds that Scotty would have added.

Danielle's answer, the possibility that her wolf is diagramming out on the collective paper of our pack, is one that comes from the heart of an engineer who has never read any of the books. A drawing that quietly, deftly lays out all of the parts and joins and junction boxes that would be necessary for the bear of poem to exist.

If he wants to.

My sentinel gulps as he sees the fullness of what she's laying in front of pack. System schematics that make a polar bear useful, that use him to warm a den and fill soaking pools with joy and bring safety to all of our shadows. Those parts aren't scary. Ronan has always known how to do those things, and this pack is already letting him.

The breath-snatching part of Danielle's design isn't in the outcomes. It's in the guts. In what she's hooked up to the heat exchanger. Ronan has always chosen to flow through the pipes of a pack as the embodiment of kindness. A quiet, sturdy, cautious wolf is asking him to do it with his power, too. With his full size. With his true shape.

A practical, pragmatic, searing offer that is about to run smack into the brick wall of Ronan's biggest fear.

I reach into the earth and brace as the collision happens.

Danielle's song doesn't lose. Searing answers never do.

But the wall that crumbles has a polar bear's heart trapped under the rubble.

15

HAYDEN

I hate it when Lissa glares at me. Especially when she's right.

I shrug helplessly. "I don't know." It's a sucky answer, but it's the best one I have. I've been trying to come up with a better one as I supervise the building of snowmen so that they don't end up with pups rolled up inside of them, but I'm not making a hell of a lot of progress.

She leans against me and makes a face. "This alpha gig needs to come with a manual."

My wolf hides his nose under his paws.

I pat his head. At least she didn't wish for a spreadsheet. "We'll figure it out." The question that we thought was on the table might have been left to two consenting adults to sort out. This one, there's no chance. Not when Reilly's eyes are full of painful hope that's been holding its breath for hours, already.

There is no doubt about how a grizzly cub would vote.

I look over at the ice bridge that Ronan built from river water and all the snow we could gather and magic pixie dust. It gleams, translucent and lightly orange in the setting sun, with Braden curled up on its ramparts. Or whatever you call the castle tower that somehow got added to a bridge. One of the more tangible aftershocks of Danielle's steady laying out of a vision so daring that my wolf is still gaping.

It blows my mind that it feels possible. Whistler Pack, guided by my mother's deep and sophisticated understanding of pack structure, has been working on building a big enough space for a polar bear for most of my life. It seems utterly insane that a small, ragtag pack of wounded wolves who are mostly missing their dominants could even contemplate doing such a thing.

Except a sturdy wolf who likes raisins in her oatmeal and order in her toolbox drew us a set of freaking instructions. A road map to a polar bear's most deeply hidden wish—or to all of his biggest nightmares. Whistler Pack makes space for Ronan with checks and balances. Counterweights. The rock-solid assurance that there are always forces big enough to contain his bear. Danielle's diagram didn't even try.

The part of me that is one of Ronan's closest friends would place every single poker chip he owns on Danielle's bet and fight a polar bear to keep them there. The part of me that will always be my mother's son quakes at the thought of trying something that she never dared, even with the might of the largest pack in the continent at her back.

Even after decades of work putting those checks and balances and counterweights in place, Ronan could hurt Whistler Pack.

He could destroy the wolves of Ghost Mountain.

Lissa's hand taps on my chest, right over my heart. "Are you going to be done thinking quite so loudly, soon?"

I sigh and wrap my arm around her shoulders. "I don't know which way to push this, Liss. I just know that my weight needs to be on the scales." Every fiber of my alpha being says so.

She keeps her fingers over my heart.

Strength comes in so many forms, and sometimes my wolf is a dumbass who forgets that. "What do you think?"

Her words come slowly. "I know the risks. I can feel them. He's so huge. Not just because he's a bear. His energy, his power—my wolf measures those as his dominance, and it's gigantic. No matter how much I believe that he would use all of it to serve pack, and I do, it would be like dropping a new planet into our solar system. A really big one."

I carefully don't comment on what it means that she can read the forces of gravity in the pack through an alpha's eyes. "Yeah."

Her fingers curl into a fist on top of my sweater.

Damn. I wrap my hand over hers. "I love his furry ass, but I love this pack, too. Tell me the rest."

Her smile wobbles. "He learned sign language so he could speak to my son."

My eyes close. Fuck. I'm making this complicated. Maybe it isn't. Maybe we do exactly what Danielle said and we believe in our patched-together, supposedly temporary systems schematic that put belonging at the center of our pack, and we trust that a polar bear isn't going to break anything that can't be fixed with a blow torch, duct tape, and diligence.

Lissa's head tips against my chest. "I know what my answer would be if Ronan asked me, but he won't. He'll ask you, and he'll be really pissed off if you don't put everything on the scales."

Always, she sees. "I don't know if he'll ask." In words, anyhow. In a profound way that neither friend nor alpha can ignore, he's already asking.

Because he hasn't said no.

Lissa glances over at the white bear sitting in shadows, sorrow in her eyes. "Any idea how he's doing?"

No. Which is why we're still standing here in the snow as the sun sets, avoiding the hell out of the eggshells we need to traverse to get everyone safely back to the den. I don't know exactly what happened at the end of Danielle's explosive song. I just know that Rio swooped in looking as fierce as I've ever seen him and he's been guarding a polar bear like he would a newborn pup ever since.

I sigh. "I'll talk to Rio when we get back." I've tried already, but it's really hard to hide in a wonderland of snow with a gigantic black wolf. Especially one who won't get more than a dozen paces away from his current charge.

I look over at the ice bridge that a polar bear managed to construct even as he trembled, because emotional firestorms should never get in the way of keeping promises to pups. It's beautiful and structurally sound and incorporated at least one item from the wish list of every member of this pack shorter than Myrna—and it's going to melt in tomorrow's sun.

Fuck.

RONAN

I should be helping to carry the little ones or the bedraggled gear or the remnants of a dinner that somehow emerged from rucksacks that were only supposed to have contained lunch, but all of those things got taken from my hands.

A pack well aware of what I'm already carrying this night.

A pack kind, and fierce, and determined that it is mine to hold.

I tried to converse with Bailey to see if ice bridges might be added to the provincial curriculum, but she turned into a red wolf at dusk, and when she came back from her time in the shadows, she had a very strange look on her face. One that a bear carrying his own weight this night needs not to touch. I would not do harm, and Bailey stands on the ramparts of some of the most dangerous wounds of this pack.

Which is just one item on the long list of reasons that the burden I carry should be so very easy to set down. This pack does not need a polar bear. Especially one who has a wondrous place in a pack of his own, not so very far away, where he is needed and loved and appreciated and permitted extra space in the yarn cupboards.

My bear croons softly, growling some kind of wordless lullaby to the wish inside me that is more fragile than the smallest cub. The wish that I wasn't aware anyone had ever seen or heard until Danielle's song insisted that it had a right to exist.

Tears prick at my eyes. She has not come near this whole afternoon, not once, even when Hoot's snowball hit Fallon's video camera and made it stop working. But she hasn't gone far, either. And every time I dared to look her way, the notes of her song reverberated in the part of me that doesn't know how to stop shaking.

I hold more tightly to the small beaded feather that Kelsey set into my hands as we began our journey back to the den. She wears several just like it in her hair. It smells of ice and snow and home.

A home I must not claim as my own—except I can't seem to let it go. I am a bear of patience and generosity and good humor. I am not a brave bear. Brave bears are reckless bears, and I've never wanted to make anyone pay the price of a polar bear's courage.

Today, a wolf offered to be brave on my behalf.

One other time in my life, a fierce and brave wolf

looked into my eyes and saw my soul and offered me a gift of such magnitude, but she was the alpha of all alphas. Danielle didn't offer me the bravery of a leader. She offered the courage of a repair bot. A breathtaking gift from a wolf who looked into my soul, not to feed it and grow it and bend it to service of pack—but simply to invite it to be seen. To become. To belong.

Adrianna Scott offered a lost polar bear hope. Danielle tried to give him a chance to come home, and I can't seem to contain my trembling long enough to give her the only possible answer.

I am not brave enough to snuff out my most fragile wish.

Adrianna taught me that a polar bear can dare to hope—but it must be hope scaled to the pack in which he wishes to fit. Today, Danielle sang of hope scaled to the auroras that dance in the winter skies of my birth.

In the face of such grandeur, even polar bears tremble.

Footsteps. Ones trying to be quiet, but still missing a woodcraft lesson or two, at least by the standards of Kelvin Nogues.

My bear gladdens. He knows those feet.

Reilly's hand slides into mine.

I close my eyes and let his warm fingers anchor me as I walk in the dark night. I don't know how to do this—but perhaps he does.

We walk for a long while before he speaks. "Do you want raisins in your oatmeal in the morning?"

My bear blinks. "Perhaps. Why do you ask?"

A smile that I can hear, even if I can't see it. "I'm on breakfast duty. Ebony's the team leader, so that means we'll be making oatmeal because she thinks bacon can only be cooked by experts and pancakes with berries look too much like zombies."

My fragile wish grabs onto promises of oatmeal with newborn-cub claws and hangs on tight. "What are her feelings on berries in oatmeal?"

A happy sigh. "That's my favorite. With extra honey because I'm a growing bear."

Any courage I might have been mustering flees into the dark night. "I might still be growing. A little. We could measure."

Tired giggles. "Myrna will sneak you extra honey because she likes bears a lot, even the growly ones."

The trees thin, and I can see the face of my walking companion. The kindness that's the very foundation of who he is shines in his eyes. "Your forests make good honey. The flowers and the bees must be very happy here."

Reilly looks up at me, his eyes suddenly careful. Careful and brave. "I'm happy here, too. My mom is really smart. She brought me here because she knew this could be a good place for a bear."

The trembling things in my bear shake harder. "She is very wise."

He nods, as if that settles something important between us. "She doesn't always remember that. Myrna says that it's good to remind her, and all of the other wolves who sometimes forget that they're really smart, too. Glow, and Adelina, and even Hayden, sometimes."

This pack wields swords of clarity as easily as the rest of us wield butter knives. I take a steadying breath. "Myrna is also very wise. And scary."

Reilly snickers. "You're not supposed to say that last part. You're supposed to say that she's an intrepid reporter and her ginger beef is the best you've ever tasted and you already knew that curse word."

This conversation is undoing every part of me that an ice bridge managed to cobble back together—and I can't let go of it any more than I can set down Kelsey's feather or the magnificent, impossible gift of a repair bot. "I know some Klingon curse words."

More of the delightful giggles. "All Klingon words are curses."

If the universe had set out to design a bear cub to steal my heart, it would have designed this one. "Maybe Myrna is Klingon."

A pinecone bounces off the back of my head. "I heard that, foolish peon."

Fingers that have learned sturdiness from their mother squeeze mine. "She's tough, but you can take her. It helps if you make her laugh, first. She has worse aim that way."

I hold tight to those fingers and try to swallow the words rising up unbidden through my cracks. I don't want Myrna's aim to falter. I want her to charge straight at the ramparts of a polar bear's most fragile wish and win him his freedom.

I close my eyes and try not to squeeze Reilly's fingers too tightly. I need to end this. I just don't know how. And the one wolf who could help me do it has been flatly refusing to lift a claw all fucking afternoon.

If I can't manage to get this right, Rio had damn well better be the first wolf charging into the breach to sit on my bear.

A hand pats my arm. "You're growling. Do you need a snack?"

I need this pack to have so much less faith in my goodness.

If I were a brave bear, I would say so. I would call on their wolves to remember what they know of apex predators, and tell them the stories of innocent flowers crushed under my big, well-meaning paws, and remind them of their painfully earned right to caution and care and prudence. I would thank them so very much for their faith in my goodness—and then I would set it all down, very gently, and walk away.

But I'm not a brave bear, and there's a schematic, drawn by a sturdy wolf, that showed exactly what their faith could make possible.

And so, I tremble.

CLEVE

My hip is tired. A sensible wolf would be curled up on a warm kitchen floor or under the blankets that keep appearing on all of the ledges that overlook the den, but I was never the sensible one. That was Aaron. I got whatever patience was tucked into the womb with us, and most of the cooking skills, but he came out holding tight to the responsibility.

The most awful part of the day he died was that he tried to hand it all to me.

The pain in my hip flares, sharp and guilty. It didn't take long to learn why I never should have had it.

My wolf snaps at the dark thoughts.

I sigh. Fair enough. That one wasn't helpful. But I do need to do some thinking. He can use his teeth when I veer too deep into the shadows, but I'm out here because something is nipping at me, trying to herd my thoughts in a direction that they need to go, and I've spent far too much of the last six years refusing to think at all.

Aaron would have told me that was foolish, plain and simple.

He likely would have been right.

Not all the memories are dark ones.

My wolf sighs and heads off down a rabbit trail that might be fresh enough to convince me to stop thinking and do some chasing, instead.

I snort at him, amused. I did some chasing today. Threw a snowball at Myrna, too. She'll probably get even for that. Put onions in my coffee or something. Yanking her tail, even in good fun, has always come with consequences.

Still felt good.

Not all the memories are dark ones.

My hip twinges again. Not so painfully this time, but still plenty uncomfortable. It matches the mess in my mind. A lot happened today, and some of it is refusing to clear out and let me be. I'm not alone in that, but unlike most of the others, it's not the big, dramatic lines of Danielle's song that are keeping me awake. It's one that was tucked innocently in the middle. One where she said that this isn't a good pack for all bears—but it's a good pack for kind ones.

Brown will be spluttering about that for the next month.

I shoot a quick, sideways glance at that word I've been trying to avoid.

Kindness.

People always said that I was kind. Dolores, right up until she left to head back to the city and broke three kids and a wolf who couldn't offer her anything more than the contents of his heart. Ruby as she laid newborn Grady in my arms for the first time. Eamon as he yanked Stinky out of them.

My wolf snarls at the dark fingers. They always come when I walk the valleys of memory.

I shake my head. It isn't the darkness hunting for me this time. It's something else. Something that doesn't carry traces of blood and remnants of fur from my previous passings.

Something that has its beginnings in a polar bear's trembling.

My wolf wrinkles his nose. He doesn't like new things. He's old and cranky and set in his ways, and voyages of discovery are meant for young wolves with dumb luck in their bellies and fire in their eyes.

I roll my eyes. Such flowery words. He's been listening to too many of Ronan's bedtime stories.

He sniffs. The bear tells a good tale.

The thought occurs, unbidden, that maybe the polar bear's most important stories are the ones he doesn't tell. The ones that explain why he's frightened of his own power and welcomes what he hopes will make him weaker.

I slow to a walk, following the scent of a truth that I can't see.

The bear's kindness isn't weak. And when Danielle howled the song of how this could be his pack, she used our kindness and she didn't let it be weak, either. She forged it into something beautiful and strong that can hold a polar bear and keep the pups safe.

My head bows. There it is, the thought that has been hunting me all of the long run back from Rennie's caves. My daughter wasn't curled up in the warm, dry dark like a sensible wolf, either. She was out in front of her favorite cave, her eyes on the night sky. When my hip aches tomorrow, I will remember her eyes.

The rest of the thought spools out more easily, now that I've found its beginning.

I know why Rennie watches the moon tonight, her wolf content and her eyes free of pain. It's the same reason that Grady is out walking amongst the trees, touching the ones that smell of a polar bear's passing, and why my granddaughter sang to the bear inside her heart as she fell asleep.

Kelsey is the strongest of the psychic Dunns, but the rest of us can feel it, too. The last polar bear to visit our territory was a hunter. A predator. A soul who could have become like Samuel or Eamon and chose another path, and because he chose that other way, we can trust Ivan Grigori.

The polar bear who walks our lands now is something different. My wolf can feel what he is, right down deep in his bones, and it soothes the parts of me that I thought evil had shredded forever. Ronan is not a hunter, or a predator, or one who could ever let evil root inside him.

He is balm to a scarred, psychic soul.

He is power welded to kindness.

He is a guardian.

If he stays, perhaps those of us who failed to guard can finally rest.

16

HAYDEN

I smile gratefully at the green-eyed wolf who just brought me a cup of coffee as big as her head. It's not my usual mug, so clearly she's taking pity on the bedraggled guy she curled up with last night. "Any fires that I need to put out before I drink this?"

She grins cheerfully. "Shelley took care of the fire."

I don't ask. I smelled the early-morning smoke coming from the kitchen, but Kel got there before I could even get my head out of my sleeping bag, and it's not my job to ruin all of his fun. "Ronan is sorted for the next few hours. He's teaching. Bailey didn't show up for work this morning and Ravi was looking entirely panicked about trying to explain the physics of castle drawbridges."

Lissa nods. "Good."

She doesn't offer up anything else, and she doesn't look at all surprised that Bailey has gone mysteriously missing. Which is the kind of breadcrumb trail that even a caffeine-deprived alpha can follow. "I take it that those of you who intend to interfere have a plan?"

She smiles at me sweetly. "Yes."

It takes me a heartbeat too long to follow the path of her eyes. When I do, it somehow doesn't surprise me to see the shark squad quietly standing in a line. I gulp coffee and wait. This clearly isn't my time to be speaking.

Layla clears her throat. "Is Ronan going to join our pack?"

Definitely not enough coffee. "I don't know."

She studies me for a long time before she nods.

Miriam takes her mate's hand. "Would your wolf handle it if he did?"

I stare at them. I fretted about a lot of things in the predawn hours. That didn't even make the list. "You're worried about *my* wolf?"

They look at each other and then at me. More silent nods.

Lissa snickers.

Cori rolls her eyes. "We had to ask. It's only polite. You're alpha, and all."

I remember when she could hardly meet my eyes. And when she definitely didn't calmly help plan pack insurrection. I shake my head. "You had to ask before you do what, exactly?"

Her dimples flash. "We're going to make Ronan a nice invitation and hand-deliver it."

Miriam snorts. "*You're* going to deliver it. It's hard to

refuse adorable pregnant ladies who might puke on you if they get too upset."

Amusement gleams in Cori's eyes. "I might."

My wolf wants to lick them all.

Dumbass. He needs to remember the predawn list. It was really long. "That's it? You're just going to ask him nicely to join our pack?"

They all look at each other again. It's Eliza who finally answers. "Yes. It matters to know that you're wanted."

I stare at the wolf who has no idea that Ronan went to town two nights ago to pour that exact invitation over the head of her grown pup. "He would affect every single atom of the hierarchy in our pack. You get that, right?"

Four quiet smiles.

Lissa elbows me. "This is the part where you tell the nice submissive wolves who are asking their alpha for permission that they have it."

Smartass. "They already asked her."

Miriam and Cori hide their grins. Layla and Eliza don't bother.

Lissa makes a sound that falls somewhere between a sigh and growl.

Right. The really big mug of coffee wasn't just the green-eyed wolf being sweet. It was a caffeine injection to make sure that I didn't fuck this up. I squeeze the shoulders of the woman who holds me to a higher standard, just by breathing, and look into four sets of eyes. I let them see their alpha's doubt and worry and fear—and his trust. This is a pack where submissive mamas get to lean on the scales of really big decisions. "Threatening him with the puke of a pregnant wolf is a nice touch."

Cori grins at Miriam. "She's sneaky like that."

Eliza's lips quirk. "Says the woman who helped Myrna change this morning's lesson plan from the math of musical chords to the physics of castle drawbridges."

I blink. That's Kel-level sneakiness. "Is somebody going to tell me what Myrna is up to this morning? Or Bailey, for that matter?"

Four innocent smiles from the team of women who once took the leadership of their pack out at the knees.

I glance at the general of that particular water fight. "Do I need to be doing anything different than drinking my coffee and trying to figure out how many more wolves are missing than usual?"

Lissa grins up at me. "Nope."

Trust isn't about what you do on the easy days. It's about what you do on the tangled, complicated ones with no right answers. "Can I make a request?"

It does wondrous things for my wolf's ego when five heads nod instantly.

I don't let my wolf answer them, though. This isn't a request from their alpha. It's one from the small boy who laid eyes on a nervous polar bear and decided to be his friend. "Can I be there when the invitation is delivered?"

Five sets of eyes soften.

Yeah. They don't miss anything, these mamas.

Miriam nudges Cori. "He just wants to see you puke on a polar bear's paws."

Cori makes a face. "I'll be really happy when that

isn't a credible threat anymore. I don't think my belly appreciated Wrinkles's new tea blend this morning."

My wolf belatedly realizes that she's looking a little green. I reach frantically into my pockets for the ginger cookies we've all taken to carrying like talismans. "Tell Wrinkles to stop messing with your tea. Alpha's orders."

Eliza chuckles. "Like that will work."

My pack is so unruly. I finally dig up a ginger snap. It's a little squished, but nauseous wolves generally aren't very picky.

Cori smiles at me as she takes it. "The last time I was pregnant, I was scared for the whole nine months about what was going to happen and about the kind of world this was going to be for my baby. This time is really different."

I look at her open, heartfelt smile—the one that will never take a single moment of the good in this pack for granted.

My wolf grins. The shark mamas are fighting dirty.

That smile is going to slay a polar bear.

KEL

The women of this pack have clearly already sorted out the dividing and the conquering. I look at the crew that's come to sit on me. Teesha, Bailey, Wrinkles, and Fallon. Ghost arrived at the same time as they did, but she's just here to report.

I nod her way. She might as well say the damn thing where everyone can hear it.

She smiles faintly. "It's recess. Reilly is walking around with Kelsey on his shoulders. Danielle is in the kitchen fixing the video camera that broke yesterday. Ronan is acting completely normal except for his eyes, and sometimes he breathes a little weird when we don't ask him another question about drawbridges fast enough."

Damn bear who's trying to hide inside his shredded heart. Almost as dumb as a soldier who once tried to hide inside his pride. "So we don't need to muck with anything, yet?" I point the question at the four who came to interrogate me as much as at our youngest beta. All packs have shadow leadership to go along with the formal kind. I'm looking at almost all of them.

I assume Myrna is busy keeping her eyes on a couple of bears. There's no way I'm the only one who has a spy in place.

No response from the rest of them. Which is interesting, even though I don't think they're here to dig anything out of me besides an answer that I don't have for them. The beta wolf might have one. The soldier definitely does. But Ronan is my friend, and that thoroughly fucks up all the other answers I might have.

I take a deep breath and meet the eyes of the members of this pack who know how to stare down hard choices and ugly answers, and will in a heartbeat if it serves those they love. "I assume you have an agenda for this meeting. Are you good with Ghost listening in?" She might as well learn young that betas get their asses kicked on a regular basis.

Wrinkles snorts. "You think we arrived here when she did by accident?"

We both tactfully ignore Ghost's surprised gulp and rosy cheeks. She needs to occasionally be reminded of just how much her pack values her. It's also good for a wily healer to know that an old soldier is on to at least some of her ways.

Wrinkles's lips quirk. "Is Ronan dangerous?"

That's a loaded question. I glance at Bailey, surprised that she's not the one asking it. We trip over each other doing unofficial perimeter runs most nights. She's almost as paranoid as I am.

She raises an eyebrow that carries almost as many messages as one of my scowls. "We know our answer. We want to know what yours is."

I sigh. I hate it when the questions that I don't want to answer are reasonable ones. "Yes. Every polar bear shifter is exceedingly dangerous. Most of them don't ever leave the north because of it." The ones that do find other very dangerous people to hang out with, but they didn't come here to talk about soldiers and war.

Teesha holds out her palms and moves a set of invisible scales up and down. "Because a bear is hard for their human to balance, right? Even Brown has to work at it, and his bear is cute and cuddly compared to Ronan's."

Wrinkles's eyes dance with merriment. "Please say that where my mate can hear you."

Teesha snorts. "I know better than to poke even a

cute and cuddly bear."

Teesha pokes at growly animals just fine. I've never seen a human dance along a wolfpack's sharp edges as well as she does. "In some shifter forms, the animal is almost always the submissive presence. For wolves and ravens and cats, it's generally more balanced. For bear shifters, it takes a lot of skill and control and compassion to navigate that inner relationship without the bear coming out mostly on top."

Ghost's eyes narrow. "Brown handles that by spending a lot of time in the woods. Reilly handles it by leaning in to his wolf side so that he can use pack to help."

Smart wolf. Let's see if she's got the rest. "Yup."

She doesn't even miss a beat. "Most polar bears handle it by living somewhere that they can mostly be a bear or a really intense kind of human."

I've never heard a better explanation.

Teesha nods slowly. "The intense stuff for their humans really matters. It's part of how they get tough enough to handle their bears."

Oh, hell. "Do I want to know which polar bear you're chatting with?"

She grins. "Reina."

Ah. Phil's daughter. The human orphan Ivan picked up out of the rubble of a war zone and took to live with the polar bears. I met her, once, along with half of my platoon. There was a lot of vodka and swearing involved. "Watch yourself. She's at least as dangerous as the average bear."

Teesha snorts. "No shit."

I roll my eyes. "Just so that we're clear when we're playing with fire."

Fallon reaches into the pocket of my shirt and steals my spare granola bar. "Polar bears seem more like ice than fire."

Not once there's vodka involved. "Are we almost at the part where you people tell me whether you're recruiting me or about to kick my ass?"

She just looks at me, unblinking. Which is a trick she must have learned from a damned owl. Or maybe Kendra. She likes staring contests with wolves.

I roll my eyes again. "You think I'm new at this beta stuff?"

Ghost grins. "I am."

There isn't a single teenager in this pack that I would trade for an adult with five times the experience, and she's right at the top of my list. But I explain, because making Kel say obvious things is clearly part of the game this morning. "When the unofficial leadership of a pack closes ranks like this, they either have a job for us to do, or they disagree with us on something important and we need to think really hard about whatever position we've taken."

Ghost nods solemnly. "Which is what, exactly?"

Bailey chokes off a laugh.

My life was so much simpler before I took a walk in the woods with a guy carrying a backpack full of watermelon. "I haven't decided, yet."

Wrinkles snorts. "Bullshit."

Excellent. Just what our newest beta needs—coaching from one of the pack's most troublesome elders. I make shooing motions at Ghost. "You can go back to class, now. Recess must be over."

She just grins and leans against Fallon's shoulder.

Fallon hands over half of the granola bar she stole and shoots me a look that's pure street and really damn effective.

She'd make a fucking fantastic beta if she weren't quite so useful as a pack rebel and quite so allergic to the idea of being officially in charge of anything important. I eye the healer who got her here anyhow. Bailey is the strongest wolf in this bunch, but I don't think this meeting was her idea.

Wrinkles's lips quirk again. "You've told us why polar bears are dangerous. Now tell us why Ronan is."

The answer to that is the reason that I don't yet have a position, official or otherwise, on where I think one of my best friends should spend the rest of his life. "He's less dangerous than he thinks. And more dangerous than you think. This pack stirs up some of his most primitive instincts."

Wrinkles smiles slowly. "We know."

Of course they do. I sigh and give them the answer of a guy who would chew off one of his limbs if this particular polar bear needed it. "I want to say that Ronan has a right to feel all of those things, but he's like a high-grade weapon. No matter how gentle and sweet and generous he is, and he's all of those things, he's also deadly."

Bailey shrugs. "He has better control of his bear than I do of my wolf. Maybe more."

That's getting perilously close to acknowledging something that she's never said out loud. "Yes. Adrianna taught him that. I helped some."

Four heads nod. Two who know what it is to ruthlessly contain their animals, and two who love others who have that fight.

I finally get it. They're not just here as shadow leaders. They're here as the ones who most fully understand the risk that Ronan would be to this pack.

And they've made a decision.

RIO

I shake my head as the earth offers up more updates.

It's been a big day. The women of this pack are gathering us up. Pulling us together. Getting us ready so that we can stand for a polar bear and anyone else who wobbles as he contemplates the enormity of his own deepest desire popping out of a genie's bottle and trying to come to life.

Wise women, every last one of them. They're also very specifically steadying up around the three of us who are Ronan's closest friends—and who have been trying awfully damn hard to keep our weight off the scales. Which is an error that my sentinel named bright and early this morning, but he hasn't let me do anything about it.

He wanted to see who came to adjust my thinking.

They've made him wait very patiently. The sun is only an hour or so away from setting, and school is about to let out and open the door of the cage that Ronan has very gratefully sequestered himself in all day.

I thought that was about to make me a lot busier, but the thrumming lines of tension in the fabric of our pack suggest that I might be wrong. Yesterday they let me do my actual job. Today I suspect that I'm mostly being relegated back to my usual pack role as the cute, oversized wolf with a candy addiction.

I smile as Shelley joins me with two mugs of steaming cocoa in her hands. "You're my emissary, are you?"

She snorts. "Yes. Which means that you had to wait until the stew was bubbling properly on the stove and Mikayla got back from Dorie's camp to supervise it."

My wolf grins. He likes stew.

She holds out one of the mugs. "Yours has some gummy bears added for extra flavor. Jade thought you would like those better than marshmallows."

I take a careful sip. I'm not sure whether gummy bears dissolve in hot chocolate or not, which seems like a notable gap in my education. "Did she put some in the stew, too?"

Shelley chuckles. "Mikayla convinced her that spinach was a better choice."

I make a face, even though the tiny leaves of baby spinach are the first crop from our new greenhouse and every wolf in this entire pack will eat their helping with fierce gladness, including mine. "This pack is developing a disturbing fondness for putting leafy green things in my dinner."

"You'll survive." Shelley pats my arm. "Besides, I hear that Ronan likes vegetables."

Shelley Martins is not a wolf who beats about the bush. So a sentinel won't, either. "He's more fragile than he looks." Which is saying something, because to wolves as hyper-observant as the ones in this pack, Ronan looks plenty shaken.

She nods quietly. "We figured."

Of course they have. Which is why they've spent most of the day reinforcing the threads of pack so that our fabric is strong enough to catch a polar bear if he falls. An act of stupendous courage and generosity, and if I say so, she'll likely dump her hot cocoa on my head.

I lean against her shoulder. "You think he belongs here."

She takes a long sip from her mug. "I do."

I inhale the scent of chocolate and steady friends. "Why?"

She's silent for a long time, taking my question as seriously as I meant it. "Because of our history and what it made us, we can give him what he needs."

That's an achingly beautiful answer—and she's not done.

"The rest is the same answer as I would have given about you." She rests her cheek on my shoulder. "Whistler Pack loves him. This pack needs him."

17

DANIELLE

"That wiring isn't going to be needed until next spring at the very earliest." The hand that reaches in and takes my pliers away also closes the door of the small locking cupboard that acts as one of our temporary electrical sheds. "Come. We're going for a soak."

I look up at Eliza and sigh. I have no idea when the sun went down, I'm starving, and the look in her eyes says that she knows both of those things and likely more, besides. "Okay. I need to grab some food, first."

Glow steps out of the shadows and holds up a picnic basket. It smells good enough to make my wolf drool. Indrani is right behind her, carrying towels and a bowl of something that smells almost like food, but not quite.

She nods her chin at the bowl in her hands and grins. "Mikayla mixed up some goop to put on our faces. She looked up a recipe on the internet. It's supposed to relax us and make our skin recite poetry, or something."

I stare at the bowl suspiciously. "I'm not sure that's a good idea. It might clog the pipes."

Indrani snorts. "If the pipes can survive wolf fur and pinecone wars, they can survive a little goop." Glow, who is the one who actually has to deal with clogged pipes, nods definitively.

Eliza hooks her arm around my elbow. "This isn't a choice, team leader. It's an intervention. You've been fussing with your wires and junction boxes all day. We figured that you needed time to think. Now you need a hot soak and peach Bellinis and goop on your face and friends who will set you straight if you haven't gotten there, yet."

I move my feet, because she's a strong wolf when she's got a mind to be. "What's a Bellini?"

She chuckles. "Something else from the internet."

Glow makes a sign that I have no trouble interpreting. "We're drinking? In the hot pools? Who's supervising the pups?"

Eliza pats my arm. "Someone who isn't you, dear."

I eye Indrani and Glow as I walk. "Are either of you even old enough to drink?"

They roll their eyes.

I used to drink a little. Before. Way before. Back when it could be a nice way to relax with friends instead of a prelude to ugliness. I take a deep breath. Maybe if I have fancy stuff in a glass, I can keep the fancy stuff in the bowl off of my face. "A soak sounds nice."

Glow holds up her basket. "Stew. And apple pie. The pie's good."

Her gravelly words make my eyes feel hot and itchy. "Do we get to start with the pie?"

Indrani grins. "Heck, yeah." She sets the goop bowl down carefully on the edge of the largest hot pool and considers its contents. "We should probably eat before we put this stuff on, anyhow."

I look around. The pools are entirely deserted. There's no way that's an accident. My stomach turns over. I'm not sure that I'm ready for an intervention. I'm not sure that I'm ready for anything besides a bowl of stew and my sleeping bag. I need to read about grounding wires in freezing temperatures. A couple of the junction boxes are worrying me.

Eliza gently squeezes my shoulder. "Let it go, sweetie. You've let your hands work all day long. Now let's see what your heart has to say."

I'm suddenly acutely aware of just how tired and cranky and hungry I am. "I'm not feeling very talkative."

Glow shoots me a sympathetic look. Then she makes a sign that isn't sympathetic at all.

I try not to growl, even though she works with Brown plenty and can absolutely handle my wolf's bad moods. Instead, I reach into the picnic basket for one of the warm bowls of stew nestled inside. It smells like comfort and wholeness, and my entire world suddenly narrows down to the need to find a spoon.

Eliza chuckles. "Here. Bring your bowl and come with me. We'll get situated somewhere that's good for eating. Then Glow can set out all of the pretty accessories that Shelley sent and we can all discover what a peach Bellini tastes like."

I'm glad I'm not the only one who has no idea. I follow her meekly over to the steps and set my stew bowl down on the bench long enough to discard my clothes beside hers. Then we're in the water, letting it soothe away the sudden chills of our fragile human skin.

I sink my nose nearly into my bowl and spoon up some of the stew. It's full of carrots and potatoes and big chunks of onion. I smile. Reilly chopped up the potatoes —I saw him hard at work with Shelley's big kitchen knife before school this morning, concentrating fiercely and listening to a podcast on black holes.

He's such a sweet bear.

I take another spoonful of stew. I chew slowly, letting the work of my son's hands steady me. Then I look into the eyes of my friends. The ones who know that sometimes I need to spend quiet time with my wires—and sometimes I need to step away and face what I did in front of my entire pack under the daybright moon.

Eliza smiles. Glow settles a glass of something cool and orange in my hand. Indrani just watches me with her raven eyes that see everything.

I sigh. "Did I make a mistake?"

Eliza raises an eyebrow. "Not yet, so don't start making one now."

I stare at her as I eat my stew.

Indrani clears her throat. "Your song was beautiful. Eliza told me what it meant after, but even when I didn't understand all of it, it made me want to move here and never leave."

Glow looks over at her carefully. "You could stay."

Indrani ducks her head. "Thank you. I need my flock, but Rio says I can come work from here as often as I want after my internship is done."

My wolf snaps her teeth. She doesn't understand internships and jobs and flocks. She wants her packmates to stay where they belong. Even the ones with feathers who can't understand her songs.

I don't tell her that Indrani has another pack. My wolf needs more stew in her belly before she's going to handle that kind of news well. Instead, I smile at the cheerful young raven who has somehow become my friend. "You'll be welcome."

She smiles happily. "That's the same thing you said in your song to Ronan, right?"

Eliza chuckles. "Mostly. It's the part she didn't say that I thought was the most interesting, though."

My stomach lurches.

She smiles. "Drink your Bellini. I think you might need it."

I take a cautious sip of the orange concoction in my glass. It's delicious, in a way that smells of danger and voyages into brave new lands. I set it down carefully on the side of the pool. I'm not sure I'm ready for either of those things. "I said plenty."

"You were a team leader," says Eliza quietly. "You showed us how we could take what we need and what Ronan needs and what we already know how to do, and use them all to fit a polar-bear-sized part into our pack system."

I can't look at her. I stare down at my stew instead.

"You left out one part, though." A weight settles gently on my shoulder. "What does your heart want?"

My hands flail, desperate for something to hold that requires more of them than a bowl of stew. "I want a strong pack. A good pack for my son. A place where he can learn and be safe and become a good man who knows how to walk well with the bear inside him."

"And?"

Eliza puts so much love in that single word. My eyes fly up, because apparently they aren't listening to me anymore. "That's all. That's enough. The rest doesn't matter. Ronan has three degrees and I can't even understand the first page of most of his books and he has a job doing important work all over the continent and he's a bear." My words jerk to a sudden halt. A very temporary one that jars loose again with a vengeance. "Bears don't want the same thing as wolves."

Three friends gather around me. Catching me as I fall. Collecting up my words. Drying my tears. Eliza nuzzles my cheek. "I think that maybe this one does, sweetie."

My head shakes violently.

Her chuckles are watery. "It doesn't matter. That part isn't up to us to decide. What matters right now is what you want. What the woman and wolf inside you want when you're not busy being a team leader and a packmate and a mom."

"I don't know. How can I know?" My words are more of a wail than anything else. "There's never been any time. Any space."

"You made some." Glow's gravelly voice is close to my ear. "That's part of what you put in your design. Time and space for a bear to stay and for you to consider who you might want him to be in your life."

My head swivels to stare at the young wolf who just spoke more words than I've ever heard her say at one time. "What?"

Indrani giggles. "Even I figured out that part, and I don't speak wolf."

I hold tighter to my stew bowl, like it might somehow anchor me in a world where my friends are calmly talking about things inside myself that I'm only beginning to see. "I didn't howl about anything like that."

Eliza grins. "We're engineers, sweetie. There was a really obvious part missing in your design. Did you think we wouldn't notice?"

The crazy truth, the one that I spent all day trying to leave tangled inside a junction box along with the wiring that we won't need at least until spring, unspools and floats naked in the hot pool under the stars. I swallow. And swallow again. No words come out. None even try.

Eliza rests her head on my shoulder. "Do you remember what you said to Reilly right after Adrianna talked to him about going to university?"

I try to gather up the floating bits of my brain and fail miserably. "No."

She chuckles. "You told him that this was a pack

where we could have dreams, now. Where it was okay to wish for crazy things because the bad times were done and it was okay to believe in wild ideas and have big dreams."

I do remember. His eyes got so big. I sniffle and swipe at my cheeks. "I was talking about the dreams that cubs have. We're adults."

She pats my arm. "We're adults who can wish for time and space to at least consider whether we might want to drag a polar bear into the woods and have our way with him."

I gape at her, utterly speechless, while Indrani sinks underwater spluttering with laughter.

Glow clears her throat. "If you need tips, I bet Wrinkles has a lot of them."

Eliza bumps her shoulder. "Good one."

I shake my head as Indrani surfaces and leans against Glow's other shoulder, still giggling helplessly. I'm about as in charge of this team as I am in charge of Mellie when she's chasing a squirrel. "I was worried about the drinks and the goop. I guess I should have asked what Shelley put in the stew."

Indrani grins. "Truth serum."

I can't stop the giggles. I don't know if I caught them from Indrani or found some of my own, but they pass through the four of us like an electrical current. Then a different signal passes through the three of them, and the energy quiets and begins to smell of little more than stew and easy friendship.

Intervention complete.

Eliza ripples her hand over the surface of the water. "I do like these hot pools. We did good work."

Glow nods silently. She picks up two bowls and hands one to Indrani, her words evidently tucked back into storage for the evening.

I lean back against a rock that's perfectly contoured for my head and contemplate what to do with the truth they dragged out into the dark night. And I eat my stew.

RONAN

The teenagers of this pack have their noses in everything, but it isn't one of them who comes to find me as I fill yet another wheelbarrow with pea gravel. Kennedy deigned to let me use the one with a functional wheel today. Convincing her to let me work alone was harder.

It was a quiet nod from Brown that finally did it. He understands that bears aren't wolves. Sometimes we need solitude to work through our inner landscapes.

Apparently, my time is up.

Dorie drops down from a tree onto the precarious top of pea-gravel mountain and barely displaces a handful of pebbles. "Bear."

I dig out my poker face so that I don't grin at her. Cats don't like you to get amused when they've barely begun their shenanigans. "Elder."

She snorts. "Are you trying to make me mad?"

It rarely takes much with a cat, but my bear isn't

looking for games this evening. And he's curious that she's the one who has come to interfere with his solitude. Not that he had much left, anyhow. The sun is going down on his wheelbarrow filling. "Did Hayden send you?" He knows that I've got a fondness for feisty elders.

Dorie glares at me. "Do I look like a wolf who does my alpha's bidding?"

From what I've seen, he rarely has to ask. This pack reveres him. They also treat him like the overgrown pup he generally pretends to be, but some at Whistler Pack didn't see through those antics. Here, Hayden Scott is known.

My bear rumbles, restless. Wolves share too much. Danielle sang to the pack of private things.

I meet a cat's eyes. Bears aren't wolves, but those of us who choose to live amongst them have to give up some of our desire for private things. Especially when we didn't manage to hide them well enough.

I walk over to the basket that Shelley had Stinky deliver earlier this afternoon. It's full of many things covered in honey, but there's likely something inside that will tempt a cat. "How did you come to join this pack?"

Silence.

I look up, my bear scenting an interesting story. More than interesting. One with private things that the cat is considering sharing with me, and that's a trust I know better than to take lightly. I lift out a glass jar of sun tea and the cookies that are tucked in beside it. It's too dark to tell what they are by sight, but they smell of cinnamon and spice. "Join me?"

Dorie grins. "You could come sit up here with me."

My poker face almost slips. I'm a more agile bear than she gives me credit for being, but clambering up a mountain of pea gravel while carrying drinks and snacks isn't going to be anything other than a thundering mess and we both know it. I'd do it anyhow, just to play with her kitty, but I won't be the only one filling wheelbarrows of gravel in the days and weeks to come, and I don't like to make messes that I don't clean up.

I hold out a hand for Dorie to take, instead.

She does, using it to lever herself down to the ground in an elegant leap that is as much monkey as it is cat. "I'm not shoveling. Just so we're clear."

I've no doubt that she could do it all day long if she were so inclined. "Noted."

She takes a seat on a convenient rock that puts her ears level with mine. Her head tilts, her eyes shining bright in the evening dim. "You're an interesting bear."

I don't know if she means that as a compliment or not. "I try to be a simple bear. And a helpful one."

Her lips quirk. "You're one of those things."

I know better than to ask which one. I pour two cups of the fragrant sun tea. "I hope you like honey." Whoever made the tea added a good-sized dollop to the jar.

She snorts. "It makes my teeth ache."

Cats rarely admit to liking anything sweet, even as they line up to trade for Shelley's cookies and Mellie's drawings and Eliza's wee knitted things. I hand Dorie a cup of tea. I don't know all of her story, but I know that a number of the teenagers in this pack are here because she brought them. Which means she has an oversized supply of another trait very typical of cats.

They're prickly, volatile, tricky, temperamental softies.

I bump gently against her shoulder.

She takes the cookie out of my hand and gives the edge a good lick. "I came to Ghost Mountain because I found a tiny wolf pup chasing cars on the side of the highway. When I pulled over to see if she was hurt, I found myself holding a naked, squalling toddler with a heck of a set of lungs and lost brown eyes."

I exhale carefully. She won't want a bear's gratitude.

She shrugs. "This was the nearest wolf pack. I stayed a while to make sure she was settling in all right. Left a few months later and barely made it to Vancouver before I found another pup curled up in an alleyway."

Whistler would have been the closest pack to Vancouver, and Adrianna Scott has always had a reputation for accepting strays—even ones the size of fully grown polar bears. It means something important that Dorie didn't bring that second pup to Whistler. "So you brought that one home, too."

She shoots me a loaded glance.

I brush my hand down her braided hair, following its trail down her spine. "You brought them to a good place. This is a pack that knows how to shape itself around newcomers."

She leans ever so slightly into my touch. "They weren't bad at it, back then." A pause. "We're better now."

My bear quietly, helplessly yearns. "Yes. You're magnificent."

She looks over at me, and there are hints of prickly, volatile, tricky, temperamental softy in her eyes. "Are you going to let us shape ourselves around you?"

My eyes close as the breath whooshes out of my bear. Brave elder cat. Cunning claws, discerningly applied. I give her the answer she's earned. "I don't know how I can."

She snorts. "You can get your head out of your ass, for starters."

My eyes jolt back open.

She shakes her head. "Stop weighing how big and dangerous you are, bear. You're not a cat. Selfishness isn't your way. Neither is sorting through how you could serve, although I'll give you that you're a decent wolf in that heart of yours and this pack could really use you."

This is what cats do. They put you in a dryer and watch you tumble around. "Thinking like a bear earns me a one-way trip back to Ivan's territory."

She snorts. "He's an interesting bear, too."

Comparisons to Ivan are an old discomfort. I brush them aside. Dorie is old and wise and she understands those of us who were lost before we belonged. I would like to hear what she's come to say, claws and all. "He is. But you've come here to speak of me."

She studies my face for a long time. Then she nods a little. "Some bears are hunters. You're not. Some are hermits or fighters or drinkers, and you're mostly not any of those, either."

I swallow. I wanted to be all of them, once. Felt the yawning lacking of none of them being my truth. "What do you see in me?"

She shrugs. "Storyteller, some. Collector of stories, more. Force who breathes life into the stories of others, most."

If you're in a dryer, you tumble. "Yes."

She reaches out and touches my arm, her fingers kneading it like a cat. "Let your story take a breath or two, bear."

Gentle claws are so much worse than fierce ones. "I can't. I could cause too much harm."

"That was true, once. Back when you were a bear with lost eyes." She looks straight at me, and I feel as naked as the squalling baby she held on the side of the highway. "But the right people found you and helped you and breathed life into that bear's story. You're not him anymore."

I can't move. She has hunted me right to my cave.

She kneads my arm one last time. "You're the bear they helped you to become. It's time to find his story. He'll know where he belongs."

18

KEL

I grin as Mellie charges over my toes with the standard reckless abandon of a dominant pup on a mission. One who figures that anyone standing in her way should move, and likely will.

Ebony chuckles. "I'm taking a beta vacation when she's a teenager."

I try not to think about things that will turn my fur more gray than it already is. "Kennedy will need something to do by then."

Ebony rolls her eyes. "She's not going to be able to keep up with the hawks."

I look up at the circling pair. Apparently Finn and Kendra decided to take this delivery run personally. Possibly because we have some very nice hot pools and one of Kendra's few vulnerabilities is her love of a warm soak. The fledglings in her flock generally only try interrupting her bubble baths once, but their attempts are the stuff of legend.

Mellie runs in excited circles around where they'll land, yipping.

Ebony shakes her head as Finn executes an elegant dodge so that the large messenger bag he's carrying doesn't whack her on the head. "Belay that last concern. She won't live long enough to become a teenager."

Every wolf in this pack, including the two of us, would die before we let that happen, and probably several hawks, too. I nod at Finn as he looks around for the recipient of this particular delivery. "I sent a runner to find her. She should be here shortly." I know better than to deprive him of the joy of seeing one of his deliveries opened.

Especially one that's going to be this epic.

Indrani arrives first, her cheeks flushed and her eyes bright. "They're coming. Glow tried to fix a pipe that bent except the new blow torch is really big and the pipe overheated and then Danielle threw water on it and the hissing made Glow's wolf run away and Ronan got his finger stuck in the pipe."

Finn grins. "Sounds like a regular day in a wolf pack."

Indrani nods cheerfully. "Pretty much."

Danielle and Ronan working together is an interesting addition to the day. They've been tiptoeing around each other all morning. I keep that thought to myself, however. If I have a part in this play, it's a very small one.

Kendra lands beside her mate and ruffles Mellie's head. "Soon, chickadee. I saw some pretty mountains with new snow on the top. Maybe I'll take you for a ride and see what happens if I drop a pup in a big snowdrift."

Mellie yips happily.

I don't bother to snarl. Kendra will lose Mellie shortly after she lets Finn clip her wings. "Come have a soak after you're done playing in the snow. The pools were drained and cleaned this morning, and they're almost full again." So say the reports from the dozen pups and teenagers hanging their noses over the pool edges, anyhow. "We'll even chase out the riffraff if you want."

Hayden has this silly idea that the pups need to learn about privacy. He'd be way smarter trying to impress that lesson on our elders.

Finn laughs. "What fun is a swim if you can't drown a wolf or two?"

Indrani shoots him a look that says if he tries, he'll discover that she's got a few settings that aren't entirely cheerful.

My wolf grins. He likes this raven. He wants to keep her.

I pat his head and remind him that she'll visit often and he'll have all the ravens he can handle after Fallon's baby arrives.

Glow pulls up beside me, her eyes glued to Kendra's and Finn's delivery bags. She doesn't reach for them, though.

I smile. They'll be hers soon enough. Just as soon as the lead designer of our den systems blesses their use and installation.

Danielle arrives a lot more hesitantly than any of her

teammates, but she's got nothing on the polar bear on her heels. I've never seen Ronan look so cautious, or so torn. I look around for Rio, in case this is one of those situations that requires a sentinel—or a hand grenade—but he's nowhere to be seen.

Danielle clears her throat. "Are those the parts from Scotty?"

"Yup." Finn holds out his bag and bows. "Some very pretty, specially machined pipe joinery from the master of the blow torch himself, to be delivered into the hands of the lady that he says will do them justice."

I take a readying breath as she opens the bag. I don't know what's about to happen—but I do know the tiptoeing is about to end, and that generally means beta wolves need to be ready to make themselves useful.

Danielle stares into the bag for a very long time. Then she lifts out one of the parts gingerly, holding it like it might explode. "These aren't the parts we ordered."

Ronan clears his throat. "They are."

She shakes her head wildly. "These aren't right. They're art. They're covered in those fancy welds that Scotty does. The ones that cost the earth." She reaches into the bag for a second pipe fitting and pulls it out, the colorful decorative weld of a sleek wolf gleaming as it meets the sun. "We can't afford these."

A bear's eyes twist in the wind.

Fuck. Ronan pulls stunts like this every day of the week and knows how to help them land, but today, he's clearly got nothing. "Ronan has enough stored poker winnings in his ongoing duel with Scotty to have paid for those four times over. Don't worry about the money, Danielle. Worry about whether or not they'll work."

Her eyes zip from me, to Lissa, to Finn, to the parts in her hands.

Anywhere except to a very still bear.

I do what betas do when there aren't any good options left. I pray to whatever deities might be listening.

It takes a long, ticking time for the panicked caution in Danielle's eyes to soften. "I'm sure they'll work." She crouches and carefully sets down one of the fittings so that she can stroke the sleek lines of the multi-colored wolf. "They're beautiful."

They're the embellishments that a bear finds as necessarily as breathing. I wait to see if Danielle understands how much that matters to the man who upgraded her order—and who had no idea that they would arrive today, because a couple of betas intercepted the delivery notification and decided not to pass it along.

I've made less fraught calls on a battlefield.

Danielle's fingers trace the wolf, every bump and line of the metal that melted and reformed under the hands of an artist with the soul of an engineer. When she finally looks up again, this time her eyes go straight to the very still bear. She swallows, but she doesn't look away. "Thank you."

"They're sturdy and functional. Just like you ordered." Ronan's dark cheeks turn several shades that I've never seen them go. "But we thought you deserved beautiful, too."

I wince. His bear is never going to let him get away with that dodge.

He clears his throat and looks down at the ground. "*I* thought you deserved beautiful."

DANIELLE

I'm looking at the pipe fittings, but I can't see them. I can only see the words that Ronan just said, the ones that just melted every part of me and I don't know what shape I'm going to be when I harden up again.

The silence scrapes at me. I need to say something, I know I do, but I can't. My wolf won't let me. She's too busy looking at the gorgeous rainbow wolf, and at the raven beside it with vibrant eyes and wings that look like they flew through a storm.

Just once, I would love to have eyes like that.

More pipe fittings settle on my knees. A skunk, which makes my wolf snicker. An adorable baby bunny who looks just like the troublemaker that took a bite out of every single one of Shelley's late summer zucchini.

My breath catches as I see the last fitting—the one that will go right in the middle of our den where the main pipes branch off to the school. It's gorgeous work, and instantly recognizable. A gangly bear cub with eyes I would know anywhere.

I touch the fur that's somehow smooth and cool under my fingers. I know what to do with this bear. It's the one who gave him to me that has me quivering in confusion. I build sturdy things that get tucked away inside walls and under floors and into dim electrical sheds.

These don't belong in any of those places. I can already feel my hands redrawing the schematics. These belong in the open where they can be seen.

I gulp. I'm taking too long, and this is the kind of gift that deserves a response, that needs one, because these parts are for pack, but they're also for me.

The words were definitely for me.

RONAN

Damn Scotty and his timing. I've never been a bear who struggles to tell the truth, but I'm struggling mightily now. I expected this to be a gift of significance, but I never expected it to arrive right after her song that changed everything—including what some pretty welded parts could mean.

I watch her hand as it strokes the bear that looks so very much like her son. Her fingers tremble. My head tries to melt into my shoulders. Once again, I've made myself too big.

Her head comes up, as if her wolf has scented my inner shrinking. Her eyes focus on mine, not in the usual careful way that she has, but the other way. The one that happened right before she began her song to the daybright moon. "This one isn't the way I drew it in the schematics."

My engineer scrambles to his feet, alarmed. She's right, it isn't. Because there's a leap she needs to make. Because Scotty jumped a step she hasn't gone, quite yet. It's the correct part, or it will be once she makes the adjustment he casually assumed that I would have already made.

I must be careful. So careful. The systems of this den are her work, not mine—and they're beautiful. I would not have this gift diminish her sense of her own worthiness. Parts can be switched out. Remade.

She looks down at the pipe fitting again. Studies it. Traces the functional parts with her fingers this time, not the silly, gangly, perfect bear cub. When she looks up again, amusement flickers in her eyes. "Were you going to tell me that we needed to make that change before Kennedy and Glow buried all of the pipes, or after?"

My bear has never done bashful in his life. Until now. "Before. Mostly."

She nods slowly. "We're going to have to change some things around anyhow. We can't hide these inside utility cupboards like we were planning."

Her eyes are saying something so very different than her words. "You could, but the welds are pretty, and they'll handle the weather just fine."

She looks back down at the welded bear with the mussed fur and delighted eyes. "Will you help me think it through?"

I'm not going to be capable of rational engineering thought until at least next winter. "I could do that."

HAYDEN

Thank fuck. I suck in air, along with the rest of the pack that has been collectively holding its breath. Lissa's grip on my hand eases, along with her equally tight one on Robbie's scruff. None of us entirely relax, though, and all eyes are still on the wolf with the pipe fittings in her lap and the polar bear who is sitting on the ground beside her with his entire heart on his bright, knitted sleeve.

Which Danielle seems to understand. Somehow she sees through all of Ronan's many layers into the ones that matter most. I don't think either of them has a freaking clue what to do about that, just yet, but at least I don't have to try to reassemble a polar bear after our den systems designer threw a bunch of really ostentatious pipe fittings at his head.

That would have made my wolf sad. He thinks they're pretty.

A raven screeches overhead. Danielle and Ronan look up just in time to catch the falling tube instead of getting beaned by it.

Kendra rolls her eyes. "If she wants messenger work, she needs to work on her delivery skills."

Finn elbows her. "Jules says we can't have that one, remember? She wants to be an engineer."

The hawk alpha's sniff says exactly what she thinks about where engineers fall in the hierarchy of the world. Which does the job she means it to do, and helps to amuse my pack while a bear and a wolf very gingerly find their footing again.

I should probably be helping with that, but I'm having trouble taking my eyes off of the main action. I watch as Ronan tugs some papers out of the tube as delicately as he would handle a fragile ball of yarn. Those are Danielle's systems designs. Apparently the rest of us don't handle them nearly reverently enough.

Kendra smiles faintly as a polar bear spreads papers out over his massive knees and a smaller head leans in to get a better angle. "I can't believe that I flew skunk art up here. What kind of pack are you running, Hayden Scott?"

Kennedy snickers, right on cue, and elbows the bear cub wedged between her and Rio. "Is it the cute skunk, or the mean one that sprayed Stinky?"

Finn rolls his eyes. "They're all mean."

Says the guy who can flee in the one direction that skunks don't usually aim. I watch Reilly's eyes. The rest of him hasn't moved since the first pipe fitting came out of Finn's delivery bag, but his brain is working as hard as one of Scotty's imaginary supercomputers.

Given that he's nearly swaddled in big, black wolf, his heart is clearly doing some pretty major work, too.

Rio's eyes meet mine. Not alpha business. Not yet, anyhow.

Kennedy elbows her favorite grizzly cub again,

tucking him a little deeper into Rio's ribs. "The bear totally looks like you, except I don't think your paws are that big."

Myrna, who is never slow on the uptake, braves the bubble around Danielle and Ronan long enough to steal one of the pipe fittings. "His paws will grow. Just you wait. This wolf looks like me when I was a pup, don't you think, Cleve?"

An uncomfortable guy in a flannel shirt and pants that are several sizes too big clears his throat. "I think it looks more like Ben. Or maybe Molly."

Myrna snorts. "You're a blind old man. This pup has mischievous eyes, not kind ones."

My wolf growls his approval as several heads bend over the purloined pipe fitting and start a swelling debate over whose tail is that bushy and whose ears are that big. Smart elder. More cover for the dance of wolf and bear.

I look over at Danielle and Ronan and snort. My wolf might be hoping for a mating dance, but that seems unlikely to happen while they're buried in engineering schematics, even highly irregular, poetic ones.

My wolf grins. The green-eyed wolf thinks columns of numbers are romantic.

I sigh. He has a point.

He eyes Ronan. The bear should stay. He would make pack stronger and he would be a good father for the cub.

I blink. That's not just the yellow-gold wolf who likes chasing Ronan in the woods talking. It's his alpha instincts. The ones that wouldn't hesitate to send one of my best friends packing if he thought this was a bad idea.

He shrugs. The elders have spoken. The mamas are issuing the invitation. The cub is willing. The bear is welcome.

I raise an eyebrow. He left one major player out of that list, and there's no way that was an accident. He has a special fondness for Danielle and her ability to fix everything that the pups and teenagers break. But I'm not having that conversation with him when he's in a possessive mood. Instead, I head toward the one that he's long since learned to expect from me. The bear put a skunk on our pipe fittings. And a cute, inedible bunny.

He grins. The bear is funny. The skunk pipes go to the showers.

I stare at him. He never paid a second of attention in engineering class.

He snorts. He doesn't know anything about pipes. Those aren't for wolves. But he knows the hearts of his pack and the heart of his big, white friend. He knows what the fittings that the hawks delivered will do.

I roll my eyes. He's a wolf who doesn't know shit about engineering, no matter how smart he thinks he is.

He rises, alpha strong inside me, confident and certain. The metal wolf who looks like none of us and all of us will feed water to the main den building. The bear cub will guard the pipes for the school, because installing him there will make Danielle's heart sing, and the raven will stand watch over the heat running up to the viewing ledges. The skunk will sit at the entrance to the showers because it will make small, stinky boys laugh, and the baby bunny will water the outside gardens and the timid hearts that seek solace in the den's quiet places.

I gape at my wolf and wonder if I've somehow completely forgotten a conversation that I had with Scotty or Rio.

He shakes his head regally. He is a smart wolf. This isn't about design or pipes or engineering. It's about telling stories. The bear, he tells very good ones. Important ones. I should listen.

I look at my friend. At the generous, boisterous, sensitive man who has always fought for space for himself and his bear and then given it back up again.

And then I phrase a very careful question for my wolf.

19

ADRIANNA

The call isn't an unexpected one. Neither is the young face that pops up on my laptop screen. "Hello, dear. I presume that you called to tell me why the entire web of Whistler Pack is shaking?"

Kennedy winces. "Crap. I don't think anyone thought about that part."

Oh, I imagine a sentinel did. And my son, if he's got his alpha head screwed on at all straight. That neither of them placed this call is to their credit—and interesting. "We're fine. Most haven't felt it, yet. Just the ones with highly tuned pack sense." Including my daughter, who can't figure out if she should tap dance on a mountaintop or scream from one.

Both may well happen.

A baby alpha who has lived through more pack

turmoil than anyone should see in fourteen years studies me for long enough to be disconcerting. Most shifters take the alpha of Whistler Pack at her word. This one doesn't think I'm lying—but she's considering that maybe I haven't noticed all of the important bits of the truth, just yet.

I let her look. All alphas need such wolves at their sides.

My wolf grins. If Ronan moves to Ghost Mountain, maybe we can steal a couple of packmates in return. She would choose this one. And Mellie, because she is fierce and fearless. And—

I stop her before she names every shifter in Hayden's pack. This pack is more than enough to handle, and besides, even if Mellie were available, we'd have to fight Kendra for the privilege of taking her. "Has Ronan come to a decision?"

Kennedy raises an eyebrow. "If you know that much, how come you don't know the answer?"

Oh, she would keep me on my toes. "A wise alpha listens to her instincts. A smart one also collects data from eyes on the ground."

She grins at me as Braden crawls into her lap. "Tell Scotty that the metal wolf is really pretty, but we don't understand why it has Ebony's paws and Moon Girl's tail."

If she thinks she's the first scout who's tried to distract me with juicy gossip and cute pups, she's sadly mistaken. I wave at Braden, who looks remarkably unsticky at the moment. He must like the hot pools. "I thought it had Hoot's paws and Kenny's tail, myself."

Kennedy rolls her eyes. "That's what Myrna thought, but she's just trying to cause trouble."

It's what elders do best. I eye the baby alpha who doesn't think the antics of her elders are enough. "Was it your idea to call me, or hers?"

Hesitation. A loyal lieutenant weighing her options. "Neither. It was Hayden's. He said to tell you that you're not supposed to interfere. This is ours to do, or some of us, anyhow, because the dominants are supposed to sit quietly and not throw our weight around. But we can gather information. Hayden says that's a good job for me because he has to stick to being alpha or Ronan's bear might get weird."

I take a berry from the bowl that a thoughtful pack-mate left on my desk and chew slowly, processing all of the clues that I was just neatly handed by a young wolf who probably recognizes most of them. The clear understanding that she's walking a very fine line of loyalty, one that, even with her alpha's permission, would tear up most dominant wolves. The careful work, fluent in both wolf and bear, that my son is doing when he doesn't yet know what Ronan's answer will be. The wolves who, yet again, are choosing their submissives to lead them.

The first conclusion I come to is pride. Hayden and his pack are doing something that I would have imagined impossible, and they're doing it in the only way that they can—and perhaps in a way that only *they* can do. The claws and teeth of Ghost Mountain would never be enough to contain a polar bear. Their tested, wily love just might.

The second conclusion I come to is that Ronan has fallen into one of his blind spots. For a bear with a PhD in psychology, one that he took simply to try to be a better packmate, sometimes he's remarkably unwilling to see the obvious. "Interesting. What information are you seeking?"

Kennedy's lips quirk. "The kind where you're really smart and tell me any thoughts you have so I can go whisper them in Shelley's or Lissa's or Wrinkles's ears."

Somebody has been listening to the interviews I sent her. I chuckle and eat another berry. "Are you capable of whispering, my dear?"

She takes a very silent bite of a honey berry bar and offers the rest to Braden.

Darn. Those are really delicious, and we somehow can't seem to get the recipe quite right. Our berries must grow on the wrong side of the mountain.

I look into the eyes of a young woman who reminds me so very much of myself at fourteen, and wonder how I can help her navigate the gravity beams she's preparing to reorganize on behalf of her pack. Because no matter what she might go off and whisper into wise submissive ears after our chat, Kennedy is also on my laptop screen because a baby alpha wants to know where to apply her weight.

It won't do to start by swallowing hard that her alpha

trusts her with both of those jobs. "I don't have a solution for you, but I do have a couple of thoughts."

She digs underneath Braden and comes up with a pad of paper and a pencil in an eye-searing shade of pink. "Reilly gave me a notebook. Shoot."

I don't even want to think about the swirling waters a bear cub is currently swimming in. My wolf is having enough trouble staying put as it is. "Someone is taking good care of him, yes?"

I get a glare truly worthy of an alpha.

I let my sheepish wolf show in my eyes. "Sorry. Grandmothers need to ask these things."

Kennedy's face softens. "We've got him. Rio says he's doing big work inside his heart, but he'll be okay if we feed him extra honey and love him lots."

If a sentinel and a fierce baby pack are holding watch over Reilly, then I can probably keep my wolf from hitchhiking north for another day or two. "Thank you."

She shrugs, and hints of my own sheepishness echo back at me. "If you wanted to maybe send him some honey or something, Kendra said that she could find one of her restless juveniles to come collect it."

My eyes fill. A young friend, and an old and cherished one, scheming together to help me with the gargantuan task of sitting on my hands. "Thank you for arranging that."

More sheepishness, maybe even reticence. "Ronan likes honey, too."

I shake my head, mostly at myself. I missed that angle, and I shouldn't have. Honey is exactly the sort of message that a very large polar bear needs from his alpha right now. Fourteen-year-old Adrianna Scott didn't have a fraction of Kennedy's fluency with gravity beams. Fifty-eight year old Adrianna might not, either. "I'll go see what I can bargain for in our kitchen."

Kennedy grins. "Good luck with that. I hear that you make terrible deals."

I make wonderful deals. Anyone who thinks otherwise doesn't add proud eyes and slowly dawning grins and wolves making tentative steps into their own power as they stare down the alpha of all alphas into their math. "I'm an excellent dishwasher. That's usually decent currency in the kitchen."

A baby alpha, who I happen to know washes plenty of dishes, snorts, as she should. "Hand over those thoughts before you go, in case they chain you to a sink in the dungeon."

Braden sits up, looking concerned.

I grin. Ronan must be telling stories of castles and their basements, again. "Not to worry. I practiced my dungeon escape skills just yesterday." A variation of them, anyhow. Some of the betas thought that their alpha might be getting slow and lazy without Kel and Ronan to put me through my paces.

Kennedy looks intrigued by that notion. Which means I need to give her a direction to head, because restless baby alphas are never a good thing. I pause a moment to collect my thoughts. They're not quite advice. The beginnings of guidance, perhaps, translated as best as I can into the unique language of her gravity beams.

"You're looking to build a pack shape that can hold a polar bear, correct?"

She nods like that's the kind of thing that fourteen-year-olds and packs that have lost most of their dominants do every day before breakfast. "Danielle has an awesome plan for how we do it. But it could maybe be stronger. In some way that engineers maybe don't think about."

It takes every millimeter of self-control I possess not to gape at her. I knew they had a plan. I didn't know of its architect.

I take a steadying breath and a firm hold on my wolf. She didn't truly believe that she might lose her polar bear. Until now. "You might start by considering how your pack contained you."

Kennedy peers at me, her head tilted like an owl.

I leave it there. Too much more and I risk limiting the wonderful imagination of a pack who thinks so very differently from me and mine. "My other thought is that you might consider talking to Ivan. I did, once."

Her eyes widen. Then they narrow. Then the part of her that's loyal to her bones kicks in and adds daggers.

My wolf grins. She really does want to steal this one. "I knew how to do that without betraying the confidences of pack or of a young polar bear who mattered to me. You know how to, as well."

She makes a rueful face. "Sorry. It's just that I really like Ronan, and Reilly already talks to Ivan some, and it's kind of complicated."

I open my mouth to comment on the truth and opportunity of that—and then I see Kennedy's eyes change.

I don't get to see what happens after that. I only get blurred visuals as a phone and a pup both tumble unceremoniously to the grass. But I heard the same owl hoots that she did, and I've walked the perimeter at Ghost Mountain enough to know what they meant.

Incoming. Friendliness uncertain.

20

RIO

Crap. I snarl at my sentinel. He's not supposed to let this kind of mess sneak up on us.

He snarls right back. He was busy with the bear cub. I have a nose. I was supposed to be using it.

It's a little late for that. I can already see Damien's pale face, walking in on the path from the old den with a bravado that his eyes can't match and a rucksack over his shoulder that holds a whole lot more than his spare underwear.

Ghost skids to a halt beside me, holding onto Kelsey with one hand and Kenny with the other.

I eye them all. Kelsey is vibrating, Kenny is brimming with guilt and indecision, and Ghost is quite possibly the most dangerous wolf in the den. I deal with her first. "Nobody will successfully order Kelsey to shift ever again. I promise you."

Her rage stands down a notch. "You can stop it?"

I plunk a firm hand on the shoulder of the guy whose guilt just tried to go supernova. "I could, but I won't have to." I smile down at the pup who stole my heart so many lifetimes ago that I can't remember not loving her. "You've got this, don't you, sweet pea?"

She nods, her eyes solemn.

Kenny lets out an inarticulate gurgle.

Shelley shoots him a look of disgust as she arrives with all of Ghost's speed and none of her rage. Not on the surface, anyhow. I'm looking at the Shelley Martins who lived as Samuel's mate. Glass, reflecting whatever the viewer needs to see.

My sentinel reaches for the earth. Not to calm their rage, nor to fuel it. To honor it. I don't think it will be needed today, but it's righteous and holy and I wouldn't take it away from them, ever.

Kelsey's wolf sniffs at what I put into the ground beneath her.

I snort. *Let me do my job, little wolf.*

Her answer is all prim attitude. My job is to help with the rucksack.

I roll my eyes. My sentinel happens to agree with her, but neither of them are giving me anything more than that to work with. I look back over at Damien as Hayden steps out of the wall of pack that has formed and our visitor crashes to an ungainly halt. Not because of the alpha theatrics, which would normally be pretty effective, but because of the low, communal growl emanating from the wall.

Hayden's lips quirk for a fraction of a second. Then he makes a hand signal that stops the growl dead in its tracks.

My wolf watches, curious. Hayden let pack handle the last incursion from town. This time he's clearly choosing the far more traditional bossy-alpha route. Which he only ever does for careful, well-thought-out reasons. Or on pure alpha instinct. Given how closely Lissa is watching him, this time it's probably the latter.

Damien clears his throat and tries to speak, but utterly fails. His wolf won't let him. He's too busy getting ready to be kicked in the ribs.

Fuck. I have no idea what shit the guys in town have been filling his head with, but it's got the kid shaking in his boots. Which isn't how anyone deserves to come home, even if he spent years apprenticing to become an asshole.

Not unless he plans to continue that tradition, anyhow.

My sentinel shakes his head. The kid's body language isn't what matters. None of it. Not the bravado and not the fear. It's all about the rucksack.

My eyes narrow. I consider whether I need to move into Hayden's line of sight so I can send him a discreet hand signal or two about the damn rucksack. Or maybe Kel is in position to do it. I scan the invisible wolves in the woods who are stalking a scared kid as he tries to get all the way home without crawling. Kennedy. Bailey. Ebony. Kel. Brown. Dorie. Fallon, with a grave, focused Ben patrolling below her.

That's insane overkill for one slouching wolf.

Ah. They're worried he's not alone.

I send Kel some quick sentinel shorthand. The kid is as alone as anyone I've seen in a long time.

The answer I get back is succinct and pithy. He's going to damn well make sure. And our visitor is not a kid.

I consider that, because Kel's instincts are rarely wrong. But everything in me says that the wolf currently shaking in his boots in front of his alpha never made it out of an extended version of middle-school hell.

He's here. He's trying. And he's just a kid.

A kid who did a lot of damage. I take a quick read on the wolves and the bear cub that I'm watching most closely. There are too many of them, but I need to suck it up and deal. Reilly is nervous, but fine. Kenny is settling, probably because Ghost shoved him toward Reilly with fire in her eyes and Kennedy's growl at her back. A baby pack giving him one job, and one job only. Eliza is tucked in behind the first row of the wall with Danielle glued to one side of her and Glow on the other.

Hayden makes a quiet noise and yanks every set of eyes in the pack to his, even mine.

My sentinel blinks. That's hella bossy alpha.

He tips his head down the bare fraction required to be polite to a visitor. "Damien. We weren't expecting you."

Gulps from the kid. No words.

Hayden backs his wolf off a fraction.

My sentinel approves. No matter what is streaming off of the kid, his wolf is a dominant. The worst possible thing his alpha could do is make this too easy.

It sounds like an avalanche of tin cans when Damien clears his throat again, but he manages to speak this time. "I know the requirements. I'll sleep in the woods. And work if you'll give me something to do."

The wall softens. A little.

Hayden studies him. "You're asking for the right to earn a chance to live back at the den."

Good alpha. The kid doesn't have a lot of words left in him. Not until someone claws a few holes in the miasma of despondence he brought in with him, anyhow. Which Hayden needs to do, because there's something else buried inside that cloud of black—and it packed the rucksack.

RONAN

I expected this to be hard. I didn't expect to remember, quite this vividly, what it was like to be standing in dusty boots, looking into an alpha's eyes and feeling entirely inadequate to the task of asking for what I wished for so deeply.

It isn't Damien's trembling that's pouring acid on my soul. It's his conviction that nothing he's carrying in his heart or his backpack will matter. I ache as he nods numbly at the question Hayden just asked him, the one an alpha opened up with his claws so that all of pack will see this moment clearly.

Hayden keeps Damien fixed in place with his eyes. They're not hard, exactly, but they offer nothing of home to a young man who needs one so badly that he can barely breathe.

I hold mine. I know that Damien needs to choose, here, in front of his pack and not just in a sad and solitary bedroom as he filled his backpack for this journey—but I also know that it's so very hard to choose when your soul is starving.

A bear cub leans against my side. Wary. Watching.

I have a moment of worry that he's escaped his baby pack and then I feel Kennedy's shoulder bump hard against my ribs on the other side. I wrap my arms around two sets of narrow, wiry shoulders. The young bear I once was wasn't smart enough or humble enough or experienced enough to accept such supports.

He learned.

Damien is capable of such learning.

I keep watching him. Aching for him. Daring the hope that he can't. I said many words to him two nights ago. Perhaps some of them made a difference.

KEL

Fuck. I have no idea what's in that rucksack, but I know what was in mine the day I came home. Arrogance. Bleakness. Guilt so deep I couldn't remember how anything else smelled.

Damien isn't as arrogant as I was, but the other two are riding heavy in that load on his shoulders, and his mother's eyes are sending a plea into the universe that would have my feet moving even if Adrianna Scott's grace all those years ago didn't demand it of me.

Besides, I think this kid is smarter than I was. Smart enough to have maybe listened to the fiery words of a polar bear who spoke every single one of them from the depths of a soul that knows what it is to have the contents of his rucksack taken out of his shaking hands and shared with pack. I was too damn stupid for my hands to have trembled. Judging from the fists in Damien's pockets, he's not quite so far gone.

I step out from the shadows long enough for Hayden to see me and derail my intentions if he has other plans. When he doesn't, I make the racket necessary to get the kid's attention.

Damien jerks to attention, clearly expecting fangs in his neck any second.

I move to where he can see me. I don't bite stringy kids. Not until I've tried a whole bunch of other methods, anyhow. "What's in your backpack?"

He turns several shades of sickly green.

Hayden folds his arms across his chest.

Hardass alpha. Good. "Empty it. Now."

Scared gray eyes jerk away from Hayden's gaze to mine.

I hide a smirk. Drill sergeants know how to outrank generals when it matters.

Hayden rolls his eyes and says nothing. Which is fine. Drill sergeants also know when we have the permission of our generals. "Your right to have secrets ended when you crossed into this territory. You can show us what you brought, or you can leave."

A shudder—and then Damien's wolf finds the very edges of one of the vertebrae he's going to need if he actually intends to walk this walk. His eyes come up slowly.

I dial the drill sergeant down sharply. This next part, the kid needs to do alone.

Damien sucks in a shaky breath and pulls the backpack around to his chest, cuddling it like a little kid on his first day of kindergarten. "He said to come back as the wolf that I mean to be. Not the wolf that I was." His gulp travels visibly all the way from his shoulders up to his chin. "So I brought some things."

Hayden's eyes light with interest. So do those of the watchful, waiting wolves.

A very large bear tries to hide himself behind all of them.

Dumbass. It's not going to take them ten more seconds to figure out who spoke those words where an errant son could hear them.

My wolf grins as Myrna's head turns. Make that three seconds.

Damien reaches for the zipper to his backpack.

Between his shaking hands and his wolf's intractable need to hold his alpha's gaze, it's not an easy task to pull out whatever he packed in there along with his meager belongings, but he manages.

When Hayden gets a good look, his wolf blinks in surprise.

The drill sergeant I once was grunts his approval. Points to the kid.

Damien holds up an opaque plastic bag with lumpy contents. "Hazelnuts. One of the vacant lots in town has a tree. I shelled them myself. With a hammer, so there might still be some bits of shell, but I tried to pick them all out."

The kid talks too much when he's scared. Good.

Shelley steps forward, the poker face that survived six years with Samuel firmly in place. "I'll take those." Her eyes soften a fraction. "They'll be welcome. The pups like them in their muffins."

Damien soaks up every drop of softness like a cactus in the first warm rain of summer. He reaches into his backpack again, his hands a little more steady. "I have something for the pups, too. I've been collecting them." He pulls out a handful of very well-used board books. Then his face falls and his entire body deflates.

I put drill sergeant into every silent line of mine.

He jerks and looks somewhere between Hayden's eyes and mine. "I, uh, know that they didn't used to have very many books. And that we poured beer on Kelsey's favorite."

No one says anything for a long time. It's Lissa who finally nods her head. "What else did you bring?"

I wince. Not at her tone—he needs that if he's got any chance of making it through to the other side. At what it's likely costing her submissive wolf to use it on a dominant.

Damien's hands close into fists. Not aggressive ones. The ones of a young wolf trying to hold it together and coming very close to failing. He reaches into his backpack one more time and holds out another lumpy plastic bag like it might be radioactive. He glances over at where his mom is standing and then his eyes skitter away. He has to clear his throat three times before he manages to speak. "I went to a river in Lonely Peak territory with Evan. He says that you're polishing pebbles up some and selling them. I don't know if these are the right kinds. I still have a job in town on the weekends. I clean up a bar after hours. That money can go to pack."

REILLY

I stare at the bag in Damien's hand. Collecting pebbles is hard work. So is shelling nuts with a hammer, but I bet the rocks were harder because Evan probably told Damien that the wolf who polishes rocks is his mom. Sometimes she cries when she does it.

Evan might not know that part.

I cuddle in a little closer to Ronan's ribs. He isn't in

his fur, but sometimes I can still feel it even when it isn't really there.

I don't know what to think. Damien was mean to me. And really mean to Kelsey. And he talked to Shelley in that way that made her eyes sad when nobody important was looking. Lots of the guys did that, but Damien is the one who wants to come home and live at our den and see all of our special things and have Shelley make him birthday dinners.

I don't know how I feel about that.

I lean into Ronan's ribs some more. I know he went into town two nights ago. Ghost saw him leave and Kennedy tracked them for a while and we had to give Kenny his special tea for breakfast the next morning because Wrinkles says it isn't good for a wolf to drown himself in self-pity.

I don't know exactly what that means, but the tea smells pretty awful, and Kenny didn't even complain before he drank it, and his eyes looked that way that they do when he sneaks into town to spy on the guys who live there because they're stupidheads who are making bad choices.

I stare at the bag in Damien's hand again and wonder what stories Ronan told him, because this is maybe a good choice. It feels like an apology, and maybe a promise, too. Or the start of one, anyhow.

The feeling inside my belly isn't sure whether it believes him.

I swallow. Ronan says that a bear needs to trust his gut. And that he needs to make sure it isn't just hungry.

I'm not hungry, though. I had a whole honey berry bar for snack and then Adelina gave me most of hers because she eats like a bird, even though she isn't one.

Ghost leans in and kisses the top of my head like she does when she's being really sweet with my bear. "Watch Kel."

I look over at where Kel is standing, because Ghost is really smart and she sees things that sometimes I don't notice. Kel is just standing quietly and watching Damien, but he's got a strange smile on his face and a look in his eyes that helps my bear to steady some, even though I don't know what it means.

Kel raises an eyebrow at Damien. "Do you want to work at the bar?"

My bear feels kind of sick. If he goes back to town, the other guys will find him.

Damien gets a look on his face that he used to get a lot, mostly when Baird was being really mean to him. "I want to contribute."

"Not that way." Kel's voice has a sound in it that makes my bear want to do things right away, even if the words weren't for him. "If you want to be here, you're done hanging out with drunk assholes." His next smile is his really scary one. "You get sober assholes, now."

Damien's shoulders squeeze up to his ears. "I want to earn the money. To pay back what I used up without considering anyone else."

There's a scuffle over behind Lissa. Fallon steps up to Hayden's shoulder. "Show me the rocks."

Damien looks at her like she's speaking Klingon. Kel

looks a little confused, too, but then he gets his strange smile, again.

Lissa walks forward and takes the bag from Damien's hand and gives it to Fallon without speaking. Her eyes are really fierce, but she winks at Hayden as she walks back. Which is good. His wolf is kind of jumpy because Fallon has a baby in her belly and he hasn't decided if Damien is really ready to be a good packmate, yet.

That makes me feel better.

Fallon pours out some of the pebbles into her hand and studies them. Then she tips her head and shrugs. "These aren't bad. And you did okay with the books, too. I'd be willing to take you on as an apprentice trader."

Hayden makes a growly sound. Lissa elbows him. Ronan chuckles. He doesn't make any noise, but I can feel his ribs bouncing against my cheek.

Fallon rolls her eyes at her alpha. "If he's dumb enough to make a pregnant raven cranky, Wrinkles will put stuff in his tea that will make his balls fall off."

Damien turns white. Then his mouth opens and his eyes glue themselves to Fallon's belly.

My bear gets fired up and ready, because that baby is sort of like my cousin and she's going to be really tiny and Damien doesn't get to be an asshole to any more pups, even ones with feathers.

But his eyes don't want to be mean.

They don't want to be mean at all.

They look kind of like Kelsey's when she sings songs to Fallon's belly.

RIO

My wolf rolls his eyes. Trust a raven who lived on the streets to give her whole pack a collective nightmare without even trying hard. But it's a good solution. Damien needs watching, and he needs to be under the eye of someone who's heard a lot of crap and knows better than to take it personally—and who will peck out his eyes if he's too much of an asshole. It takes time to retrain those kinds of behaviors, and he needs a chance to do it with someone who understands what it is to have put on that kind of armor in the first place.

It's an answer I might have come up with myself if my wolf could get past the blinding need to protect the unborn packmate in her belly. I let him add his two cents. "Just so you know, after your balls fell off, Ivan would eat you. He considers Fallon a friend."

Fallon rolls her eyes again.

Ben shoots me a grateful look. He's the guy who's going to be living closest to the nightmare.

Eliza just watches silently, wrapped in her friends and letting us do our job of sanding off her son's roughest edges so that he can start making his way back to a comfortable place in his pack.

Sometimes silence is the fiercest kind of courage.

My sentinel sends her quiet words through the earth and gently, reverently touches the memories that she's clutching to her heart. The ones of a small pup with happy eyes. A boy who picked flowers in the woods for his mother's birthday. The afternoon she showed him how to crack nuts with a hammer.

I smile. There are so many ways to come home.

The kid picked good ones.

21

DANIELLE

I set down my armful of wiring and tools on top of the electrical hut and sigh. I'm doing work that we won't need until at least spring, again. I needed something to keep my hands busy.

So does everyone else, apparently. Damien is scrubbing pots. Glow is helping Dorie rig a new ladder into a tree for wolves who can't just walk straight up its trunk. Eliza is sanding an enormous boulder that Brown rolled in on the rock cart this morning. It's huge and jagged and has purple streaks running over its surface like lightning. Just the kind of gaudy thing a polar bear might want for his den, or at least that's what Brown muttered before he dumped the boulder in Eliza's lap and fled.

If Ronan doesn't end up living here, I have no idea how we're going to get it all the way down to his apartment at Whistler Pack, but it doesn't matter. It gave Eliza a way that might be big enough and shiny to begin to say thank you to the polar bear who just gave her everything. Even if she's been polishing it all morning with tears streaming down her cheeks.

Which is still easier to think about than Ronan maybe living here.

I sigh again. Today isn't about me and the strange ideas roaming in my head. It's about Eliza and her son who has come home.

Her son who came home because a polar bear roared. Damien hasn't said a word, even when we fed him spaghetti and meatballs for dinner and made him sleep on the schoolhouse porch, but Kelsey sat herself in Kel's lap at breakfast and smiled sweetly and he groaned and told her the short version of what happened in town while Rio and Hayden tried really hard not to laugh.

Kel's eyes looked happy after, too.

Ronan looked kind of embarrassed, especially when he heard about how many wolves tracked them through the woods. Ebony even followed them all the way into town on a motorcycle she borrowed from Reese. It wasn't working very well when she borrowed it, but I fixed the rattles last week and she hasn't had time to return it, yet.

Or that's the story we're all sticking with. Including Reese. We're probably going to have to pay him in information, though. He's a very curious cat.

I pick up the new wire pliers he sent me. They're the really good kind, except they're smaller than any pair I've ever seen and they fit in my hand perfectly. I don't know where he got them, but I need to trade repairs for more of them. Indrani's hands are even smaller than mine, and Hoot was watching really closely the last time I repaired one of the video cameras.

I start stripping and bending wires, getting them ready for a junction box. It's mindless work, or it would be if it didn't still feel like a small miracle to get to do this every day. I did some work around the old den when the dominants weren't looking, but it mostly got done in the middle of the night when my fingers were cold and clumsy and lost small parts in the dark.

My wolf prowls inside my ribs, restless. She wants a lot more than my repair work to emerge into the light. Wolves are night creatures. Human hearts need sunshine to work right.

I smile at her assessment. We're deep into the gloomy days of fall and early winter, but she's not wrong. Fortunately, this pack has a lot of sunshine. Enough to shine on a pot-scrubbing wolf who never really had the chance to grow into a decent man, and maybe the polar bear who somehow convinced him to give decency another chance, too.

Because Kel's story at breakfast wasn't just about Ronan's roar. It was about kind words spoken by a polar bear who understands what it is to feel hopeless inside, and who knows that sometimes the only way out of that place is to take tiny baby steps that feel as big as the world.

I remember my walk home. I was tired and dusty and carrying a cranky Reilly in my arms and so much grimy despair inside me.

I had no idea how many more steps there were to take, back then. Coming home is only the first one. Sometimes that home changes and sometimes it doesn't have what you need and sometimes grimy despair finds you in the middle of the night and steals the breath from your ribs as you watch your still-too-quiet cub sleeping.

I start bending wires and attaching them. I don't feel like that when I watch Reilly sleep these days. He's not too quiet anymore. Ronan gave him that. Others, too—Kennedy and Ebony and Hayden and Myrna with her wild-hoyden yells. But it was a big, loud bear with a generous, ear-filling laugh who was the most convincing.

I swipe at the tears that have somehow found my cheeks. Reilly is a full-sized bear and Damien is scrubbing pots and Grady was up on the ledge with Grandpa Cleve yesterday, wearing a shiny welded wolf medallion on a leather cord around his neck. Cleve said the leather cord smelled like polar bear.

Ronan isn't just helping Eliza's son come home, he's making enough space for all of them to be here. And that's making a space inside of me that I don't know quite what to do with. I just know that it's decorated with schematics and ice bridges and shiny welded art that will look gorgeous in the rain.

RONAN

I write down another measurement that's changed since the first time I took it, and snort. Schoolhouse doorways don't change shape without help, so the bear taking the measurements is almost certainly to blame. He's having trouble paying attention. To the measurements, anyhow. He's too busy eavesdropping on the happenings in eighth grade.

Reilly enrolled Damien this morning and sent Kennedy down to the kitchen to spring him loose from pot scrubbing for long enough to learn why drawbridge chains creak and the implications that has for space elevators and other big equipment under heavy loading.

Scotty got pretty geeky on that last part, but his audience still watched the video attentively. Judging from their current conversation over the assignment questions, however, none of the eighth graders understood nearly as much as the bear cub in fifth grade who is carefully explaining some of the more technical details.

One who is consciously, intentionally displaying the smarts that were a big part of why he got bullied. A bear cub making it very clear that things are different, now.

He's also casting cautious, assessing glances at the newest kid in the class while he does it.

For good reason. Damien looks more ready to crack by the second. I can sympathize. The bear I once was would have managed scrubbing pots under Myrna's brisk supervision. He crumbled the first time he was issued an invitation into belonging.

Which is what Reilly did this morning, even if his eyes are wary and measuring.

A decision that I believe he made while talking solemnly to his mom over bowls of oatmeal with extra honey. I growl under my breath. I will match Danielle's courage in this, no matter how much I want to hide a bear cub behind a much larger polar bear's bulk. I pick up my measuring tape and apply it to the part of the door frame that has me suspicious. The door squeaks, and such an embarrassment to HomeWild's engineering team cannot be tolerated.

Reilly gets up from his chair and heads over to a bookshelf in the far corner. He slides one out, looks something up, and then reshelves it with a conviction that rings in the sudden, uneasy silence.

The wolves of eighth grade might have a questionable grasp on physics, but they read their favorite bear cub just fine.

Damien swallows hard as Reilly heads in his direction.

I don't stop with my work, and neither do any of the others who are keeping an eye on things, but Reilly's body language would have our attention even if he wasn't walking toward an edgy wolf who hasn't slept since he got here.

That part is Kelsey's fault. She gave Damien a pillow that smells of small girls who smile a lot and sing pretty songs and sometimes still have bad dreams.

I cast a quick glance at the sentinel sitting at the low table. He has a better angle on the wolf who's thoroughly overwhelmed by the science of drawbridges and everything else that has gone on in the last sixteen hours. Rio's still working on a map of North American shifter alliances with Adelina and Hoot, though, so Reilly probably isn't going to claw Damien just yet.

Although Bailey has Kel's field kit tucked under her chair, so maybe that possibility can't be entirely ruled out.

I believe we are all in agreement that the young man who just came home has earned such a response a hundred times over. And that a smart, sensitive bear cub has the right to choose whether or not he will deliver it.

Reilly stops by Damien's chair and folds his arms.

My bear blinks. That's classic dominant wolf posture.

Bailey's lips quirk.

Reilly speaks quietly, but his voice is full of steady strength. "I have something I want to say to you."

Damien's head jerks like he can't figure out which way to move it.

Adelina and Hoot start to get up from their chairs, but a hand signal from Kennedy has them sitting back down again.

Smart wolf. In some very important ways, she has turned herself into a bear for the cub in her baby pack. She would know how important it is to him to do this alone, even if Reilly hasn't quite figured it out, yet. Because it was his bear who was made weakest by the evil that came to live in his pack—and his bear who most needs to reclaim that power.

Bailey lays a hand on Kel's field kit. A wish, maybe—and a promise. From another who lived six years with much of her power wrapped in voluntary chains.

I send her the silent respect of a bear. Her way of

freeing herself will involve claws, and I don't think the wolf who will wear some of those marks has any idea, yet. But Reilly is the shifter looking to cast off some of his chains today, and he doesn't have the heart of a fighter.

Which doesn't mean there won't be blood.

I hold my bear steady. It was an act of fierce trust for Danielle to send her cub to school this morning. He must not be the one who gets in Reilly's way.

Damien looks ready to puke up all of the single pancake that he ate for breakfast, but he nods silently.

Reluctant empathy flickers in Bailey's eyes.

Compassion also rises in my bear. He knows just how hard this will be for a young wolf who thought he was fully grown and is about to discover just how far he has to go. Perhaps some day Damien will understand just how much it matters that Reilly was willing to deliver this blow.

"You were mean to me." Reilly's eyes are the dark brown of his bear. "You said things to make me feel small so that you could feel bigger after Baird and Sean and Eamon kicked at you."

Damien's hackles rise. He is not yet mature enough to understand the nuances of the bear cub's opening volley. One that carries the pawprints of the wolf who shares his soul. Bears don't volley. They swipe and leave guts hanging and let truth bleed out into the snow.

Bailey's fists tighten where Damien can't see them.

None of the others move, and it isn't the adults in the room they're taking their cues from. It's Kennedy, casually leaning against the back of her chair with pride shining in her eyes.

She understood the nuances.

I take a shallow breath. A deep one would disturb too much of the air in the room.

"You need to talk," says Reilly sternly. "You need to say what you did. Otherwise it will feel like a bad secret inside you and then you won't be able to become a better wolf."

Kennedy's pride ratchets up several notches.

The bear cub isn't watching the alpha of his baby pack. He's looking at the hackles of a dominant wolf so weak and lacking in proper guidance that he picked on a little kid. "How did you feel when they were mean to you?"

Damien can't hold on to the thin sheen of bravado that was allowing his hackles to stay up. "They were assholes. I was, too."

A decent admission from a dominant wolf. One look at Reilly's eyes says that it won't be enough.

He shakes his head. "I don't want you to talk about the part where you were a big, dumb jerk. I want you to talk about the other part where they made you feel small and weak and like you didn't matter."

Bailey's fists have turned to mottled marble.

My bear knows why. Damien was hers, once. Good leaders feel every single one of their failures.

I look at Kennedy, who is young and powerful and surely feeling some of the same, but she hasn't wavered from her singular focus—ensuring that Reilly's heart is wrapped in the armor of an alpha's pride.

Damien swallows hard. "It wasn't so bad. What we did to you was worse."

Reilly nods solemnly. "I was little and I didn't have choices. You did."

That one gets all the way through to Damien's innards. He shrugs painfully. "I tried. For a while. Then it got too hard." He looks down at his hands. "I'm sorry. I know that doesn't actually make anything better, but I walked all the way from town thinking about what it must have felt like to be a kid or a submissive when Samuel and Eamon were in charge."

A task worthy of a long walk. And one that catches Reilly's attention. His head turns side to side like a raven evaluating a new shiny. "Do you want to know what it feels like here now?"

Damien blinks. "Uh. Okay."

Kennedy's poker face slips just long enough for her lips to twitch.

Reilly stands taller. "I used to think that I had to be a really small, quiet bear, even when you were mean, because that's how I kept my mom and my friends and my pack the safest."

Every last bit of air left in Damien comes out in a single, awful whoosh.

"It's not like that anymore." Reilly's eyes glint with love and fierceness. "I don't have to hold on to my bear so tightly because now he knows when to be big and wild and when to be slow and gentle. He knows that he can be all of those things. He just has to pick the right places and times."

Damien looks as shellshocked and confused as a wolf can get.

It doesn't matter. This chapter of the story isn't really about him. It's about a magnificent young bear cub who is naming his power as he reclaims it. A naming that has spilled a much older bear's guts out onto the snow. I can feel them bleeding, and I can feel the truth that a bear cub spoke throbbing inside them.

He knows when to be big and wild and when to be slow and gentle.

He can be all of those things.

Reilly takes a big breath, large enough to disturb every molecule of air in the room. "That's what you need to learn. It's okay to be a bossy wolf if you do it for the right reasons. Until you know what those are, you probably need to be a wolf who scrubs pots and does a lot of physics homework. I can help you with that part. I'm pretty good at homework."

Kennedy's eyes fill with the love she's been heroically containing. "Hey, now. Don't go promising all of my help to other wolves. I need to pass physics, remember? Or I'll still be in eighth grade when you and Stinky get here."

Hoot and Adelina snicker. Which is the first sound they've made since Reilly stood up.

Damien glares at them.

A short, sharp growl cuts him off at the knees.

I blink, because it wasn't Kennedy who took him down, even though she was expecting it to be her job. It was Bailey. Which in the language of dominant wolves means that in addition to her very clear threat, she also just made a promise—and judging from the disgusted look in her eyes, it's one she didn't actually mean to make.

Kennedy grins.

Damien deflates right back down to pancake wolf. His eyes flick briefly to Hoot and Adelina. "Sorry. I don't really remember how to be a decent guy."

Reilly's dark brown eyes don't waver. A bear who has learned to be hard when it will serve his pack. "That's not a good excuse."

It isn't just Kennedy's eyes that are full of pride, now. The entire room is fairly crackling with it. Damien nods slowly and manages to lever himself up from his chair, moving like a very old man. "I think I'll head back to the kitchen. There's probably more stuff to scrub."

I believe Shelley and Ravi were making burrito fillings with the younger students for just that purpose.

Bailey gets to Damien's side before he's taken three steps. "I'll go with you. We can review the basics of angular biomechanics while you clean up the lunch dishes."

He scowls fiercely. "None of that shit used to be in eighth grade."

She claps a hand on his shoulder. "It's there now. Suck it up."

He groans—and walks a little taller with the dominant air she's just blown into his lungs.

I grin at a bear cub who knows just which parts of Scotty's university courses got plundered for the new

Ghost Mountain science curriculum. "Maybe don't tell him about the next unit for a while." I helped with that one myself. Medieval weapons have all kinds of interesting physics applications.

He snickers, his bear sliding back into easygoing eleven-year-old with surprising grace. "Myrna says that we can't build the catapult until she finishes seventh grade. Which might take a couple more weeks because Katrina is having trouble with chemistry equations."

I make a mental note to see how much chemistry I can dig out from under the engineering in my brain. Right after I go walk in the woods for a while. I need to think about songs to the daybright moon and sturdy, competent hands and conversations over oatmeal that are shaping a bear cub into a man. And I need to retrieve a polar bear's guts from the snow.

I don't have to hold on to my bear so tightly because now he knows when to be big and wild and when to be slow and gentle. He knows that he can be all of those things.

It's only been a few months. Just a few short months of a pack able to give a bear cub the kind of space and time and packmates inviting him to play and be and live as he needs—and yet he feels different, both human and bear.

I've had years to change from who I was when I left the north. Decades. I've embraced the changes of the man. Honored them. Been grateful for the willingness of the bear to be small so that the man could have those experiences.

I've never really fully considered what has become of my bear.

Dorie is right. I need to find that bear and pick up his guts off the snow and listen to his story. I need to ask if he knows how to be all of those things.

22

HAYDEN

I dodge as Hoot hurtles by me, chased by Sierra and Indrani and a raven youngster I haven't seen before. Once a month, the blended teenage forces of all the local packs spend the day wreaking as much havoc in Ghost Mountain territory as possible and eating all of our food.

The invasion is clearly in full gear.

I look at the hawk who just landed. She's young and bright-eyed and not wearing nearly enough warm clothing, but saying so will just make the big alpha hawk coming in behind her cranky.

Finn shifts into a pair of really gaudy Hawaiian shorts and shakes his head. "Kezzie, darlin', that was a glitzy landing, but you almost dropped your courier pouch. Safety first, of you and the goods. It's not just about impressing the ladies."

She rolls her eyes. "I *am* a lady."

He grins. "Some of you like impressing the ladies, too."

More eye rolls. "Can I go play? Sienna brought her new video camera and we're doing a flash mob in Dorie's trees."

I shake my head. That's probably something a couple of alphas should go check on, but I'm guessing neither of us is brave enough. We've already learned that young wolves who live in a cat pack can come up with the kind of shenanigans that give my mother's teenage reputation a run for its money. I raise an eyebrow at Finn as Kezzie runs off. "Do I need to keep an extra eye on any of yours?" Hawks generally deal with wolves and mayhem just fine, but Kendra is like Dorie. She collects strays.

Finn shakes his head. "Nope. Kendra headed over to the ravens with our newest addition. The three who came here can handle whatever your claws and teeth decide to dish out."

"Claws aren't allowed." Kennedy skids to a halt, sounding thoroughly insulted. "Is that the new tiara that Eady sent for Myrna?"

My wolf winces. He really doesn't want to know why my grandmother is sending royal headgear to my pack's most troublesome elder.

Finn grins and tosses his bag over his shoulder. "Maybe. But it's not for you, either way. I'll just go see if I can find the intended recipient."

Kennedy rolls her eyes at his back as he strolls off. "He knows about the teenager-pack rules because I told him. No claws, no chasing birds, no yanking tails, and no bossy juice."

The devilry of leadership always lies in the details. "How are those working out?"

She sighs. "Bossy juice is tricky because the cats mostly just use snark and we can't really make a rule about that or we wouldn't have any fun. But Finn can send any hawks that he wants. We'd be nice to them." Her eyes flash a message about just what would happen to anyone who didn't temper what they dished out to what the recipient could handle. Which is her only real rule, and it's an inspired one.

I put my arm around her shoulders. "He knows that."

She huffs out a sigh. "Yeah. I know. I just want this to work for everyone. Sierra and Sienna brought Devlin today, and she's having a really great time."

Devlin is the cats' most recently minted teenager, and unlike most kitties, she's shy, and if she has claws, I haven't seen any sign of them. "Who did you buddy her up with?"

Kennedy grins. "Maybe I did it differently this time."

Quite possibly. She likes to keep the kitties in the teenage pack on their toes—and the watching alphas. I rub my cheek on the top of her head. Leaders of chaos sometimes need soft places to land.

She leans in. "I'm good. Glow and Katrina have Devlin, and Molly is hanging out with Ree and the new ravens, and Reilly is doing something with Sienna and Mikayla to see if they can make mud blow up."

The upper end of what constitutes a teenager in this

large and unruly baby pack is a very bendable rule. "Is Damien back in the kitchen?" Kennedy got him to help set up the buffet table so he could meet some of the incoming teenagers as they arrived. He lasted until Sierra gave him a friendly hug.

Kel got to have some fun catching him and chasing him back to scrubbing duty.

Kennedy nods, her shoulders tensing a little.

I nuzzle a teenager who doesn't seem to be inclined to leave her alpha's easy affection, just yet—and who will need an excuse to stay there. "I heard about what Reilly did this morning. How much did you have to do with that?"

She snorts, her shoulders easing. "Nothing. I thought Reilly should just whack Damien and boss his wolf."

A baby alpha who understands that a bear cub wasn't forced to a side under Samuel's reign—he chose one. "What were Reilly's reasons for doing it differently?"

Her sigh is one of bedraggled alphas everywhere. "He said that Kelsey couldn't do that and his bear didn't want to be bossy and there had to be a better way. And then he sat alone quietly and thought up a new plan."

He might have been sitting quietly. He wasn't alone. This morning was the act of a bear cub who felt his whole pack wrapped around him, and the one who was doing most of the wrapping is currently stealing my last honey berry bar and cuddling against my ribs. "Some of your baby pack wasn't in the schoolhouse."

I wasn't either, but someone had to amuse the pups while they did outdoor lessons and stayed thoroughly out of potential harm's way. Which mostly looked like chasing their alpha though some old leaves while Ravi made up some new verses to his latest silly song.

Kennedy wrinkles her nose. "My wolf didn't like that part, but Ghost said we couldn't all be in there because bears are like that, so she stayed outside with Kenny while he growled."

I knew about that part. I had to throw a pinecone at Kenny's head. "You took care of Reilly's bear and his wolf. That's complicated. Rio was impressed."

Kennedy makes a face. "I'm just trying to pass physics."

My wolf huffs out a quiet breath. That's why she's cuddled into my ribs. A baby alpha, worried that she got too big again. "Is that going to happen?"

She snickers. "Bailey says that miracles might come to pass."

I'm not entirely sure why we've decided to make eighth grade harder than second year university, but nobody has ever asked my opinion. "I know some people, if you need help. With physics, or herding teenagers, or that other secret thing you're planning." Because apparently she doesn't see the irony in trying to convince a polar bear that he's a perfectly reasonable size to fit in this pack.

She pats my chest. Almost done with needing her alpha. "You're not supposed to know about that."

I grin. "I bribed Rio with purple gummy bears." And carefully didn't tell him what Shelley put in them to make them purple.

Kennedy scowls. "He's not supposed to know about it, either."

It's really hard to have secrets from a sentinel. Especially when you're conspiring to remodel the foundations of his pack. Which is all the information he was willing to give me, even for the very last purple gummy bear. I elbow the teenager who is ready to go back to being a force of nature. "I hear there's a flash mob in Dorie's trees."

Her eyes light up. "Really?"

I snicker as she runs off. Nobody ever tells alphas anything.

KEL

Idiot bear. I duck the obvious jab he tosses at my chin and the far more subtle blow aimed at my knees. "Do I look like I got old and gray while you were gallivanting around the Arctic?"

He huffs out something that might have been a laugh if we weren't exerting ourselves so hard. "You've been gray forever. The rest of you is just catching up to your fur."

I try a version of the knee takeout he just deflected and don't get any further than he did. The hazards of fighting with someone who's been a sparring partner for several decades. I follow it up with one of Kennedy's flamboyant roundhouse kicks just for giggles.

Ronan snorts. "When did you start fighting like a girl?"

That isn't an insult. We both get put in the dirt regularly by girls. When it doesn't happen frequently enough, Adrianna comes to sparring practice. Leaving Whistler Pack and moving several hundred kilometers away hasn't changed that. She's the one who taught Kennedy the flamboyant roundhouse kick. "When did you bury your brains in the dirt and decide to leave them there?"

His eyes flare as his bear momentarily tips the balance in favor of a hunt. One with my guts as the reward.

I don't help Ronan wrestle his bear back into balance. I don't win when I fight fair, and most of those decades of sparring were to force him to rebuild the balance between man and bear, over and over and over again.

If he stays, he'll need people besides me to help out with that. I'm getting old.

He calls a pause for long enough to drink more water than my belly could hold. "When I got off Ames's plane, I think."

It takes me a second to remember that I asked him a question. It's an interesting answer. I lean into a stretch that makes my knees creak. "Keep talking."

He shrugs and towels some of the sweat off his face. Polar bears don't like to drip hot, salty water. "My bear caught one sniff of Danielle and he was a goner. You know that."

The entire pack knows that. Then it got complicated. "Which you tried to bury."

He snorts. "Of course I did."

I wipe the sweat off my own face. I'm allowed to get delicate in my old age. "So you never really thought through any of the steps that might come after that. Instead, you let your bear have his fantasy about becoming her friend and romancing her and cozying up in a desolate cave together some day."

He winces at the tone of my voice. As he should. He doesn't get to steal the only person who knows how to keep our oven running. "I didn't look at the obvious logical pitfalls. I never considered that it would actually happen."

A man who never set his engineer to working on a tricky problem because he assumed that his bear wouldn't get what he wanted. I take up a fighting stance again. We're finally getting somewhere. The only way to keep that happening is to continue fucking with Ronan's balance.

He dodges the lazy punch I throw at his nose and tosses his towel onto the ground. "Got any wise advice, old man?"

He knows how to fuck with my balance plenty, too. "I don't do advice. Especially about romance."

His dark eyes bore into mine. "This is about way more than that and you know it."

It's plenty about that. It's also about longing and belonging—and terror, because he's still not throwing his punches full strength, and with Ronan, that's always a sign that he's crawled into his darkest place. The one where he's so damn certain that he risks breaking everything he touches.

I know that feeling. I used to believe that everything I touched would blow up. "I was worried about Danielle for a while."

Ronan's eyes narrow. "Why? She's strong. And smart. And careful."

He's so gone. "She's all of those things. None of which changes the unrelenting pressure that even a very meek polar bear can apply just by existing."

The blood drains from his head as I land my blow right on the very tenderest part of his bear.

I aim a fist at his chin, next. Sometimes fast and hard is the only way. "I had it wrong. She's solid, and her friends are applying duct tape as needed. Sadly for you, I suck at that engineering crap, so you're just going to have to go with what I can do decently well."

It takes far too long, but his eyes eventually glint with amusement. "Kick my ass?"

I'm doing my best. He's faster than I remember. I pivot and jab and wait for what should be coming right after the amusement, because Ronan is not and has never been a dumb bear, even if he's temporarily buried his brains in the dirt and left them there.

His eyes darken as he parries a kick that should have gotten through. "Wait—you think that *I'm* the fragile one?"

The dirtiest word in a bear's vocabulary. I land my last blow. The best and hardest one that I saved for last. "In this pack, you might be."

MYRNA

I set the phone down in my lap and take a deep breath. The video would be easier to see on Lissa's laptop, but I need to watch it a time or two in private, first. Not that I'm keeping any secrets by sneaking off into the woods.

My pack knows that Xander sends me messages when he can.

I used to have to take Ebony's creaky old phone to the far side of Moss Rock to get the videos to play, but it was always worth it. My wolf doesn't understand words on a screen. She needs to see her boy's face. Both of them, maybe. Sometimes Xander manages to get a shot or two of Milo's wolf.

I take another deep breath. It doesn't help, just like the first one didn't. When you've lived for six years with your ribs squeezed in tight, all the breathing in the world can't put them back to right. I tap on the small arrow that will launch the video. It doesn't start with Xander's face like it usually does. I squint at the small screen on the phone. That looks like snow. Snow, and a pair of thoroughly irritated boots.

A blur, and then my youngest son's bearded face comes into view. His normally mild eyes are blazing. "Mom, what the hell is happening up there? All I've been getting from you are messages about knitting and muffins. I'm not Greg."

He certainly isn't. My oldest never questioned the

pablum I sent him as the pack he was born in lived through six years of hell. Xander has never been nearly that easy to placate. I stroke the screen as he stomps through the snow. "Check the other account, sweetie. I sent all the good stuff there." Editions of *GhostPack News*, and photos, and a sketch Brandy did of his favorite tree. Which isn't fair, but I only have one son who can still hear the call of pack, and I'm weak enough to want him to hear it.

Xander's face comes back into view. "Sorry. You probably sent more to my email, but I managed to scramble my password somewhere in the Andes." He directs a wry glance down and to his left. "A big paw accidentally landed on my login screen."

My wolf perks up. She can hear Milo breathing if she listens very carefully. They must be climbing.

I frown. There's no cell reception in the mountains of South America.

Xander snorts. "Yeah, we're not there anymore. Which you've probably figured out."

I shake my head. Always, he does this. His videos are like conversations, ones where I get to fill in my part after they arrive.

He huffs out a breath, and I can see it misting in the morning sun. "We're somewhere in the Sierra Madres, I think."

He knows exactly where he is. He just doesn't know the human names for all of the places they travel through.

His eyes bore into the screen. "We seem to be heading north."

Hope blazes in my wolf—and terrible, consuming fear.

Xander makes a face. "Don't panic. It will take us months to get to you, especially if Milo keeps chasing every fucking rabbit he scents along the way."

Terror beats in my chest. As wolves, they could travel the distance in weeks. The extra time will be needed for Milo's episodes. The ones that will get so much worse if he tries to come home. I try to reach my fingers into the screen, desperate to touch my son's face. His beard has grown wild again. Mountain man. They mustn't come.

Xander scowls at the screen, which is exactly what he's always done when I tried to tell him what to do, even as a boy. "Which brings me back to asking what the hell is happening up there. A couple of days ago, we were meandering our way through a pretty patch of Mexican forest and I was trying to convince Milo to head to a nice beach for the winter, because I was really tired of having my ass chewed on by jungle bugs."

He often travels human. Trying to help Milo remember.

He walks into a patch with more shadows and tall trees overhead. "So there we were, minding our own business, and then Milo's wolf stops dead and turns around and points his nose due north and howls. Which has probably started a bunch of new legends, because there aren't supposed to be wolves in those particular woods."

My eyes widen. Not at the legends.

Milo howled.

Lone wolves don't do that.

Xander raises an eyebrow that is so much sterner than when he left. "Know anything about that? Two days ago, middle of the morning?"

I count—and my heart clenches.

Two mornings ago, Danielle heard a polar bear's silent whisper under the daylight moon and gave us a song—one of pack making room for something big and terrible and dangerous. My fingers scrabble on the phone screen. Milo, the protector, always. Of course he heard, but he didn't understand. Danielle wasn't singing of a threat to pack. The polar bear is good. Evil does not stalk us again.

Xander stops in the snow, and his eyes fill—but not with what I expect to see there. Not with fear or helplessness or the intractable need to save his broken brother or the stoic determination he's grown in six years of walking beside Milo as they traveled everywhere that a wolf's paws can go.

On the small screen in my shaking hands, I don't see any of those things in my youngest son's eyes. Instead, they're full of cautious, tremulous wonder. "He sang to the moon, Mom. About that freaking rabbit we chased when we were boys. The wily brown one that eluded us the entire fucking winter. Remember that one?"

I nod and swipe at my nose. I remember. An old hare that amused himself tormenting a couple of small wolves on their first hunt. It could have forged a sense of failure. Instead, it forged a brotherhood.

I breathe. My wounded boy, my broken one—he howled a story of happy things.

My whole face trembles.

"He headed north after that. Nothing I say or do is changing his mind. He's okay. He's eating. Sleeping. He's just determined." Some puffing as Xander climbs over rocks into more sunshine. "We seem like we're headed your way, so I need to know if it's okay if we get there."

A pause, a blur, and then hints of a dark wolf trotting in the trees.

He's moving smoothly. Easily. Ears forward. Eyes bright.

My wolf quivers. She sees him. She sees her boy.

Xander's face again. "If it's not okay, I might need some help heading him off."

My throat closes. Xander's courage has always been a match for anything, but his wolf has never been a match for his brother's fiercely dominant claws.

Which didn't stop him from trying.

I touch the screen again, stroking the beard that hides the scars that are the least of what Wrinkles patched back up that awful night in the woods. I see the lingering wonder in his eyes, but there's still something missing. He doesn't dare hope, even now, that his brother might make it all the way home.

I don't know if I dare to hope, either. These woods broke Milo, and I don't know if he'll ever be able to set foot in them again and keep the last pieces of his soul. But I do know three things.

They need to try.

I need to ask an enormous favor of a big, black wolf.

And I need to go talk some sense into a polar bear.

I tap into the app that will let me send a text to the emergency contact beacon that can reach Xander with a short message no matter where they are. It costs the earth and I've only used it twice in six years.

I have no idea what to say, but my thumbs do.

I knit you a new hat. There are muffins. Come home.

23

RONAN

She walks silently through the forest to my side.

I don't ask how she found me. This elder is a very good hunter.

She takes a seat on the log beside me and studies the view in the distance that has been charming my bear for the last hour while he thinks.

I look over at the top of her head. It's wearing a wool hat that Stinky and Jade knit. It has several endearing holes and my bear hopes that one day he might earn one just like it. "Most people wouldn't dare to interrupt a polar bear's thoughts."

Myrna snorts. "We're a pack of submissives and teenagers and pups. We don't fight the way that other packs fight."

They surely don't. I have some defenses against those ways.

She pats my arm. "Our fiercest skill is holding each other while we tremble. So you go right ahead and keep doing that. I'll just sit here a while."

There's a note in her voice that catches my bear's attention. I wrap a big arm around her shoulders. "When do you tremble, wise elder?"

This snort is a lot wetter. "I'm going to be doing it all winter." A breath flutters in and out of her like a falling leaf. "Some of my boys are coming home."

My bear freezes. It can't be the one in Montana. He does good work on the wind project and has an annoying fondness for rules and paperwork, and he would not make her tremble. "How can I help?"

She sniffles and wipes her nose on her sleeve. "You can help me knit Rio that sweater he wants. The one with the fancy colorwork that Brandy designed."

My bear stares, mystified. It's a gorgeous, tricky pattern, but Myrna is more than capable. "Of course. Why?"

She swallows. "I'm thinking that he's going to need a warm sweater while he's off doing the very big favor I'll be asking of him."

My brains scramble to catch up, but apparently a lot of them are still covered in dirt. Sentinels don't need bribing, but she knows that. "I know where to get mango-flavored gummy bears. Those might be faster."

She chuckles and leans her head against my ribs. "We have time. My boys need to get closer before I send a sentinel to hunt them down."

My bear finally catches up. Of course. One of her

sons was badly damaged in the blast that took out most of Kelsey's family, and he would need Rio's care. But that isn't the sharpest point of this particular conversation. The sweater she speaks of will take weeks to knit properly, even with two sets of hands.

The small, fragile whisper inside me trembles.

Perhaps she asks for more than my knitting skills.

She sits up and draws her knees against her chest in a pose that would have me falling off of the log. "You aren't answering our questions."

I proceed carefully. Everything about her body language says that caution is warranted. "I'm not sure which ones you mean."

She studies the intricacies of something off in the distance. "Shelley needs to know your favorite kind of cookie and what you like for your birthday dinners. Miriam wants to know if you like greens, because they're about to plant some new kinds in the greenhouse. Cori needs to know how you feel about fake fur and googly eyes on pillows."

I stare at her, mystified. I have heard such topics discussed around the campfire and the schoolhouse table, but they were never directed at me. "My birthday isn't until March."

Her eyes bore into an entirely innocent tree. "You're missing the point, and you're a smart bear who doesn't miss many of them, so I want to know why you're missing this one."

I'm most certainly missing something. I sit quietly.

It's what smart bears do when the ice under their paws is suddenly no longer solid.

"You maybe don't have a grandmother."

I wait, still puzzled, but not failing to scent the importance of the moment that has found me. Elders are revered in the north, too. The very few that survive the long nights and vodka and lack of purpose, anyhow.

Life has not been kind to the elders of this pack, either.

Myrna nods, like something important has been decided. "I'm not old enough to be your grandmother, but I have a frying pan and I'm pretty tough and we're just going to have to make that work."

My bear stares down at the top of her head, stunned.

She wraps her arms more tightly around her knees. "This is my daddy's pack. The land he chose."

A long pause that sets my bear's fur to trembling.

Her eyes gaze fiercely at the horizon. "It would never be the same again if you joined us."

The small, fragile whisper inside me cracks. She knows. She feels, in her wise bones, why I can't be here. "I don't know if everyone fully understands that, just yet."

Her eyes flick in my direction. "Don't underestimate us. We saw our pack demolished by the evil of two men, and we know what it is to be shrapnel. We aren't innocent, and neither is our invitation."

Something hot and acidic pours into my newest cracks. "I don't understand."

Her lips quirk. "That would be why I'm out here with my frying pan."

My bear tries to string together some words that might make sense and eventually subsides, entirely lost.

She pats my arm. "We've launched an offensive, silly bear. One we'd hoped you would recognize, given how much time you spend with the submissive wolves of Whistler Pack. But since it's failed to get through your thick fur, here's the version from the business end of my daddy's cast-iron skillet. We want you to stay."

Things spark in my brain that aren't hooked up to any wiring. "What? Why?"

She rolls her eyes. "Because you fight like we fight. Because I need help with that sweater so my eyes don't bleed. Because every ghost wolf in this pack is doing better since you got here. Because someone needs to keep up with Reilly. Because who you are offers protection to some of our most broken places. Because you give wonderful gifts that see right into hearts and you're going to save me from seventh-grade chemistry and you use the wheelbarrow with the dinky wheel. Because you're helping our boys to come home." A pause, and then the faintest of smiles at the horizon. "But mostly because we see you and we see your bear and we love you."

My ice cracks. All of it.

She pats my arm, more briskly this time. "I interrupted your thinking. I'll go now so that you can finish."

She doesn't speak again until she reaches the tree line. "Don't take too long."

24

HAYDEN

Bears don't slink. Not unless they've done something horribly wrong or they're so wretched that they can't hold up their heads any longer, and I've never seen Ronan in either condition.

Which is why his careful walk into the den catches my full and complete attention, along with that of every other shifter in the vicinity.

He doesn't look at any of us. He just makes his way over to the bear cub who's sitting in the dirt trying to build a space elevator out of twigs and forks and knitting yarn.

Ronan takes his first breath as he crouches down beside Reilly. "That looks interesting."

Reilly's eyes finally look up from what he's doing—which is when I can see just how much fear and hope he's been hiding. "It's just a conceptual model. Scotty's sending some balsa wood and wire so I can make a better one."

Ronan nods like a bear who isn't quite sure his head is going to stay in place. "That's good. I won't get to see him as much if I'm living up here, so maybe he can deliver the supplies in person."

The punch that lands in my gut isn't from Ronan's words. It's from what flares in a listening bear cub's eyes.

Twigs snap in Reilly's hands. "You're staying?"

Ronan nods slowly. "I want to try. But I'm scared. My bear is very big. Bigger than yours will ever be."

Joy blazes from an eleven-year-old's face as he rolls to his feet. "That's okay. We know how to help with that."

RIO

I knew what they were planning. I knew, and I'm still not ready when Ghost and Kennedy come to stand beside Reilly.

They look at a blinking polar bear and then at each other, and in that look, I finally understand. They aren't daunted at all by what they're about to do. They've been ready since the moment this plan was hatched. They were just waiting for a polar bear to choose.

Reilly faces Ronan, and the look in his eyes steals my sentinel's breath. "You're scared that you might do something bad one day. That you might hurt your pack because your bear doesn't remember quite fast enough that we're smaller than he is. Right?"

Truth spoken by a young bear who has lived and breathed that fear.

Ronan very carefully nods.

Reilly smiles at him gently. "We don't want you to have to be scared about that, so we talked to Ivan."

I knew that part. I wasn't ready to see it land—on a polar bear, or on Hayden, or on the rest of us as we watch the face of a bear cub who somehow calls gentleness out of the fierce northern alpha who has none.

"I was on the call," says Kennedy quietly, which gets Ronan's lungs working again. "Ghost was, too."

Reilly nods. "Smart bears know when to have a team, right?"

Ronan doesn't have enough control of his head to nod anymore. My sentinel doesn't help him. Nodding isn't necessary. Reilly isn't looking for reassurance. He knows the full power of what he holds in his hands.

Reilly stands up a little straighter. "Ivan said that polar bears are the fiercest and most dangerous when they hunt, but the one thing that could stop even a hunting bear would be a cub. Not all bears, but the right kind of bear, and he says you're that kind."

Ronan sways.

My sentinel gives in and sends a small pulse of support to a polar bear's paws. This story will be a lot better if the big man at the center of it stays conscious.

Ghost and Kennedy step forward together.

Shock skitters across Hayden's face. An alpha who

has just figured out where this is headed. Kel's breath hitches a heartbeat later.

The first hints of uncertainty surface in Reilly's eyes.

My sentinel doesn't do anything about those, either. This is the act of a bear cub who knows how to be wild and knows how to be gentle and knows the time and place for each, and this moment wouldn't be fully true if it didn't tremble a little.

Ghost speaks first. "Ivan said that cubs don't have to be bears. Phil's cub is human."

Kennedy shrugs. "We don't have dads. So we got you a shirt, if you want it." She unrolls the scrunched-up fabric in her hands and holds it up. It's lime green and wrinkled and big enough to fit a bear, but it's the bold letters on the front that matter.

World's Best Dad.

The universe stops turning or moving or breathing while a polar bear's eyes make their way over the big, black letters and process their casually offered, deadly serious invitation. It doesn't take sentinel woo to know when it lands like a ton of bricks on the small, terrified whisper inside him.

Hoot, her eyes streaming tears, steps forward to join Kennedy and Ghost. "I had a dad and I won't ever forget him. But I could use one who can give me hugs."

Stinky, his eyes solemn, steps forward to join her. A growing pup who remembers little of the father who once was, but who didn't hesitate when he was asked if he wanted to stand at his sister's side on this day.

A mournful, diffident howl sounds from the woods.

My breath stutters as Hoot clutches Stinky's hand. Grady wasn't part of the plan.

With a careful look at his mom, Reilly takes the single step forward to join the others.

The wolves of Ghost Mountain take a collective breath. Then they exhale and move their feet. Eliza raises an eyebrow at her son, who is standing in the shadows of the cook shack doorway with a pot scrubber in his hand. Miriam and Layla look at each other and smile and hold up their two pups. Adelina and Katrina and Glow walk over to lock elbows with their fatherless friends.

Robbie smiles sweetly and makes the dad sign at Hayden. Then he makes the uncle sign at Ronan.

My sentinel chuckles. Way to reduce two grown men to rubble, tiny alpha.

Jade holds up her hands and copies Robbie's sign. Kelsey smiles and repeats it. Twice. Once for herself, and once on behalf of Fallon's baby.

My wolf senses a part of the plan that he's been waiting for. He sends a hand signal to a bear cub. One we worked out in advance. Just in case.

Reilly gulps and turns very slowly toward the trees.

My sentinel carefully wraps his gentlest woo around the wolf he's been traveling with ever since she woke up this morning. Twice on this short walk, she's turned back. And twice, she's managed to turn herself around again.

Molly steps out of the trees, shaking, her eyes very carefully on Ronan and none of the other big men. She doesn't say a word as she joins the others.

She doesn't have to. A shaking polar bear heard her just fine.

KEL

A smart soldier knows when a battle is absolutely unwinnable.

I'm looking at one. A dozen fatherless pups and an extra handful looking for an uncle just in case Ronan wasn't already thoroughly shattered by the first assault.

An overwhelming victory led by a gentle, sensitive, careful bear who is absolutely his mother's son. He didn't go at this like a fighter. He looked at an engineering problem and recruited a team and found a solution.

He's also a very green general who still isn't sure whether it was enough.

My wolf shakes his head as he watches his friend of several decades shake. That isn't a polar bear contemplating what his answer should be. It's one who's trying to figure out where to land his massive bulk because all of the bones in his body have turned to goo.

Which is why green generals have sergeants.

I fire a signal at Kennedy, because she's the only one who might spare some attention for a beta who wasn't smart enough to have figured out their plan in advance, even when he stumbled on the pups practicing the signs for various family members.

I'm definitely getting old.

Her eyes widen a fraction. Message received. She unlocks her elbows from Ghost and Hoot and marches over to a crouching bear, giving him a good, solid shove with her hip. "I'm pretty sure you can't be this quiet if you want to be a good dad. Even Ravi yells, because sometimes Jade doesn't turn on her brain before she moves her feet. Fair warning, I'm totally going to be that kind of kid."

Mellie grins up from her new seat on Ronan's lap.

Kennedy snickers. "Never mind. She's definitely going to be your biggest problem."

A big hand, moving on automatic pilot, gently pats a small, feisty head.

Reilly closes in on Ronan's other side, bumping him hard just like Kennedy did. Smart bear cub. "Braden always smells really good, but we're not supposed to lick him because that just encourages him to wipe his fingers on his belly. But maybe the rules are different for bears who are dads."

"Nope." Myrna grins as she ruffles Braden's hair. "The rules are only different for grandmothers. Dads need to eat their vegetables and censor their curse words and help with homework and generally set a good example."

Fallon leans into Ben and bats her eyelashes.

He snorts. "I like vegetables."

The part of Ronan's brain that likes carrots and zucchini manages to pull itself together. The rest of him is still sitting like a robot that nobody bothered to attach to its battery pack.

I shake my head. He'd already decided to stay. We probably could have held him just fine with lots of knitting and spicy food and extra patrol duty and Danielle's careful, sturdy plan. But the youngsters of this pack have clearly been paying attention to Ronan and his need to embellish every damn thing. They've just neatly taken Danielle's design and added shiny metal wolves and bear cubs and ravens—and by the time Kelsey is done with him, I have no doubt that there will be baby bunnies and skunks in the fatherhood mix, too.

They brought overwhelming force to a battle that a polar bear didn't actually want to win. Ronan never had a chance.

RONAN

I've spent my whole life walking on a tightrope stretched over a canyon with nothing but sharp rocks below. That's what it is to be a human who shares his body, heart, and soul with an apex predator.

I have no idea what to do with a rope that suddenly feels as wide as a highway. This isn't just a nice offer by a bunch of sweet pups and teenagers that I would have been happy to love anyhow. It is something far more, and they engineered it precisely and with purpose and with knowledge of all of the parts that live inside me.

I can already feel it steadying my bear. The man need not fear the rocks below any longer, because he can feel the truth. The bear would never hurt those who are his. He is already studying each of his new cubs. Wondering what they need. Pondering how to best be their soft place and their fiercest champion.

In design, it's not all that dissimilar to what Adrianna did for me at Whistler. She made sure that I had special relationships with many of the pack's most vulnerable. Friend, mentor, confidant, defender, companion.

But to be a father is different for a bear.

So different.

I snuggle my nose into the softness in my lap. Adelina is on one knee, cracking jokes about a dad who is big enough to hold her. Jokes that are allowing her to stay. To be held. To feel what it is to be absolutely safe. A trio of pups are on the other knee, squishing themselves cheerfully into a single organism with many limbs, as pups do.

Kennedy and Reilly lean against my shoulders, sheltering Jade, who perches on one of them like a raven. Kelsey hasn't come to me, yet, but she sits where I can see her, radiant in her puffy green coat and purple rain boots, softly humming a song for my ears. Hoot is not here, and my bear can feel the lack of her. She's gone to deliver a small gift for her brother in the woods.

I glance over at the other cub who will need a polar bear's gentlest touch. Molly sits against the trunk of a gnarled, windblown tree, wedged between Ghost and Glow, with a watchful Dorie in the branches overhead. They're eating sandwiches, and Molly managed to hold her ground when Kel delivered them.

The pride that rose in my bear was a living thing—

and it stretched the tightrope yet wider. Eased, yet further, the tightly clamped control that man has always had to have over bear. Made yet wider the possibilities open to him if he doesn't have to spend every waking moment being that bear's keeper.

I shake my head. My brains are definitely still covered in dirt, acres of it, but I am awed by the wild beauty of what has been built for me. A leadership role would have called to all of my bear's hunting instincts. Instead, they've called to all of his soft and protective ones. It's genius—and it required only the gifting of what already existed.

This is a pack with more fatherless cubs than Whistler Pack has ever seen.

My bear whiffles contentedly into Adelina's hair. It *was* such a pack. They are not fatherless any longer. He is home.

DANIELLE

He has just agreed to be a father. Not to one small bear cub that he helped to create. To a dozen pups and juveniles and nearly grown adults, simply because they asked. Because they need. Because he has that much love and loyalty and responsibility in him to give.

I'm trying not to stare, because Reilly is already giving me strange looks and I am so very proud of him and my wolf is dancing around inside my ribs like someone set her tail on fire and I don't know where I put my extinguisher.

My wolf grins. She ate it.

I don't even know what that means. I just know that a polar bear is going to be part of this pack, part of Reilly's life, no matter what. My cub will have a father, one who clearly intends to take that role very seriously, and while my human is still blinking about that, my wolf knows it is a promise made for all of the right reasons and it will strengthen family and it will strengthen pack.

She whispers a wild suggestion in my ear.

I gape at her.

She grins and repeats it.

I grab for her scruff. She's lost her everloving mind. I'm not that kind of wolf. I didn't even want to turn on the water to the hot pools before all of the new pipes were ready, and this is a far crazier idea than that one.

She dances around with her tail on fire and sings her wild suggestion to the daybright moon.

Rio's head turns my way, his eyes curious and amused.

Myrna follows suit, because she can smell a crazy idea from miles away.

Kelsey makes signs with her hands as she sings. *Happy. Love. Play.*

I glare at all of them. Well, not at Kelsey, but definitely at the other two.

They both chortle.

My wolf tugs me to my feet.

I pull in the other direction. Tomorrow. I can

consider this tomorrow. This isn't a good time. He's covered in pups, and his eyes are fuzzy in that way that says his bear is still dazed, and he probably can't even hear himself think.

My wolf dances me merrily over in Ronan's direction.

I freeze when dark eyes lift to mine.

My wolf pauses. She puts her paws on the ground, steady and sturdy and true. And then she whispers, one last time.

My fingers clutch at the air, but there are no tools to be had. No wires that need stripping or cameras that need fixing or fuses that need replacing. I can't think this problem through with my hands.

Ronan's eyes gentle. Soften. Question.

No—I can't do it that way, either.

I swallow and close my eyes and make myself into a very small repair bot and burrow into my heart, because even if that isn't the proper way to build anything, it's the only way I know how to find that place of rightness where I can see what needs to be done and how to do it.

My wolf is waiting patiently for me when I get there.

Her eyes shine. It's time.

I shake my head. I'm not ready. The pipes will leak.

She grins. That's why humans invented silly things like duct tape.

I shake my head again, even though I no longer mean it. I brush my fingers over the metallic, multi-color bear cub that my repair bot stashed in here days ago. I look up at the schematics on the wall, and the sketch of the ice bridge, and the poem in Eliza's fancy writing that somehow got hung while I wasn't looking. *Friend. Safe. No harm. I like muffins.*

I pat my persistent, lunatic wolf on the head and scratch behind her ears.

Then I open my eyes, lean in, and kiss an astonished polar bear.

25

HAYDEN

"I think this might be a pack where the girls do the kissing."

"That's not how it happens in most of the stories."

"Those stories are stupid."

My wolf listens, deeply amused by the young ones of his pack. Especially the bear cub, who groans and throws his hands over his eyes dramatically every time anyone mentions kissing. He keeps sneaking looks at his mom, though. And he doesn't groan when she kisses the polar bear.

That makes the bear cub feel all warm and squishy and happy inside.

It makes a lot of us feel that way.

Danielle turned the color of a fire engine right after she did it the first time. The last couple, her cheeks have only gone fiercely pink.

Ronan, like a smart bear, is sitting very still and waiting for her to come and kiss him again. Which the teenagers of this pack are observing with loud, talkative glee.

Well, the teenagers and my loud, talkative sister.

Jules arrived yesterday about ten seconds after the first kiss, cursing a blue streak that she missed it and neatly creating enough chaos to let Danielle and Ronan stare at each other for almost an entire minute before they got pelted with a whole bunch of questions that neither of them can answer, yet.

The questions and commentary haven't stopped since. I might have to go break some pipes for them to fix pretty soon.

Kennedy shakes her head at whatever Katrina just said. "Nope. Girls definitely do the kissing around here. Lissa kissed Hayden, and before that, Layla kissed Miriam, and Ruby kissed Cody."

A collective wince at her last words—and then watery smiles.

My wolf swallows. Good baby alpha. Brave baby alpha. Making sure that those who came before are not forgotten.

Myrna clears her throat. "It started earlier than that. Tara definitely kissed Aaron. And I'll place my bets on Wrinkles, too."

The old healer grins and says nothing.

I'm not so sure about that one. Brown is a very interesting bear. He's also one who would never let facts get in the way of a good story, so we probably won't ever find out.

Kennedy scans her pack and zeroes in on the poor guy holding his guitar like a shield. "Did Cori kiss you first?"

Ravi's head tucks into his shoulders, but his eyes are pleased. "She did, actually."

Cori splutters from her blanket nest over with the knitters, who are already casting on more tiny baby things. Our pack does not lack for optimism. "Only because you were so shy and polite."

Jade clambers up her daddy's arm and gives him a kiss.

Kennedy grins. "See? I rest my case."

Katrina, who is only arguing to help her baby-alpha friend stir the pot, looks over at Ben. "There's no way that Fallon kissed you first."

My wolf agrees.

Ben's eyes glint with mischief. "Well, I kissed her first, but only after she fell out of the sky into my arms, so I think that counts."

Kennedy high-fives with Hoot. "We are so winning this."

Hoot rolls her eyes. "That's not actually the point of every conversation, bossy wolf girl."

This has nothing to do with winning and everything to do with celebrating the insane victory that they already snatched from the jaws of a stunned polar bear. A victory that even my mother, who walked in yesterday somewhat more sedately than my sister, is still shaking her head over.

Even though I can feel her fingerprints in it somehow.

My wolf licks my cheek. I can be a wily alpha later. Right now, I should find a green-eyed wolf and do some kissing.

I snicker. He's so not paying attention. Lissa is supposed to do the kissing. Which is fine by me.

Robbie walks over to Kennedy and signs rapidly.

She picks him up and delivers a big smooch to his cheek. "I will kiss you any time you like, munchkin. Unless you've been playing with the skunks. Then there are no kisses for you."

He giggles and makes the signs for kissing a skunk.

Hoot rolls her eyes. "Stinky, don't even think about it."

Her brother, currently safely ensconced with the knitters, just grins.

I look over at our betas, who absolutely need to be on the job of talking anyone out of trying to kiss the local wildlife, just in time to see Ebony grin. She leans into Kel. "I like this idea that girls should do the kissing."

He looks equal parts alarmed and confused.

She chuckles. "I'm not kissing you, idiot. Although this new pack rule clearly needs an exemption for our gay men."

Reilly nods solemnly. "I can put that in the article. Adrianna says I should write one because this is an important pack innovation and other shifters might want to think about trying something similar."

Ebony somehow keeps a mostly straight face. "I would never argue with the alpha of all alphas."

My mother snorts from under her usual pile of pups and teenagers and various food items covered in ketchup. "You argue with me all the time. You're a very troublesome northern liaison."

There are six new internships kicking off next month. Adrianna Scott is about as annoyed as a toasted marshmallow.

Myrna bangs on her frying pan. "Argue later. Right now, we need less talking and more kissing. Especially from Ebony. Inquiring minds want to know. Reilly's doing the serious reporting. I'm writing the gossip column."

Our lanky beta's cheeks go a little pink, which fascinates my wolf. Then he stares, dumbfounded, as she strolls over to the knitters, crouches down, and meets Eliza's lips in a soft, dreamy kiss.

When she finishes, there's panic in Eliza's eyes—and deep vulnerability in Ebony's.

The moment stretches between them, taut and potent and teetering toward misery.

"Maybe it has to be the girl submissives who go first." Reilly's whisper is laced with distress and a budding engineer's need to help—and comes out way louder than he intended.

Ebony's lips quirk, her eyes still on the woman she

kissed. "Are you kidding? Have you seen her wield a chain saw?"

The panic in Eliza's eyes slowly dims—and something enchanted rises instead.

Grins bust out all over the pack. Damien looks ready to blow away on the next puff of wind.

Myrna cackles. "Well, that took long enough. Anyone else?"

My wolf shakes his head. Troublesome elder. One who knows just when to pull the attention elsewhere.

Kennedy leans against Reilly's shoulder, always happy to be a distraction. "I think that means that dominants can go first, but only if they're kissing an engineer. Because they have really big tools and stuff."

Reilly nods solemnly and adds more scribbles to his notebook.

ADRIANNA

I lean against Myrna and try to keep my helpless laughter quiet enough that it doesn't disturb the conversation swirling around us, because it's hilarious and poignant and unimaginably precious. And sadly, about to segue to other topics. Which will please my daughter. She still feels mostly like Reilly does about kissing.

I watch as Indrani strolls over innocently with a tube that I'm quite sure is about to turn this den upside down. Ronan might have been a very still and quiet bear for most of the last twenty-four hours, but there was no way it was ever going to last any longer than that.

He's never wanted to lead. To him, leadership is a lonely place. He's like a much larger version of Lissa. He holds the center and fills it with warmth and generosity and relentless inclusion and utter acceptance. Whistler Pack did our best to give him that, but we never truly needed him there. This pack does, and his gratitude for that gift is going to be endless.

I watch the tube as it travels. If I don't miss my guess, and with him, I rarely do, the glaciers of his gratitude are about to break off and land in the ocean.

He smiles at his excellent accomplice and takes the tube. Then he looks at Danielle, and what lives in his eyes nearly brings my wolf to her knees.

James used to look at me like that.

Ronan pats the tube gently. "Come. I'd like to show you something."

Danielle moves closer, wariness in her eyes.

He slides some papers out of the tube. Ones that I recognize well. It's rare for Ronan to do the architectural drawings, because that's Rio's first love, but a sentinel will know why he's done these ones.

Ronan looks at Danielle again, bashful and a little uncertain. Which has my wolf gaping. They've made so much space for his softness here. He pats the papers in his lap. "I drew up some sketches. For the residences."

She blinks at him.

He swallows. "I know that you were thinking about doing the sleeping modules, so they can be added one at a time. But I had a different thought, and I wanted your input."

My wolf scootches her butt in along with everyone else's. We all make way for two scootching butts, though. Reilly and Rio arrive just in time to peer over Ronan's big shoulders as he spreads out the papers in front of Danielle.

She doesn't move for a very long time. So long that I begin to worry. Ronan's love comes in very large sizes.

Then she reaches out a single finger and touches the papers reverently.

Reilly grins. "That's so smart. It's like stacked sleeping modules, right? Where some people live in the bottom and some live up higher like birds, and some get squished happily in the middle like honey ham."

Rio nods. "Yup."

Several dozen heads squeeze in and try to make sense of the sketches in Danielle's lap.

Ronan looks around at the budding frustration of his audience and holds up his hands. "Here, I can tell you. There would be several residence buildings, each with three living levels stacked on top of each other, like this." He pulls Reilly's hands in to help illustrate.

Fallon's arm shoots up. "Dibs on one of the top units. I'll share, but I could fly right out of a window that high. So could my demon chick when she gets big enough."

Several wolves turn green.

Ronan laughs. "Yes. Birds up high, and we could build walkways for the cats to live up there if they want, and anyone else who likes to climb."

In this pack, that includes almost everyone. Wise bear, and I don't think he's nearly done.

Fallon sniffs. "I didn't say I would share with cats."

Dorie snorts. "You want help catching your demon chick, right?"

My wolf grins. She speaks street raven and cat. Those are love words.

Kel studies the drawings upside down, which won't hinder him at all. "Smart. Easier to secure with limited claws and teeth."

Ronan smiles. "Yes. Teeth and claws can live on the ground floors. And bears."

There it is. My wolf nods as she sees the glistening of his ice. There could be no possible safer place to sleep than above a polar bear's den. An offering of utter safety to the most wounded ones of a pack that has known such fear.

Wrinkles eyes Brown speculatively.

He grunts. "Don't push on me, woman. I like the woods."

Danielle's finger moves. "There's a ground floor unit here on the end that would back right up to the trees."

Of course there is. When Ronan decides to be spectacular, he does it with care and exquisite attention to detail.

Lissa clears her throat. "How many of these residence stacks are we talking about?"

I hide a smile. Like all the very best chief financial officers, she's already trying to rework her spreadsheets to make dreams possible.

Ronan shrugs easily. "As many as we can afford, to begin. More as the funds are available. We'll talk through the numbers. This is the idea. The design. The imagining. It will take the entire pack to make it real."

Smart, savvy bear. I sit back and watch him maneuver. I will miss him terribly.

Jules scowls from where she's snuck her head in beside Rio's. "There are no HomeWild offices in these drawings, bear."

Hayden's ears perk up. As they should. His sister just picked her side in this fight.

Ronan shrugs. "If you want space, I assume that a reasonable rental rate or discount on building materials could be negotiated."

Jules crosses her arms and glares.

I grin. She's going to miss him terribly, too. Which is why Ghost Mountain is about to get a satellite HomeWild office, along with all of the other changes that Ronan will catalyze as he stakes his place in this pack. The pack that finally did what I couldn't. They've given him permission to be the full force of nature that he truly is.

He's going to be magnificent.

RONAN

I almost don't hear her, at first. It isn't because of the din. It's because she's speaking so quietly. A voice that doesn't mean to be heard.

I lean in. That part of her life is done. "What needs to change?"

Danielle looks up at me, startled. Then something in her firms and becomes sturdy. "You'll need to adjust this one. You need bigger living quarters." She smiles. "You have a dozen cubs who will want sleepovers."

My bear blinks, because she isn't managing the logistics of my life. She's making sure that he has enough space—whether or not she's in it. We managed a small conversation last night as we added the new lights that Jules brought for the hot pools. I will be permitted to court her, so long as I keep my gifts within reason and give her time to consider and move slowly and feel sure she's making the right choices for herself and her cub.

My bear is entirely good with that.

He wants what we build together to be very sturdy.

Even if he has to spread his gifts out over a very long time. Drawings, first. Dreaming. Repair-bot designs. In a month or two, thoughts on how to pay for some of them.

My bear frets. He has treasures. He will sell them.

I stroke his ears. We must save some of them for the pups, and we must let others contribute their treasures. Adelina is already whispering with Indrani, and there's a light in Myrna's eyes that bodes very well.

A shy hand reaches in and touches one of the units that will be directly above a polar bear's den.

Danielle smiles at Molly. "You want that one? It might be noisy."

Katrina snorts. "We're used to listening to Dorie snore. We'll be good."

My bear grins. His cubs are bonding. They will sleep above him where he can keep them safe. It is good.

Dorie pelts Katrina with a pinecone from the stash of them she has up in her tree. "You're the chatterbox, missy. No one will get a lick of sleep. Cleve should have one of those units, too. With a way in that lets a visitor or two come spend the night without having to run a gauntlet of talkative wolves."

I hide a smile. Of course the cat elder, with her prickly softness, sees. I wanted a way for those who dwell on the ledges to come into the warmth for a while, and Cleve will be the perfect wolf to host them.

Danielle adds a bridge to one of the second-story units. She hands a second pencil to Brandy, who begins quickly sketching faces. And an ancient wheelbarrow with a dinky wheel.

My bear grins. She drew one just like it for him the other day. For his new basket.

Rio shakes his head over my shoulder. "The design I drew was just fine, you know."

I turn so that I can study his eyes, but it's not necessary. The gladness is in his voice. "It was very elegant. You can use it for another pack. And I'm sure you'll want to tinker with this one."

His lips quirk. "I might."

Kennedy bumps his shoulder. "You just want to live in the unit next to the gummy bears."

Reilly giggles. "Those are in the cook shack, silly. And after that, they'll go live in the main den with the fancy table and couches that are big enough for bears and the TV screen where we can watch *Star Trek* in between the kissing movies."

Danielle ruffles her son's hair. "I thought you were allergic to kissing."

Kennedy snickers. "That's what he says now, but I bet if Devlin tried to kiss him, he wouldn't get any hives at all."

Reilly turns the color of my favorite tomatoes—and looks sheepishly enchanted.

Danielle shoots me a helpless look as her shoulders start shaking in silent giggles.

I lean my forehead against hers. "At least you only have one cub."

Kennedy pats my shoulder. "Don't worry. Some of us don't like kissing."

Four teenagers speak at once. I don't hear any of the words. They don't matter. What matters is that my cubs know each other and tend to the hearts that need tending.

I glance at Rio and speak under the teasing. "How is Grady?" He howled in the night. And was answered by a polar bear's roar.

A quiet smile laced with more gladness. "Sleeping. Wearing his medallion. Smelling like honey berry bars."

It is entirely a mystery to me why those haven't already brought all of the missing wolves home. I have sent some to Ivan. Years ago, he cast out a young polar bear with harsh words that took away his home. With the words he offered to Reilly and Kennedy and Ghost, he helped to give home back to me.

Warm, sturdy fingers wrap in mine. Danielle, finding me even as she continues to wield a pencil in her other hand. A wider pipe for more warmth in the unit that will house Cori and Ravi and their pups. Extra wiring to the unit where the offices will live. I watch as my sketches are reshaped by her pencil. And find myself quite out of words.

Some lines in a story require no embellishment at all.

I am home.

Next up: The big den building is coming—but it won't be the only thing unloading off of the trucks... Get Elder, book seven in the Ghost Mountain Wolf Shifters series!

Printed in France by Amazon
Brétigny-sur-Orge, FR

16034448R00187